SHE WORE MOURNING

SHE WORE MOURNING

ZACHARY GOLDMAN MYSTERIES #1

P.D. WORKMAN

ISBN: 9781988390772 (IS Hardcover)

ISBN: 9781988390765 (IS Paperback)

ISBN: 9781988390734 (KDP Paperback)

ISBN: 9781988390741 (Kindle)

ISBN: 9781988390758 (ePub)

pdworkman

ALSO BY P.D. WORKMAN

Zachary Goldman Mysteries
She Wore Mourning
His Hands Were Quiet
She Was Dying Anyway
He Was Walking Alone
They Thought He was Safe
He Was Not There
Her Work Was Everything
She Told a Lie (Coming soon)
He Never Forgot (Coming soon)
She Was At Risk (Coming soon)

Kenzie Kirsch Medical Thrillers
Unlawful Harvest

Auntie Clem's Bakery
Gluten-Free Murder
Dairy-Free Death
Allergen-Free Assignation
Witch-Free Halloween (Halloween Short)
Dog-Free Dinner (Christmas Short)
Stirring Up Murder
Brewing Death
Coup de Glace
Sour Cherry Turnover

AND MORE AT PDWORKMAN.COM

To those who are broken, and yet go on

Zachary Goldman stared down the telephoto lens at the subjects before him. It was one of those days that left tourists gaping over the gorgeous scenery. Dark trees against crisp white snow, with the mountains as a backdrop. Like the picture on a Christmas card.

The thought made Zachary feel sick.

But he wasn't looking at the scenery. He was looking at the man and the woman in a passionate embrace. The pretty young woman's cheeks were flushed pink, more likely with her excitement than the cold, since she had barely stepped out of her car to greet the man. He had a swarthier complexion and a thin black beard, and was currently turned away from Zachary's camera.

Zachary wasn't much to look at himself. Average height, black hair cut too short, his own three-day growth of beard not hiding how pinched and pale his face was. He'd never considered himself a good catch.

He waited patiently for them to move, to look around at their surroundings so that he could get a good picture of their faces.

They thought they were alone; that no one could see them without being seen. They hadn't counted on the fact that Zachary had been surveilling them for a couple of weeks and had known where they would go. They gave him lots of warning so that he could park his car out of sight, camouflage himself in the trees, and settle in to wait for their appearance. He was no amateur; he'd been a private investigator since she had been choosing wedding dresses for her Barbie dolls.

He held down the shutter button to take a series of shots as they came up for air and looked around at the magnificent surroundings, smiling at each other, eyes shining.

All the while, he was trying to keep the negative thoughts at bay. Why had he fallen into private detection? It was one of the few ways he could make a living using his skill with a camera. He could have chosen another profession. He didn't need to spend his whole life following other people, taking pictures of their most private moments. What was the real point of his job? He destroyed lives, something he'd had his fill of long ago. When was the last time he'd brought a smile to a client's face? A real, genuine smile? He had wanted to make a difference in people's lives; to exonerate the innocent.

Zachary's phone started to buzz in his pocket. He lowered the camera and turned around, walking farther into the grove of trees. He had the pictures he needed. Anything else would be overkill.

He pulled out his phone and looked at it. Not recognizing the number, he swiped the screen to answer the call.

"Goldman Investigations."

"Uh... yes... Is this Mr. Goldman?" a voice inquired. Older, female, with a tentative quaver.

"Yes, this is Zachary," he confirmed, subtly nudging her away from the 'mister.'

"Mr. Goldman, my name is Molly Hildebrandt."

He hoped she wasn't calling her about her sixty-something-year-old husband and his renewed interest in sex. If it was another infidelity case, he was going to have to turn it down for his own sanity. He would even take a lost dog or wedding ring. As long as the ring wasn't on someone else's finger now.

"Mrs. Hildebrandt. How can Goldman Investigations help you?"

Of course, she had probably already guessed that Goldman Investigations consisted of only one employee. Most people seemed to sense that from the size of his advertisements. From the fact that he listed a post office box number instead of a business suite downtown or in one of the newer commercial areas. It wasn't really a secret.

"I don't know whether you have been following the news at all about Declan Bond, the little boy who drowned…?"

Zachary frowned. He trudged back toward his car.

"I'm familiar with the basics," he hedged. A four- or five-year-old boy whose round face and feathery dark hair had been pasted all over the news after a search for a missing child had ended tragically.

"They announced a few weeks ago that it was determined to be an accident."

Zachary ground his teeth. "Yes…?"

"Mr. Goldman, I was Declan's grandma." Her voice cracked. Zachary waited, listening to her sniffles and sobs as she tried to get herself under control. "I'm sorry. This has been very difficult for me. For everyone."

"Yes."

"Mr. Goldman, I don't believe that it was an accident. I'm looking for someone who would investigate the matter privately."

Zachary breathed out. A homicide investigation? Of a child? He'd told himself that he would take anything that wasn't infidelity, but if there was one thing that was more depressing than couples cheating on each other, it was the death of a child.

"I'm sure there are private investigators that would be more qualified for a homicide case than I am, Mrs. Hildebrandt. My schedule is pretty full right now."

Which, of course, was a lie. He had the usual infidelities, insurance investigations, liabilities, and odd requests. The dregs of the private investigation business. Nothing substantial like a homicide. It was a high-profile case. A lot of volunteers had shown up to help, expecting to find a child who had wandered out of his own yard, expecting to find him dirty and crying, not floating face down in a pond. A lot of people had mourned the death of a child they hadn't even known existed before his disappearance.

"I need your help, Mr. Goldman. Zachary. I can't afford a big name, but you've got good references. You've investigated deaths before. Can't you help me?"

He wondered who she had talked to. It wasn't like there were a lot of people who would give him a bad reference. He was competent and usually got the job done, but he wasn't a big name.

"I could meet with you," he finally conceded. "The first consultation is free. We'll see what kind of a case you have and whether I want to take it. I'm not making any promises at this point. Like I said, my schedule is pretty full already."

She gave a little half-sob. "Thank you. When are you able to come?"

After he had hung up, Zachary climbed into his car, putting his camera down on the floor in front of the passenger seat where it couldn't fall, and started the car. For a while, he sat there, staring out the front windshield at the magical, sparkling, Christmas-card scene. Every year, he told himself it would be better. He would get over it and be able to move on and to enjoy the holiday season like everyone else. Who cared about his crappy childhood experiences? People moved on.

And when he had married Bridget, he had thought he was going to achieve it. They would have a fairy-tale Christmas. They would have hot chocolate after skating at the public rink. They would wander down Main Street looking at the lights and the crèche in front of the church. They would open special, meaningful presents from each other.

But they'd fought over Christmas. Maybe it was Zachary's

fault. Maybe he had sabotaged it with his gloom. The season brought with it so much baggage. There had been no skating rink. No hot chocolate, only hot tempers. No walks looking at the lights or the nativity. They had practically thrown their gifts at each other, flouncing off to their respective corners to lick their wounds and pout away the holiday.

He'd still cherished the thought that perhaps the next year there would be a baby. What could be more perfect than Christmas with a baby? It would unite them. Make them a real family. Just like Zachary had longed for since he'd lost his own family. He and Bridget and a baby. Maybe even twins. Their own little family in their own little happy bubble.

But despite a positive pregnancy test, things had gone horribly wrong.

Zachary stared at the bright white scenery and blinked hard, trying to shake off the shadows of the past. The past was past. Over and done. This year he was back to baching it for Christmas. Just him and a beer and *It's a Wonderful Life* on TV.

He put the car in reverse and didn't look into the rear-view mirror as he backed up, even knowing about the precipice behind him. He'd deliberately parked where he'd have to back up toward the cliff when he was done. There was a guardrail, but if he backed up too quickly, the car would go right through it, and who could say whether it had been accidental or deliberate? He had been cold-stone sober and had been out on a job. Mrs. Hildebrandt could testify that he had been calm and sober during their call. It would be ruled an accident.

But his bumper didn't even touch the guardrail before he shifted into drive and pulled forward onto the road.

He'd meet with the grandmother. Then, assuming he did not take the case, there would always be another opportunity.

Life was full of opportunities.

2

olly Hildebrandt was much as Zachary expected her to be. A woman in her sixties who looked ten or twenty years older with the stress of the high-profile death of her grandchild. Gray, curling hair. Pale, wrinkled skin. She wasn't hunched over, though. She sat up straight and tall as if she'd gone to a finishing school where she'd been forced to walk and sit with an encyclopedia on her head. Did they still do that? Had they ever done it?

"Mr. Goldman, thank you for seeing me so quickly," she greeted formally, holding her hand out for him to shake when he arrived at her door.

"Please, call me Zachary, ma'am. I'm not really comfortable with Mr. Goldman."

Telling her that he wasn't comfortable with it meant that she would be a bad hostess if she continued to address him that way, instead of her seeing it as a way of showing him respect. He hadn't done anything to deserve respect and was much happier if she would talk to him like the gardener or her next-door neighbor.

Not that there was any gardener. Molly lived in a small apartment in an old, dark brick building that was sturdy enough, but had been around longer than Zachary had been alive. The interior, when she invited him in, was bright and cozy. She had made coffee, and he breathed in the aroma in the air appreciatively. It wasn't hot chocolate after skating, but he could use a cup or two of coffee to warm him up after his surveillance. Standing around in the snow for a couple of hours had chilled him, even though he'd dressed for the weather.

Molly escorted him to the tiny living room.

"And you must call me Molly," she insisted.

She eyed the big camera case as he put it down. Zachary gave a grimace.

"Sorry. I didn't come to take your picture; I just don't like to leave expensive equipment in the car."

"Oh," she nodded politely. She didn't ask him who he had been taking pictures of. That wouldn't be gracious. She would have to imagine instead, and she would probably be correct in her guess.

They fussed for a few minutes with their coffees. Zachary wrapped his fingers around his mug, waiting for the coffee to cool and his fingers to warm. It felt good. Comforting. He waited for Molly to begin her story.

"You probably think that I'm just being a fussy old lady," she said. "Imagining something sinister when it was just an accident."

"Not at all. Why don't you tell me why you don't think it was an accident?"

"I'm not *sure* at all," she clarified. "Maybe they're right. Maybe it was an accident. It isn't that I doubt their findings…" she trailed off. "Not really. I know they had to do an autopsy and all that. We waited for months for them to come back with the manner of death. I thought that once they ruled, everyone would feel better."

"But you still have doubts?"

"I'm worried for my daughter."

Zachary blinked at her and waited for more.

"She's not well. I had hoped that once they released the body… and after the memorial… and after the manner of death was announced… each milestone, I thought, it would get better. It would be easier for her, but..." Molly shook her head. "She's getting worse and worse. Time isn't helping."

"Your daughter was Declan's mother."

"Yes. Of course."

"What's her name?"

"Isabella Hildebrandt," Molly said, her brows drawn down like he should have known that. "You know. *The Happy Artist.*"

Zachary had heard of *The Happy Artist.* She was on TV and was popular among the locals. Zachary didn't know whether she was syndicated nationally or just on one of the local stations. She had a painting instruction show every Sunday morning, and people awaited her next show like a popular soap. Most of the people Zachary knew who watched the show didn't paint and never intended to take it up. She was an institution.

"Oh, yes," Zachary agreed. "Of course, I know *The Happy Artist.* I didn't put the names together."

"When it was in the news, they said who she was. They said it was *The Happy Artist*'s child."

"Sure. Of course," Zachary agreed. He rubbed the dark stubble along his jaw. He should have gone home to shave and clean up before meeting with Molly. He looked like he'd been on a three-day stakeout. He *had* been on a three-day stakeout. "I'm sorry. I didn't follow the story very closely. That's good for you; it means I don't have a lot of preconceived ideas about the case."

She looked at him for a minute, frowning. Reconsidering whether she really wanted to hire him? That wouldn't hurt his feelings.

"You were going to tell me about your daughter?" Zachary prompted. "I can understand how devastated she must be by her son's death."

"No. I don't think you can," Molly said flatly.

Zachary was taken aback. He shrugged and nodded, and waited for her to go on.

"Isabella has a history of... mental health issues. She was the one supervising Declan when he disappeared, and the guilt has been overwhelming for her."

That made perfect sense. Zachary sipped at his coffee, which had cooled enough not to scald him.

Molly went on. "I think… as horrible as it may sound… that it would be a relief for her if it turned out that Declan was taken from the yard, instead of just having wandered away."

"That may be, but how likely is that? Surely the police must have considered the possibility, and I can't manufacture evidence for your daughter, even if it would ease her mind."

"No… I realize that. I'm not expecting you to do anything dishonest. Just to investigate it. Read over the police reports. Interview witnesses again. Just see… if there's any possibility that there was… foul play. A third-party interfering, even if it was nothing malicious."

"I assume you know most of the details surrounding the case."

"Yes, of course."

"How likely do you think it is that the police missed something? Did they seem sloppy or like they didn't care? Did you think there were signs of foul play that they brushed off?"

"No." Molly gave a little shrug. "They seemed perfectly competent."

Zachary was silent. It wouldn't be difficult to read over the police reports and talk to the family. Was there any point?

"The only thing is…" Molly trailed off.

As impatient as Zachary was to get out of there, he knew it was no good pushing Molly to give it up any faster. She already knew she sounded crazy for asking him to reinvestigate a case where he wasn't going to be able to turn up anything new. For no reason, other than that it might help her daughter to come to terms with the child's death. He looked around the room. There were no pictures of Molly's husband, even old ones. There was no sign she had raised Isabella or any other children there. There were several pictures of a couple with a little child. Declan and Isabella and whatever the father's name was. There was one picture of

Declan himself, occupying its own space, a little memorial to her lost grandson. There were no pictures of anyone else, so Zachary could only assume Isabella was an only child and Declan the only grandchild.

"Declan was afraid of water."

Zachary turned his eyes back to her. He considered. It wasn't totally inconceivable that a child afraid of the water would drown. He wouldn't know how to swim. If he fell in, he would panic, flail, and swallow water, rather than staying calm enough to float. Molly wiped at a tear.

"How afraid of the water was he?" Zachary asked.

"He wouldn't go near the water. He was terrified. He wouldn't have gone to the pond by himself."

"How tall was he?"

Molly gave a little shrug. "He was almost five years old. Three feet?"

"How steep were the banks of the pond and what was the terrain and foliage like?" He knew he would have to look at it for himself.

"I don't know what you want to know... there wasn't any shore to speak of. Just the pond. There were bulrushes. Cattails. Some trees. The ground is... uneven, but not hilly."

Zachary tried to visualize it. A child wouldn't be able to see the pond as far away as an adult would because of his short stature. If his view were further screened by the plant life, the banks steep and crumbly, he might not be able to see it until he was right on top of it. Or in it.

"It's not a lot to go on," he said. "The fact that he was afraid of water."

"I know." Molly used both hands to wipe her eyes. "I know that." She looked around the apartment, swallowing hard to get control of her emotions. "I just want the best for my baby. A parent always wants what's best. Growing up... I wasn't able to give her that. She didn't have an easy life. I wonder if..." She didn't have to finish the sentence this time. Zachary already knew what she was going to say. She wondered if that rough upbringing had caused Isabella's mental fragility. Whether things would have turned out differently if she'd been able to provide a stable environment. Molly sniffled. "Do you have children, Mr.—Zachary?"

Zachary felt that familiar pain in his chest. Like she'd plunged a knife into it. He cleared his throat and shook his head. "No. My marriage just recently ended. We didn't have any children."

"Oh." Her eyes searched his for the truth. Zachary looked away. "I'm sorry. I guess we all have our losses."

Although hers, the death of her grandson, was clearly more permanent than any relationship issues Zachary might have.

In the end, he agreed to do the preliminaries. Get the police reports. Walk the area around the house and pond. Talk to the parents. He gave her his lowest hourly fee. She clearly couldn't afford more. He wasn't even sure she'd be able to pay on receipt of his invoice. He might have to allow her a payment plan, something he normally didn't do, but something about the frail woman had gotten to him.

He put in an appearance at the police station, requesting a copy of the information available to the public, and handing over Molly Hildebrandt's request that he be provided as much information as possible for an independent evaluation.

"You got a new case?" Bowman grunted as he tapped through a few computer screens, getting a feel for how many files there were on the Declan Bond accident investigation file and how much of it he would be able to provide to Zachary.

"Yes," Zachary agreed. Obviously. He didn't encourage small talk; he really didn't want Bowman to start asking personal questions. They weren't friends, but they were friendly. Bowman had helped Zachary track down missing documents before. He knew the right people to ask for permission and the best way to ask.

Bowman dug into his pocket and pulled out a pack of gum.

He unwrapped a piece and popped it into his mouth, then offered one to Zachary as an afterthought.

"No, I'm good."

Bowman chewed vigorously as he studied each screen. He was a middle-aged man, with a middle-age spread, his belly sagging over his belt. His hairline had started receding, and occasionally he put on a pair of glasses for a moment and then took them off again, jamming them into his breast pocket.

"How's Bridget?" he asked.

Zachary swallowed. He took a deep breath and steeled himself for the conversation. Bowman looked away from his screen and at Zachary's face, eyebrows up.

"She's good. In remission."

"Good to hear." Bowman looked back at his computer again. "Good to hear. It's been a tough time for the two of you." His eyes flicked back to Zachary, and he backtracked. "I mean it's been tough for her. And for you."

"Yeah," Zachary agreed. He waved away any further fumbling explanation from Bowman. "So, what have we got? On the Bond case?"

"Right!" Bowman looked back at his screen. "I've got press releases and public statements for you. medical examiner's report. The cop in charge of the file was Eugene. He likes red."

Zachary blinked at Bowman, more baffled than usual by his abbreviated language. "What?"

"Eugene Taft. I know, it's a preposterous name, but he's never had a nickname that stuck. Eugene Taft."

"And he likes red."

"Wine," Bowman said as if Zachary was dense. "He likes red wine. You know, if you want to help things along, have a better chance of getting a look at the rest of that file, the officers' notes and all the background and interviews. If you have to apply some leverage."

"And for Eugene Taft, it's red wine."

"Has to be red," Bowman confirmed.

"Okay." Zachary looked at his watch. "Can you start that stuff printing for me? Is there anyone downstairs?" He knew he would have to run down to the basement to order a copy of the medical examiner's report. Just one of those bureaucratic things.

"Sure. Kenzie should be down there still."

Zachary paused. "Kenzie. Not Bradley?"

"Kenzie," Bowman confirmed. "She's new."

"How new?"

"I don't know." Bowman gave a heavy shrug. "How long since you were down there last? Less than that."

Zachary snorted and went down the hall to the elevator.

As he waited for it, Joshua Campbell, an officer he'd worked with on an insurance fraud case several months previous, approached and hit the up button. He did a double-take, looking at Zachary.

"Zach Goldman! How are you, man? Haven't seen you around here lately."

"Good." Zachary shook hands with him. Joshua's hands were hard and rough like he'd grown up working on a farm instead of in the city. Zachary wondered what he did in his spare time that left them so rough and scarred. He wasn't boxing after work; Zachary would have been able to tell that by his knuckles. "Hey, how's Bridget doing? Did everything turn out okay…?" He trailed off and shifted uncomfortably.

"Yeah, great. She's in remission."

"Oh, good. That's great, Zach. Good to hear."

Zachary nodded politely. His elevator arrived with a ding and a flashing down indicator. Zachary sketched a quick goodbye to Joshua and jumped on. He was starting to regret agreeing to look into the Bond case.

The girl at the desk had dark, curly hair, red-lipsticked lips, and a tight, slim form. She was working through some forms, those red lips pursed in concentration, and she didn't look up at him.

"Hang on," she said. "Just let me finish this part up, before I lose my train of thought."

Zachary stood there as patiently as possible, which wasn't too hard with a pretty girl to look at. She finally filled in the last space and looked up at him. She raised an eyebrow.

"You must be Kenzie," Zachary said.

"I don't know if I must be, but I am. Kenzie Kirsch. And you are?"

"Zachary Goldman. From Goldman Investigations."

"A private investigator?"

"Yes."

He didn't usually introduce himself that way because it gave people funny ideas about the kind of life he lived and how he spent his time. Most people did not think about mounds of paperwork or painstaking accident scene reconstructions when they thought about private investigation. They thought about Dick Tracy and Phillip Marlowe and all the old hardboiled detectives. When really most of a private investigator's life was mind-numbingly boring, and he didn't need to carry a gun.

"And what can I do for you today, Mr. Private Investigator?"

"Zachary."

"Zachary," she repeated, losing the teasing tone and giving him a warm smile. "What can I do for you?"

"I need to order a copy of a medical examiner's report. Declan Bond."

"Bond. That's the boy? The drowning victim?"

"That's the one."

She looked at him, shaking her head slightly. "Why do you need that one? It's closed. A determination was made that it was an accident."

"I know. The family would like someone else to look at it. Just to set their minds at ease."

"You're not going to find anything. It's an open-and-shut case."

"That's fine. They just want someone to take a look. It's not a reflection on the medical examiner. You know how families are. They need to be able to move on. They're not quite ready to let it go yet. One last attempt to understand…"

Kenzie gave a little shrug. "Okay, then… there's a form…" She bent over and searched through a drawer full of files to find the right one. Zachary had filled them out before. Usually, he could manage to do an end-run and Bradley would just pull the file for him. Officially, he was supposed to fill one out. He didn't want to end up in hot water with the new administrator, so he leaned on the counter and filled the form out carefully.

She went on with her own forms and filing, not trying to fill the silence with small talk. Which Zachary thought was nice. When he was finished, he put the pen back in its holder and handed the form to Kenzie. To the side of the work she was doing. Not right in front of her face. She again ignored him while she finished the section she was on, then picked it up to look it over.

"You have nice printing," she observed, her voice going up slightly. She laughed at herself. "No reason why you shouldn't," she said quickly. "It's just that the majority of the forms that get submitted here are… well, to say they were chicken scratch would be insulting to chickens."

Zachary chuckled. "That's the difference between a cop and a private investigator."

"Neat handwriting?"

"Yeah. Cops have to fill out so many forms, they don't care. You can just call them if you need something clarified. Me… I know if I don't fill it out right, it's just going to go in the circular file." He nodded in the direction of the garbage can.

"I wouldn't throw it out," she protested.

"If you couldn't read it? What else would you do?"

"I would at least try to call you."

Zachary indicated the form. "That's why I printed my phone number so neatly."

Kenzie smiled and nodded. "It's very clear," she approved.

"You'll call me?"

"I'll let you know when it's ready to be picked up."

Zachary hovered there for an extra few seconds. He was enjoying the give-and-take of his conversation with her but didn't want her to accuse him of being creepy. He wasn't the type who asked a girl out the first time he saw her.

He gave her another smile and walked away from the desk. Maybe next time.

3

Zachary had expected that he would need to meet with Spencer Bond, Declan's father, at his office. Men tended to want to act from a position of power, so he would want Zachary to see that he was well-respected and had some kind of influence. Spencer had surprised him by inviting him to the house. In the middle of the day. Surely, so long after Declan's death, he would be working again. Men tended to throw themselves back into their jobs.

Zachary decided Spencer must have taken the day off, or at least the afternoon, in order to meet with Zachary and answer all his questions.

The man who came to the door was similar to Zachary in age. Somewhere in his mid-to-late thirties. He had a young face. Dark hair. Clean shaven. He wore a suit and tie, so maybe he hadn't taken the day off work. Maybe he worked close by and had just taken an hour off to meet with Zachary. That was a little disappointing since Zachary figured he'd need more time than that to go over all the pertinent details.

"Mr. Bond?" Zachary asked politely.

"Yes. You must be Mr. Goldman of Goldman Investigations."

"That's me. Just Zachary, please."

"Zachary." Spencer looked at him for a moment and didn't offer to shake hands. He nodded and opened the door farther, motioning for Zachary to enter.

It wasn't a huge house, but it was simple and spacious. Bigger than anywhere Zachary had ever lived. Well, any *house* he had lived in, anyway. A few coats hung on pegs at the door. A blue man's coat. A couple of short women's jackets. There were a couple of umbrellas in an umbrella stand.

Looking around as Spencer led him through a living room with deep greens and pink pastels, Zachary couldn't see any sign that a child had lived there. No toy boxes or shelves. No fingerprints or crayon pictures on the coffee table. Declan Bond had drowned months before, at the end of the summer. They wouldn't have just left everything out. Maybe for a few days, but not for months.

Spencer led him into an office. Large windows, the afternoon sun streaming in. The room was warm, so either the windows had high-efficiency ratings, or they had a good furnace.

"Have a seat," Spencer muttered, going around the desk to sit.

Zachary selected a chair. Spencer reached over to a bottle of antibacterial gel cleaner and pumped a squirt into his hand. He rubbed his hands together, distributing it. All of this was done in an automatic gesture as if he wasn't even aware of it.

"Do you work from home?" Zachary asked, looking around.

"Yes." Spencer's dark eyes met Zachary's. "Didn't you already read our police interviews?"

"No. I'm still waiting to get everything. The police haven't allowed me access to their investigation notes yet, just the public releases. I'll talk to you and any other witnesses first, and then I'll go back over the police documentation, looking for any inconsistencies or new information. Okay?"

Spencer nodded, seeming satisfied with that.

"At this point, all I have to go by is your mother-in-law's initial statement to me, and a bare outline of what was in the news. Yours is the first detailed interview."

"I'll help you all I can."

Zachary looked over the neat desk and filing cabinets. "I didn't find any mention of what type of work you do."

"I am a reviewer."

Zachary wrote a note in his notepad, considering the answer. "What kind of things are we talking about? What do you review?"

"Product reviews. Anything. Food, cleaning products, toiletries, car accessories, books... anything and everything."

"Really. That must be interesting. Companies just send you products, and you test them..."

"I test them and post product reviews," Spencer completed, nodding.

"That lets you work from home. You don't have another office?"

"No. I work from here."

"And your wife is *The Happy Artist*. Does she spend a lot of time out of the home, or are both of you generally around?"

"Normally she's gone in the mornings. Then we're both around in the afternoon. It depends. She doesn't like to lock herself into a schedule." Spencer's eyes went to the big calendar on his wall, with carefully marked starting and ending times and columns of tasks. Zachary glanced over it.

"What were your child care arrangements? Whoever was home took care of Declan?"

"I was his primary caregiver. Isabella had to be away from the home more than I did. Taping, touring, doing interviews. She had her own artwork aside from the show. Painting, attending showings and schmoozing with the right people..."

"What happened the day Declan died? Can you walk me through the events of that day?"

Spencer swiveled his chair and gazed out the window. His office looked into the back yard.

"Deck was playing out back. Isabella was watching him. In the afternoon. She looked away, and when she looked back, he was gone. She thought he was just out of sight... waited a few minutes... looked out again... called him... I'm not sure how long he was gone before she started to worry. She came and got me. We both searched the house inside and out. Then we called the police. They started a search of the neighborhood."

Spencer stopped speaking. His voice had a flat tone to it, not what Zachary expected from a father talking about his only son's last hours on earth.

"The police organized a search. At what time?"

"I'm sure their records will be more accurate than my memory. I wasn't looking at a clock at the time. Four-thirty. Five o'clock. Something like that."

"And how long did it take to... find his remains?"

"Seven-fifteen. I think it was seven-fifteen."

"So only a couple of hours. You didn't have to deal with days of searching. That's a blessing, anyway."

Spencer stared out the window. "I suppose."

"Did they attempt to revive him?"

"At that point... they think he'd already been dead a couple of hours. There was nothing they could do."

"They put time of death at five o'clock?"

"Or thereabouts."

"By the time you started looking, it was already too late."

"Yes. So they said."

"I'm waiting for the medical examiner's report, but I assume they found water in his lungs. Were there any signs of... assault of any kind?"

"No. Nothing."

"How deep is the pond he was found in?"

Spencer turned his gaze to Zachary. "I've never waded in to find out."

"Natural or man-made?"

"Natural. Why does that matter?"

"If it was man-made, it probably has a gentle slope and fairly stable sides. If it's natural, it could be more treacherous. Deeper. Eroding banks. Maybe... sinkholes. I don't know."

"Oh." Spencer shrugged. "I see."

"Did Declan like to go to the pond? Is that somewhere you went regularly? To feed the ducks, maybe?"

"No." Spencer gave a definite shake of his head, looking almost angry at the thought. "We never went there."

"Molly said Declan was afraid of the water."

"It's a normal fear."

"I didn't say it wasn't a normal fear, but it was a fear he had?"

"I suppose, yes. Molly makes it out to be a lot worse than it was."

"She's brought it up with you as well?"

"Of course."

"What is your opinion? Do you think that he would have been too afraid to get close enough to the pond to drown?"

"No. Kids are unpredictable. He might have seen something that interested him... a dog or a rock... I don't know."

Zachary watched Spencer's Adam's apple moving up and down. The man's face was blank. The newspaper articles had said that he had shown no emotion either on Declan's disappearance or on the discovery of his body. That didn't mean that he wasn't feeling anything. Looking around the office, Zachary could see a framed picture of Declan placed prominently on the desk. On the back of the printer sat a stuffed toy dog.

"Declan liked dogs?"

"He loved them."

"Tell me about your wife."

Spencer reached out to his hand sanitizer, pumped a portion onto his hand, and again rubbed his hands together.

"Isabella was a very loving mother. This has been hard on her."

"Yes, I would expect it to be. Molly is very worried about her daughter's emotional state."

Spencer nodded.

"Do you think she's right to be concerned?"

"She knows her daughter better than I do. I know Isabella is unhappy... but that's how I would expect her to feel..."

"Like you."

Spencer gave a brief nod.

"Where did the two of you meet?"

"When I moved here, I was looking for a support group. Isabella had been put into a program by her therapist. We met. We really hit it off. It's hard for people to understand what it's like…" he trailed off uncomfortably.

"What it's like to have OCD," Zachary guessed.

Spencer didn't look surprised that Zachary had figured it out. It wasn't like he had tried to hide his compulsions.

"Yes."

"You and Isabella both have OCD?" Molly hadn't mentioned what kind of mental illness Isabella suffered from. "What's that like? It must be nice having someone who understands what it's like." Zachary made a motion to encompass the room. "It's a very tidy household," he observed with a smile.

"What you have seen so far. I thought it would be easier, living with someone like me; someone who understood; but we are very different. I think probably more different than it would have been to marry someone without compulsions."

Zachary shook his head, not understanding. Spencer tipped his chair back a little. He let out a sigh.

"Combining our households was a challenge. Isabella had accumulated so much stuff. They didn't live at Molly's current place, which you already saw. They lived in a little bungalow, and it was full to the brim with things. Isabella obviously couldn't bring everything here. She did her best to only bring a reasonable amount, and we tried to make a home."

Zachary nodded, following the story, though he wasn't sure where it was going to lead.

"The dishes were a combination of what I already had and what she brought. I went through them, getting rid of duplicate items or anything that was cracked or damaged. There was a plate that didn't match anything. A chipped blue dish. I got rid of it. This was all done while she was on a business trip, so she would be out of the way and wouldn't know what all I had gotten rid of. So, it wouldn't upset her."

With a little smile, Zachary could see what was coming. "But she noticed the loss of the blue plate."

A longer sigh from Spencer this time. Almost a groan. "That blue plate was the only one she would eat off."

"Oops."

Spencer swiveled to look at him. "That isn't an exaggeration, Mr. Goldman. She really would not eat off any other plate in the house. In the eight years we have been married, she has never eaten off another plate within these walls."

"Never? Then, what...?"

"If she's out at a restaurant, she can eat off their plates. At home, she can't. She can drink out of a cup. She can eat out of a bowl or straight out of the package." Spencer wrinkled his nose at this. "But she cannot bring herself to eat off a plate other than the chipped blue plate I threw out."

"Couldn't you get another one to replace it?"

"No. Even if I got one that was identical, she would know it wasn't the same plate, and she still wouldn't be able to use it."

"Oh." Zachary knew he should be making notes about the experience, but he was too baffled to write anything down.

"Compulsions can be very disruptive," Spencer said. "They can take over your life, out of nowhere. It isn't just a comfortable ritual." As if to demonstrate, Spencer leaned forward to squirt another stream of antibacterial gel onto his hands and scrub it away. For the first time, Zachary was aware of the sharp tang in the air, and noticed how red and chapped Spencer's hands were. "It isn't just a habit; it is something you *must* do. You can't move forward until you do. Do you want to know why I moved to Vermont?"

Zachary leaned forward. "Yes, of course."

"The sign law."

"The no-billboards law?"

Spencer nodded. "Before I came here, I had a compulsion to count billboards. I knew exactly how many there were on every route I traveled. If I was distracted and missed one of them, I had to go back to the beginning of the route and start over again. I was spending hours on the highway, just counting signs. If the advertisement on one of them changed, I had to drive by it twenty times. It had taken over my life."

"And you can't do anything about that?"

"There are therapies. Some people can get over their compulsions without replacing them with something new." His chair creaked. "I came to Vermont."

"Because you knew there weren't any billboards to count."

"Does that sound crazy to you?"

Zachary scratched his head, considering it. It certainly seemed extreme. As did refusing to eat off any other plate for eight years; but Spencer wasn't claiming to be normal. He was describing a pathology. A deviation from the norm.

"I can understand how it must have disrupted your life," he said slowly. "Moving to Vermont and starting over here seems like a disruption too, though. It can't have been easy."

Spencer drummed his fingers on the desk and gave a little shrug. "Yes, it was hard to leave Ohio to come here. Sometimes, even if it's painful, you just need to find a way to get away from your triggers. If I were still living in Ohio, I wouldn't have any kind of life now. I'd be driving up and down the highway endlessly. I never would have met Isabella. Deck would never have been a part of my life."

Zachary was uncomfortably aware of his own circumstances. All that had been taken away from him that everybody else seemed to take for granted.

"Do you ever wish that Declan hadn't been a part of your life? That he'd never been born? The pain of losing him...?"

"No." Spencer's eyes strayed to the stuffed dog. "I think he was meant to be a part of my life, even if it was only for a short time. I wouldn't want to have to give that experience up, even if it was painful."

His face was still blank of any emotion, but Zachary knew

that was just a mask that Spencer showed the world. Or maybe it wasn't something he hid behind, but that he was unable to express the emotion he felt. Zachary could feel it there between them. The grief. The anger. The despair.

"Yeah." Zachary sighed and turned the page on his notepad to a clean sheet. "I will have more questions for you later. I guess I should meet your wife now."

"Of course. We'll help in any way we can."

They both stood, and Zachary waited for Spencer to take him to wherever his wife was waiting. Spencer's mouth twitched, and he didn't come out from behind his desk.

"Has Molly told you about Isabella? What to expect?"

"No, not really, just that she's going through a difficult time. That Molly is concerned for her mental or emotional state."

Spencer didn't offer up any further explanation.

"Anything you could tell me that might help this go more smoothly?" Zachary suggested.

"You will find her... eccentric. Or maybe you won't. She wears her heart on her sleeve. She doesn't have cleanliness compulsions. She may act happy and cheerful, but..." Spencer shifted his feet. "That's her TV persona. She'll put it on if she's not comfortable with you."

Zachary nodded, understanding. "Okay. Thanks."

They made the walk to Isabella's office in silence. Zachary kept his eyes open, looking around the rest of the house as much as he could. It was almost clinically tidy.

Then they walked into Isabella's studio. That was where the neatness ended.

Spencer took him up to the doorway and didn't enter. Zachary could understand why. For someone with compulsions for cleaning and straightening, even having such a room in his house must have been painful. Certainly, he wouldn't want to spend any time there.

Zachary knocked on the open door, not wanting to just barge in on Isabella. She stood in the middle of the chaos, in front of an easel with some abstract daubing, her back to the door. She turned around, and Zachary saw the face that was so familiar from *The Happy Artist* commercials and advertisements. There was one brief, unguarded moment when she looked at him, her face hollow and lined before she realized she was facing a stranger and put on the mask Spencer had warned him about. She smiled brightly, and a fan of laugh lines replaced all the deep frown lines.

"Hello," she greeted, "come in, come in."

She looked around her and found a chair stacked with canvases. She moved the paintings to the side, leaning them against the wall.

"There you go. Make yourself at home."

Zachary sat down but wasn't exactly comfortable. There were canvases and art materials covering every surface, including most of the floor. All manner of brushes, paints, and bottles filled a couple of bookcases. There were tables with a space cleared in the middle for charcoal and pastel sketches. He had the uncomfortable sensation that everything stacked around him was going to fall down in a landslide and bury him.

Isabella herself was not untidy. She had on black pants and a flowing tunic-shirt with several layers of jewelry. Her long, dark hair had been gathered into a ponytail to keep it out of her face. When she appeared on TV, it was often done up in intricate braiding or decorated buns, a nod to the fact that her back was often to the cameras as she worked. Giving the audience something to look at besides her paint work.

"My name is Zachary. From Goldman Investigations."

"I know who you are," she said dismissively, flipping a hand at him as she studied her canvas. "And I know why my mother hired you."

"You know I'm here about Declan's accident."

"Of course." She looked away from her painting and gazed at him briefly, brows raised.

"I don't want to waste your time with small talk. I know this must be very difficult for you."

"Do you want to know why my mother is so worried about me?"

"Sure."

There was a stool nearby for her to sit on while she painted. She dragged it closer to Zachary and sat down. It was higher than Zachary's chair, so he was forced to look up at her.

"The network says I have to wear long sleeves on the air now," Isabella said, pulling up the right-hand sleeve of her tunic.

Molly's concern and the words prefacing the gesture made Zachary expect to see fresh cut marks. There was no sign of self-mutilation or a suicide attempt. Instead, he was looking at the tattoo of a boy's face, with the name Declan under it.

"Do you really think my viewers would find that so offensive?" Isabella demanded. "Why is it a bad thing that I tattooed my son into my skin?"

"Uh, no…" Zachary was caught by surprise and had no idea what to say to this. "No, I think… it's sweet."

"He came from my body, and now he's returned to it," she went on, her voice loud and forceful. "The tattoo artist mixed a small amount of his ashes into the tattoo ink. His body has returned to me and will always be with me."

Zachary did find that surprising, and maybe a little morbid. He didn't know regular people did that kind of thing. In prison, all kinds of materials were burned to make DIY tattoo ink, but he didn't know anyone would mix cremains in with the ink. Was it common, and he'd just never paid attention before?

"My son is always with me," Isabella had continued, while Zachary was lost in his own thoughts. "I don't ever want him to leave me again."

She plucked up one of the pendants that hung around her neck and held it out toward Zachary. He saw, with a mounting feeling of discomfort, that what he had taken to be a vial with rough pearls inside actually contained teeth.

"These are his. Not the teeth from his body, those were cremated with him, but baby teeth I helped him to pull out while he was still alive, and I could touch him and hold them in my hand."

Zachary stared at her. This was why Molly was so concerned. Not just because Isabella was sad, mourning her lost child, but because her mourning had taken her into territory that was... morbid and unsettling.

"Maybe we could talk about what happened that day," he suggested.

"This ring contains some of his ashes," Isabella offered as if she hadn't heard him. She held out her hand toward him, showing off a large purple stone like an amethyst. "You can get jewelry where you can put the ashes into a little chamber yourself, but this one, the ashes are actually suspended in the glass. You see the sparkle inside?"

"Yes."

"This one," she tapped the ring, "the producers will let me wear on air, but the tattoo and the teeth, those are *inappropriate*." Her tone mocked their words. "Somehow those might drive the viewers away. They wouldn't be able to handle my grief." She dropped her hand to her lap. "My viewers know that I lost my child. Do they think I wouldn't mourn him? Do they think after I've taken a few weeks off work, I'm all better? Everything is fine?"

"No. I don't think they expect that. Probably your producers don't either. They're just being... cautious..." Zachary tried to pitch his voice so that it was low and soothing. Isabella was agitated, almost manic, and he didn't know whether that was her normal state, or whether he had triggered her behavior by being there, asking about her son, trying to find some different answers from those she had already received. Did she go off like that on everyone?

Isabella ignored his assurance and went on, itemizing the other bits of hair and ash that were woven or contained within her various accessories. After a while, Zachary grew numb to it. It was no longer shocking or even surprising. He'd never known there were so many ways to carry a memento of your deceased loved one around with you. Obviously, the jewelry companies were ready and eager to provide the products.

Isabella seemed to be winding down. "I sent the rest of his ashes away to a company that makes diamonds. They actually take the ashes—carbon—and add heat and pressure to form them into a real diamond. It's not just ashes suspended in a gem, like this," she indicated the amethyst ring, "or inside a micro urn, like these... but the ashes are transformed into a diamond."

"That's amazing," Zachary obliged. "But you don't have it back yet?"

"It takes a few months to make. I'm hoping to have it before Christmas."

"That would... be a nice present."

"I want Declan to be with me. Always. I don't ever want to be separated from him again."

"Yes. I can see that." Zachary took another breath, looking for his opening. "You must have been very scared when he disappeared."

"I was! It was horrible. You don't know the kind of terror... You don't have any children, do you?"

"No." Again, the lead ball in his stomach. "I don't."

"You could never understand how terrifying it is. He was *right there*. I only looked away for two minutes!"

"I don't think anyone blames you. Children can wander away from even the most diligent caregiver."

She shook her head, not believing it. She knew that it was her fault he had wandered away. It had been her responsibility. She was the one who had fallen down on the job, and the responsibility for his death fell on her. She wore that guilt just like all the leftover bits of Declan's body.

"Can you tell me about how it happened? I know this is a

terrible thing to ask of you. You've already had to repeat it so many times. Can you manage just one more...?"

Isabella looked at him, her hands wringing in her lap. Her eyes were once again hollow, the laugh lines gone.

"You don't know what it's like to lose a child," she told him again.

Zachary gritted his teeth and didn't disagree.

"He was playing outside in the back yard." She made a gesture toward it. The yard was not visible from Isabella's studio as it was from Spencer's office.

"And you were supervising him? You were outside with him?"

"I wasn't outside."

"Oh. Where were you, then?"

"I was in the bedroom. It has patio doors that look into the yard. I could see him from there."

Zachary nodded his encouragement. "I see. Do you mind if I... see the bedroom for a minute?"

Her lips tightened, and he knew she was going to say no. She thought that he was going to judge her as a negligent mother, watching her child from a distance instead of being out there with him, playing with him, talking and laughing with him. Had either of the parents really connected with Declan? Did either of them see him as a person rather than a responsibility?

"I'd like to see where the blind spots are," Zachary explained. "Areas where an intruder might have approached and seen and talked to Declan without you being able to see them."

"Oh." Her expression softened, and she nodded. "Yes, I guess that makes sense."

"Just think of it as a security sweep. I need to understand where the weaknesses in the defenses were. I'm not here to accuse you of anything."

"Some people have been very cruel."

Zachary hoped that didn't include Isabella's own husband and mother. She couldn't have been an easy person to live with, wallowing in her grief, wearing her heart on her sleeve, as Spencer had said. Or her child's face on her arm.

Isabella got off the stool and motioned briskly for Zachary to follow her. He fell into step with her. It didn't look like she was the type to hang around waiting. She led him to the bedroom.

"Here."

It was a combination of their styles. Mostly Spencer's minimalist, fussily tidy look. There were elements of Isabella as well. Her paintings were on the walls. A row of frivolous throw pillows across the head of the bed. The closet was clearly divided into his and hers.

Spencer's shirts and suits marched in neat rows across the rod, all carefully ordered, facing the same direction, looking crisp and starched. Isabella's side of the closet was a chaos like her studio. There was no apparent order to the clothing, skirts and pants mixed in with shirts and jackets and sweaters. Fancy dresses with sequins squashed in with hoodies with silly sayings. Hangers were hooked haphazardly from the front and the back. The shoes were in a jumble, not in pairs. Scarves and belts and jewelry hung on a handmade pegboard in no apparent order.

Zachary looked around. The room had big windows, like Spencer's office, and had a good view of the back yard. It was a broad expanse of unbroken white snow. No one building snowmen or forts.

"You were watching from…?" Zachary made a wide motion to indicate the room.

"Right here," Isabella positioned herself in front of the window, a couple of feet away.

"Tell me about that. You were standing there watching him? Putting laundry away?" He felt his face flush as it occurred to him that Spencer probably did the laundry and put it away. His own, anyway. "Reading a book, maybe?"

"No, painting."

He tried to envision the set-up. It didn't fit his idea of a good place for painting. The room was carpeted. There were no painting materials out. Maybe she didn't paint there anymore because of what had happened.

"Your easel would have been here...?" Zachary blocked out the area in front of the window with his hands. "That might have obscured your view."

"No, here." Isabella swiveled to indicate the area behind her. "To make the most of the natural light coming in through the window. If I had been facing into it while painting, I would have been dazzled."

"Right here. So, the light was behind you."

"Angled a little, so my shadow wouldn't fall on the canvas. Yes. Like that."

"Your back was to the window?"

"No." Isabella looked at the imaginary easel and then at the window, frowning. "Well, yes, some of the time. I would look out at him and watch him, and then paint. Then look again."

"You were checking on him occasionally. Not strictly supervising him. He was five and in his own yard. Perfectly safe."

She nodded, her face relaxing. She had been expecting him to criticize her for not watching Declan the whole time. Was that what Spencer had said? What about her mother? It had been in the news, so there were probably all kinds of people, friends and strangers, who had opinions about what had happened and her parenting skills or lack of them.

"Yes, he was perfectly safe," she agreed. "You can see. It's fenced. Gated. He couldn't get out on his own."

"Then how did he get out that day?"

"We found the back gate open," Isabella said, staring across the yard at it. "I don't know who opened it. Deck couldn't have opened it on his own. A neighbor? A stranger? Spencer when he took out the garbage?" Isabella shook her head. "It couldn't have been Spencer. He's so careful about everything. He would never have left it unlatched."

"But it isn't locked in any way. Anyone walking by could have unlatched it."

She nodded. "It never occurred to me to put a lock on it. Do people lock their gates? It doesn't seem... it doesn't seem like something people living in houses like this would do, does it? I can understand someone who lives in a rough neighborhood. Or someone who lives in a mansion with a swimming pool. But our little house?" She shook her head, eyes shiny with tears. "I don't think people here lock their gates."

"I don't know." Zachary shook his head. "I don't know what your neighbors do or don't do. I'm just trying to get a good picture of what happened that day."

Isabella sat on the end of the bed and sighed. "He loved to play outside. He'd play for hours. Take his toys out with him. Ask if he could sleep outside at night. Neither Spencer nor I are into camping; I bet he would have loved it if we were."

"How long was he outside? What was he playing with that day?"

"He was outside for a couple of hours. I don't know what he was playing. He was an only child. A bit lonely. He made games up to entertain himself."

"Are you and Spencer both only children? Or did you have siblings?"

"Spencer has a couple of brothers. I... don't have anyone. Just Mom. I know how lonely it can be, not having any brothers or sisters. I was alone a lot too."

For a moment, Zachary was awash with memories. He too had been alone. Being taken away from his brothers and sisters had been such a shock for him. It was one thing growing up as an only child, not knowing any difference, but Zachary knew the difference. He had been part of a family, and then he didn't have anyone. He was old enough that much of the time he wasn't with a foster family. It would be a group home or residential care. Surrounded by other kids, but all by himself.

He had been lonely for so long. Did that loneliness stretch out as far ahead of him as it did behind? He couldn't face that.

Zachary shook off the memories and faced the problem at hand.

"Tell me about… when you realized Declan wasn't in the yard anymore."

Isabella put her face in her hands. Zachary waited for her to brace up and tell him the story. She probably wanted to. People avoided asking about tragedy, asking about exactly what had happened and how it felt. They pretended that nothing had happened and all was well, leaving people like Isabella to grieve alone, unable to let it all out.

"I was painting. Deck was outside. I was turning to look at him, to make sure he wasn't getting overheated or tired. Or bored. All those things you're supposed to watch out for. But he wasn't. He was happy. Then I looked once, and I couldn't see him. I thought maybe he was somewhere I couldn't see him. Beside the house," she gestured, "or up against it," she indicated the angles. "I waited for him to come back to where I could see him. He didn't. I opened the window and called him." Isabella paused as if waiting for him to answer, but they both knew he would never answer. "I went outside. He wasn't there. I panicked. I was so scared. I looked everywhere in the yard. In the front. In the house. I looked everywhere, top to bottom, and he wasn't here. I went and got Spencer, and we looked together."

She started to sob. Zachary thought he should show her sympathy, but he froze in place with no idea what to do about her tears. In his experience, trying to calm a crying woman just made her cry more, or made her angry. He didn't want to do either one. So, he waited.

"Then we called the police. They got here pretty quickly. They took our statements. They started a search. They made announcements and called for volunteers to help canvass the streets around the house before it got dark."

"Do you think one of your neighbors had something to do with this?"

That was one of the problems with bringing volunteers in too soon. The police had contaminated the crime scene. Too many people had gone tramping through the neighborhood looking for him. Had someone drowned him in the pond, or had it been an accident?

Isabella was shaking her head. "No one would do that to us. Who would do that? It doesn't make any sense."

"People who harm little children rarely make sense. To anyone but themselves. Children aren't killed out of jealousy or greed, like adults. It's completely different."

"I don't see how anyone we knew could have had anything to do with it. I don't think it was one of our neighbors."

"You believe it was an accident?"

Isabella wiped away tears and sat there on the end of the bed, her eyes red and puffy, staring into the desolate back yard.

"Yes. It was an accident. Just... one of those things."

Zachary nodded. "Okay. All right. Is there anything else you think I should know?"

"I can't think of anything."

"Can I see Declan's room before I go? Or have you redecorated it?"

Her eyes widened. "Redecorated? Why would we do that? I don't think it could ever be anything but Declan's room. Ever."

"May I...?"

"It's just next door." She motioned. "So, when he was a baby, I could hear him if he cried."

Zachary took this as his invitation to see for himself. He went down the hall to Declan's bedroom.

It wasn't much smaller than the master bedroom. The walls were painted several shades of blue. He had a kid's laptop computer or gaming system. Toy boxes and shelves. Clothing neatly arranged in the closet. Zachary could see Spencer's influence more than Isabella's. He had expected at least a wall mural for her only child. Zachary walked around the room slowly, looking for anything suspicious or out of place. He wasn't really expecting to find anything. If it had been a stranger abduction as Molly had suggested, there certainly wouldn't be any sign of it in Declan's room. He never knew when he might see something that would become important later in the case.

"Until we meet again, may God hold you in the palm of His hand."

Zachary startled and turned to see Isabella standing in the doorway. She wasn't looking at him and hadn't been speaking to him. She was just looking at the room, feeling her loss. She ran her fingers over her jewelry as if accounting for each piece. She stared down at the tattoo on her arm.

"Until we meet again, may God hold you in the palm of His hand," she repeated.

Zachary walked over to her. He touched her shoulder gently as he stepped back out of the room.

"I think it's time for me to get on my way."

Isabella nodded. She looked down at her watch. "Just let me feed the cat, and then I'll walk you out."

"Okay."

He walked with her into the kitchen. Bright and airy. Zachary watched Isabella as she mechanically picked up a bowl of cat food, dumped it into the garbage, refilled it from a big bin in the closet, and put it back down where it had been. He looked around the house but didn't see any other sign of a pet. They didn't seem like the kind of people who would keep a pet.

"Do you... have a cat?" he asked Isabella, as they walked back to the front door. The food in the dish didn't appear to have been touched. No cat came running when she filled it. The cats that he had known had always come running and yowled for their food as soon as they heard a food can, box, or bag being rattled.

Isabella stopped with her hand on the front doorknob.

"Yes. Mittens." She didn't open the door. "It's been a long time. He wandered off one day and didn't come back... just like Declan."

Zachary suppressed a shudder at her tone. Was there a connection between the two disappearances?

"When did your cat disappear?" he asked. A long time ago could be months back, when Declan had disappeared. Had the boy followed the cat? Had the cat followed him? Was there some other connection between the two?

"When we first got married."

"Eight years ago?" Zachary demanded, remembering the story of the plate.

"Yes… that sounds about right. Eight years ago."

She turned the doorknob and opened the door for him.

"Until we meet again, may God hold you in the palm of His hand."

Eight years, and she was still feeding the cat.

Molly thought that if Zachary re-investigated Declan's death, it would bring Isabella some peace.

But the woman was still feeding her missing cat eight years later.

4

It was a couple of days before the copy of the medical examiner's report was ready for him. Zachary kept himself busy in the interim with his other cases. Surveillance on Pastor Hellerman's wife. A long, tedious review of the accident reconstruction he had done on the Mae Gordon accident. Running background on the interns who had applied to work with Senator Brown. There was plenty to keep him busy.

Martin Ash was running the security check-in at the police station and gave Zachary a big smile as he approached. He had always been friendly with Zachary, even when Zachary was running an investigation that was not popular with the police force, which happened more often than he liked. It had been a while since he had seen the big, black man. Martin pushed a bin toward Zachary for the contents of his pockets. Zachary put his briefcase down on the conveyor belt behind it and walked through the metal detector.

"How are you, my friend?" Martin boomed. "And how is Bridget?"

"I'm good." Zachary picked up his keys and wallet from the bin after it went through the x-ray. "Bridget is in remission."

A look of confusion passed over Martin's face. His brows drew down. "In remission?" he repeated. "She was sick?"

Zachary's heart sank. He had assumed that Martin was part of the grapevine and knew all the details or that they had talked about it at some point already. He was unprepared for Martin's ignorance. For a moment he was frozen, unable to speak. He swallowed and licked his dry lips.

"Uh—yes—sorry, I thought you knew. She had ovarian cancer."

"Oh." Martin shook his head, looking shocked. His smile was gone. He tried to meet Zachary's eyes, though Zachary did his best to avoid connecting. "I'm so sorry, Zachary! I didn't know." He patted Zachary on the back.

"It's fine. I'm sorry to spring it on you like that. It seems like everyone knows all of the details, whether I have told them or not, so I just assumed that you knew, and were asking about the cancer treatments…"

"But she's in remission. So that's good. That means she's clean and they caught it in time."

"Yes, exactly." Zachary tried to force a smile of reassurance. "She's good. She's recovering from the chemo and starting to feel back to her old self."

"Good, good. So, the two of you…" Martin tried to approach it delicately, but he had no tact to speak of, "…does that mean you won't be able to have children? Because of the cancer and the radiation?"

Zachary swore. He should have headed off that inquiry at the same time as he informed Martin that Bridget had had cancer. He should have broken it all at once instead of leaving it open-ended.

"We aren't together anymore," Zachary told Martin gently. "I'm sorry…"

"You broke up?" Martin shook his head. "How could that happen?"

There were other people waiting for security clearance, and

Zachary made a little motion toward them. "I shouldn't keep you. You have a job to do."

"I can't believe you guys aren't together anymore." Martin moved like a robot to clear the next person in line, not smiling at him or greeting him. "I thought you two were happy together."

"For a while." But even as Zachary said it, he wondered if it was true. Had they really been happy? He had loved her. He'd hoped for a long life together, but the way things had turned out... things had never been perfect. It had always been rocky. "I think the cancer was just too much for us. Too much stress."

Martin nodded, the corners of his mouth drawn down in a pronounced frown. Zachary didn't think he'd ever seen Martin unhappy before.

"Sorry," Zachary apologized again, getting on his way and leaving Martin to clear the next visitor.

After the run-in with Martin, Zachary was anxious and on edge. Not the best side to show to the new girl in the medical examiner's office. He tried to be pleasant and cordial, but he knew he wasn't pulling it off. Kenzie kept attempting to make small talk as Zachary looked down at the photocopied report in his hand, but he couldn't seem to find the proper responses to keep the conversation going and put her at ease.

"Is everything okay?" Kenzie asked finally.

"Yes... it's fine... I just..." Zachary shook his head, looking for a way to explain. "I just had some news, that's all."

"Oh. I'm sorry to hear that." Her dark eyes searched his face, and she decided not to ask him for details. She took one of her business cards out of the holder on her desk, scribbled on it, and slid it across to him. "Call me, okay? If there's anything in that report that you want to run through. Or if you want to talk."

Zachary gave her a smile that felt stretched and nodded his head. "Thanks; and I'm sorry for being out of sorts. We'll talk."

Kenzie nodded and smiled. He could feel her eyes on him all the way to the end of the hallway before he turned and was out of her sight.

Zachary watched the blond woman get out of her yellow VW. She locked it with her remote key lock as she walked away. It gave a little chirp, and she never looked back.

He knew her routine. Coffee at The Jumping Bean. Not on the terrace because it was too cold and snowy to be open, but inside where it was warm, sitting pleasantly close to the tiny fireplace. Then she would start her errands. The parking zone she was in gave her three hours. She would likely use all of that and then restart the meter.

Zachary sidled up to the car, looking casual like it was his own car. He looked around carefully before sliding the key into the lock and climbing in. He pulled the door shut and was effectively invisible to the crowds walking by.

He went directly to the glovebox for her log file. A ledger where she tracked all her mileage for tax purposes, with client codes and odometer readings noted in her precise printing. Kenzie would have approved. He scanned it for any unusual trips, any unaccounted jumps in the odometer. There was also a plastic sleeve containing all her latest expense receipts, and he thumbed through them carefully, his eyes quick. He looked up once to make sure that she wasn't anywhere in sight. Returning to her car because she'd forgotten something inside. Unexpectedly finding The Jumping Bean closed because a plumbing line had flooded the cafe overnight. Anything could happen.

He checked the visor flaps for anything else of interest, ran his fingers along the cracks of the seats to see if anything had been dropped and lodged there. Poked through the garbage, but didn't find anything other than a stray Twinkie wrapper. Her secret vice.

His search of the car complete, he climbed out, locked the doors again, and walked away.

———————

Zachary sat in his recliner, the medical examiner's report in his lap, a half-eaten lunch on the side table by his elbow. He had only done a page-flip of the medical examiner's report, seeing how detailed it was and if anything jumped out at him. It was relatively short, a cursory review of what the police had said from the beginning was an accident, not a violent death or the mysterious death of a vital person struck down in their prime. The tests and notes all seemed to be routine.

Was there any point in doing more than that? He knew that Molly didn't have much money to put into the investigation. A detailed review of the medical examiner's report, all the police notes he could get his hands on, and re-interviewing everyone he would want to talk to in order to fully satisfy himself that it had been an accident would take a lot of hours and run up the bill unnecessarily.

His discussions with Spencer and Isabella hadn't rung any alarm bells. They both seemed to be just what they were, parents grieving the unexpected loss of their only child, getting through it the best they could manage. There wasn't any sign that it hadn't been an accident.

Other than Molly's assertion that the boy was afraid of water.

Spencer had shrugged the statement off, agreeing that Declan had a fear of water, but that it wouldn't have prevented him from going near the water. Zachary didn't think that either of them was lying; they were just interpreting him differently.

Zachary ran Kenzie's business card through his fingers, feeling the smooth, sharp edge. Kenzie Kirsch. She had written another number on it; he assumed it was her home or cell number. It was kind of her to give it to him when she saw he was feeling bad. Did she want him to call, or was it just a gesture? He hadn't asked her for her number. Women didn't offer their numbers to men if they didn't want them to call, did they?

Looking down at the medical examiner's report, Zachary reached for his phone. He dialed her number quickly, already rehearsing what he was going to say. Starting conversations with women was not one of his strengths. Give him a suspect interview any day.

"Hello?"

"Um—Kenzie? It's Zachary. Goldman Investigations."

"Zachary! I'm glad you called." He didn't hear any deception in her voice. She sounded genuinely warm. "How are you?"

He listened for background noise that might indicate she was out with friends or a date or doing something she didn't want interrupted.

"I'm okay. I'm sorry for how I was earlier. I… had something on my mind."

"No, it's okay. I understand. Everybody has a bad day now and then. I'm glad you're feeling better." There was a pause. He imagined her sitting by a roaring fire, having a sip of wine before bed. It was a nice image. "Did you have a chance to look at the medical examiner's report yet?"

"Only a high-level review. Nothing that jumps out at me on a browse through. I'll have to spend a few hours going through all the details… if I'm going to pursue the case."

"I thought you had already taken the case?"

"I did. I mean… if I decide to take it any further. The grandmother, the one who hired me, I don't think she has any means of support. Maybe her daughter is helping out with the bills."

"She's that artist on TV, right? *The Happy Artist.*"

"That's the one."

"She's really popular. I bet she makes a ton of money."

"They appear to be well-off, but the grandmother isn't. If there's nothing here to find… I'd just be stealing from her."

"Dr. Wiltshire is very conscientious. I'm sure he wouldn't have returned a finding of accidental drowning if he had any doubt."

"No. I don't want to imply he's done anything wrong. The family just wants someone to go over everything one more time."

"Do you want someone to go over the report with you? That would save you some time and help you decide if there was anything else to do."

Zachary's heart gave a couple of extra beats that almost hurt. "Would that somebody be you?" he suggested.

"It might be." Kenzie's voice was light and playful.

"Could this review be over dinner, maybe?"

"That would be nice."

"Are you free tomorrow night?"

"Sure. Where do you want to meet?"

Hardly believing that such a thing was happening to him, Zachary came up with an acceptable restaurant and time, and they agreed to get together. After he had hung up the phone, Zachary closed his eyes and again pictured Kenzie all cozied up, sipping her glass of red wine.

5

Zachary slept well for once, dreaming of Kenzie, so even though he awoke long before he wanted to be up, he felt lighter and more energetic than he had for a long time. Since he was going to be reviewing the medical examiner's report with Kenzie, he didn't spend any more time on it, but reviewed his notes of his interviews with Spencer and Isabella and typed up a summary of each. He glanced over the news articles and releases he had collected.

The phone rang, and the woman on the other end identified herself as Eugene Taft's assistant and thanked him for his recent gift. Zachary almost laughed.

It had not been easy to pin down Eugene Taft to get access to the police file, and in the end, Zachary had resorted to simply sending him the bottle of red wine Bowman had recommended, with a card congratulating him on his anniversary. Zachary had no idea if Taft was married, or if he had any other anniversary in the recent past or near future, but everyone had significant dates that they celebrated, and Zachary had thought that an anniversary gift would go over better than Christmas wishes. Besides which, he didn't want anything to do with Christmas.

"Yes, Officer Fitzgerald. I'm glad to hear he got it."

There was a hesitation on the other end as Fitzgerald tried to couch her inquiry regarding the bribe appropriately. "You had called the other day to see if Eugene had some time to see you, hadn't you?"

"Oh, I don't need to take up any of his valuable time. He should have received a request through Mario Bowman about allowing me access to a file. It was pretty routine; I'm sure it's just on his desk awaiting his signature."

"Which file was this?"

"Declan Bond."

"Declan Bond," she repeated vaguely. "Oh, the little boy who drowned...?"

"That's the one."

"Are you a reporter?"

"No, ma'am. I'm a private investigator. The family hired me to take another look at the case. Just to ease their minds that he covered everything. I'm not expecting to find anything unusual in the file."

"I see."

"If the request is not there, you could ask Bowman about it. He knows me from other cases I've helped out with."

"I think I will follow up with him," she agreed. "I'll be in touch."

"Tell Eugene 'happy anniversary' for me."

"I will."

She hung up. Smiling, Zachary put his travel mug under the coffee maker and brewed up a coffee to take with him for the site survey.

The scene was bleak during the winter. The skeletons of trees and grasses were stark against the snow. There were no children playing, no dogs running, no ducks swimming. A few black birds flew overhead, the flapping of their wings loud in the silence.

The pond was iced over and had not been cleared, so Zachary could only see the ominous shape of it beneath the snow, like an animal trap waiting to be sprung.

Hopefully, there would be pictures on the police file, as it was surely a far different place during the summer. Zachary paced around the pond, breaking a trail in the snow. A couple of times he stepped farther down than he expected, into an unseen dip or hole. He scanned the yards that backed onto the property, looking for anything suspicious or out of place. Even putting on his most paranoid goggles, he couldn't see anything that indicated danger.

The last thing he did was to walk to the Bonds' back yard. He looked at it from the back, eyes alert for any hiding places, any breaks in the fence, anyone watching out their windows. He examined the gate, which could easily be opened from the back alley and still bore no lock. Anyone could have walked up to the yard and opened the gate. Would Declan have left with them? Would he have gone quietly with a stranger, or put up a fight? Had it been a stranger?

He examined the back of the house. He could identify Spencer's office, the master bedroom, and Declan's bedroom. They all had good views of the yard. A stranger would have had to be pretty bold or sure of himself to walk right into the yard in view of those big windows.

But during the summer, would there have been blinds drawn across the windows? Isabella claimed to have had a good view of Declan, but was she looking through the slats of blinds? Or was she standing in the full afternoon sun? Just because there were no blinds drawn during the winter, that didn't mean they didn't use them to keep out the full heat of the summer.

Zachary looked at his watch and started the stopwatch function. Then he walked back to the pond.

Zachary got to the restaurant before Kenzie, which was intentional. He didn't want to be the guy who showed up late for a date, especially when she was also helping him out. He wanted to show her that she could trust him to be responsible and treat her with respect. After checking to make sure she hadn't shown up there ahead of him, he went back outside and paced around a little, watching for her. Despite the weather having been only mildly cold when he had been at the pond, there was a biting wind. After a few minutes of toughing it out, he gave in and went back into the restaurant.

Old Joe's Steakhouse was a landmark. Casual, but with great service and even better food, everybody knew about it, and it was a wonder that anyone could ever get in without booking reservations three months ahead. Somehow, people knew which hours were the busiest and scheduled their dinners for quieter times, so Old Joe was able to serve a thriving population without becoming elite.

"Are you ready to be seated, sir?" the college-aged boy leaned closer to Zachary to address him over the hum of the crowd. "I have your table ready."

Zachary looked at the door. "I don't know; I was going to wait…"

"We'll bring your guest to you. You may as well sit and have a drink while you wait."

Zachary gave a shrug and followed the boy into the dining area. The tables were close together, and the room was noisy, but it didn't feel overly crowded, just busy. Zachary followed the young man to his assigned table.

"Uh… why don't you get me a beer? I'm not sure what the lady will want."

"Sure. Any preference?"

"No. Whatever's on tap."

He kept an eye on his watch, but it was still too early for Kenzie to show up. When she eventually arrived, a quick glance showed Zachary that she was ten minutes early.

"You're here already," Kenzie observed with a smile. "Neat printing *and* prompt. Have I finally found the perfect man?"

"Not perfect by a long shot," Zachary said with a sigh. "But the longer I can keep you fooled, the better."

"Ha." She sat down across from him. "Then you shouldn't be telling me!"

The waiter came over to take Kenzie's order. She eyed Zachary's beer for a moment, but then ordered a glass of wine.

Small talk wasn't the easiest for him, so after perusing the menu and ordering, it wasn't long before Zachary was digging the medical examiner's report out of his case. They pushed their chairs together so that they could look at it at the same time instead of being across from each other.

"You sure you want to discuss a medical examiner's report over dinner?" Kenzie challenged. "Do you have a strong stomach?"

"I've already been through it. There's nothing too disturbing. It's not bloody."

"Bodies in water bloat up pretty quickly…"

"I've seen the pictures already," Zachary said firmly. "I'm okay with this. Really."

It wasn't until after he said it that he wondered whether she was trying to bow out. He had assumed that she would be perfectly okay with discussing the report over dinner. It had been her idea, after all. She was around the stuff all day, so he wouldn't expect her to be squeamish. But it seemed too late to take his words back.

"That is… unless…"

Kenzie laughed. "No, I'm fine with it. Thanks for asking. Let's go through it, then."

She took the medical examiner's report from his hand and laid it flat on the table, starting in on a lecture on drowning victims, what a medical examiner would expect to find, and what might look different between an accidental drowning and foul play.

"There was no bruising," she pointed out, turning to a page with a series of photos of the body, both front and back. "If you're going to hold someone under the water, then even if it's a little child, there's going to be a struggle, and there's going to be bruising."

Zachary nodded. "Okay. No bruising."

"I'm sure you've seen this one on your favorite forensic show on TV. Someone is drowned in their bathroom, and then their body is disposed of in the river. How do you tell they were drowned somewhere else?"

"Analyze the water in the lungs."

"Right. This is the analysis of the lungs. Their weight, showing they were waterlogged. Then an analysis of the pH, the salinity, the diatoms, any particulates..."

"Diatoms?"

"They take a sample of the water in the pond, and a sample of the water in his lungs, and look for diatoms. It's a unique profile. Like fingerprinting."

"Oh." Zachary nodded. He looked at the text of the report. "And they determined that Declan drowned in the pond."

"Right. He couldn't have drowned anywhere else, or the profile of the water in his lungs would have been different."

"Particulates?" Zachary asked, trying to keep track of all that she was saying.

Kenzie pointed to the section in the report. "When someone inhales water, they also inhale whatever else is in the water. Silt, bugs, plant life..."

"Okay. Right. So that goes back to the pond as well, demonstrating that he drowned there."

"Yes."

"But why so much time spent on tying him to the pond? He was found floating face down in it. Isn't all that already established?"

"We have to double-check everything. Assume nothing."

"Right."

"The next few pages are blood tests..." Kenzie leaned closer to show Zachary. He could feel the heat of her body, and focused for the first time on the black knit dress she was wearing, which clung to her in all the right places. He could smell her scent and his own deodorant as he started to sweat.

Their waiter returned with their steaks, carrying them over on sizzling hot plates.

"Whoops, make some room, folks. Hot plates coming through."

Zachary grabbed the medical examiner's report and case off the table so that the waiter could put the plates down.

"Looks great," Kenzie told the waiter. He checked on whether they needed refills, then left them to their dinner.

"The blood tests were all normal?" Zachary asked. "I don't need to check what each measurement means?"

"Everything falls within normal parameters. Nothing suspicious."

Zachary nodded, and they both dug in. For a while, they ate in silence.

"So how far do I go?" Zachary asked. "We review the medical examiner's report. There's nothing suspicious. Everything I do is chargeable. I could interview a million people, and it wouldn't have any effect other than to run up the bill."

"Well..." Kenzie chewed, considering. "Why did the grand-mother hire you?"

"Peace of mind."

"She wants to be sure it was an accident."

"Well... no. She'd rather I found evidence of foul play."

Kenzie's cutlery clattered. She stopped eating and stared at him. "What?"

"She thinks it would ease the mother's guilt if I found evidence that there was a third party involved. She wouldn't have to blame herself for letting Declan wander off under her watch."

"Hmm."

Kenzie ate. Zachary paid attention to his own meal.

"I think, either way, they get some peace of mind," Kenzie said after a while. She was still chewing on her steak and potatoes.

"They either get reassurance that there wasn't any foul play, little Declan didn't suffer at anyone's hands, he just slipped away in a few moments. Or they get to let go of a little of the guilt. If there was a mysterious third party involved, then they weren't negligent. There was nothing more they could have done to protect him."

"You think they're going to be happy with the results either way?"

"I can't say anything for sure. What do I know? I think that it was such a shock to them, they're having a hard time accepting it. When something happens out of the blue like that... a healthy kid one minute, and then the next he's gone... they want to believe it's not true. Somebody made a mistake. You see it on TV all the time, cold cases, reversal, someone on death row who was completely innocent... It's part of our culture. So, they're looking for that 'oh, we were wrong.'"

"Could be." Zachary cut pieces from his steak and chewed the tender beef slowly. "I think you're right about the shock. They're all a little... removed from reality. Stuck in disbelief."

She nodded her understanding. "You can understand where they're coming from. It's pretty tough to lose a kid like that. You want to blame someone. Whether it's a stranger, or the police investigation, or the medical examiner. Someone to blame."

"Yeah. Maybe so. As long as they don't blame me."

"As long as they pay you, who cares? Maybe you can offer it as a service. Scapegoat for hire."

Zachary chuckled. Kenzie had some twisted sense of humor.

"Since we can't read the report while we're eating, why don't you tell me about yourself? Have you been a private investigator for long? What made you go into it?"

"My interest in photography, for one. And TV. I grew up on detective shows."

"And is it like you thought it would be?"

Zachary snorted. "I don't carry a gun. I don't break into people's houses. I don't chase down murderers every week. A lot of it is tedious desk work, but yeah, I still enjoy it. I like teasing out all the evidence and solving the puzzle. Although most of what I do isn't that puzzling... husbands and wives cheating on each other, routine background checks, that kind of thing. I don't always get something that I can dig my teeth into."

"Do you come from a big family? Lots of brothers and sisters?"

Zachary was taken aback and immediately on guard. "What does that have to do with anything?"

Kenzie's eyes flashed up from her steak to his face in surprise. "I'm wondering about your background. What makes you tick. It was just a question."

"I don't..." He had been about to say that he didn't want to talk about his past, but that would just send up flares that there was something to talk about. "I don't have any siblings."

"Only child?"

"Well, yes."

"Were you spoiled?" Her eyes were dancing. "I'll bet you were spoiled."

"No. My parents... I lost them when I was young."

"Oh." She blinked and recomposed her face. "I'm so sorry. That was a tactless thing to say."

"You didn't know."

She ate in silence, her cheeks noticeably pink even in the dimness of the room.

"How about you?" Zachary asked. "You have to tell me about yourself. How did you get into the medical examiner's office? I hear people are dying to get in there."

"Oh," Kenzie groaned and kicked him under the table. "You did not just say that!"

"What? It was an accident. I didn't mean that..."

She laughed and shook her head. "You are an enigma, Zachary Goldberg! I always loved science in school. I was fascinated when we did dissections. Couldn't get enough of it. While the boys were horsing around, throwing frog intestines at each other, and the girls were pretending to throw up or faint, I was enthralled. I mean, there I was, for the first time, actually seeing an animal's organs. I'd always understood they were there, and what they did, but I was actually seeing them and holding them in my hands. It wasn't abstract anymore."

"And that's when you decided you wanted to be a death doctor when you grew up"

"It was either that or a serial killer. I thought I'd make more as a doctor."

Zachary laughed. As long as the spotlight wasn't on him, he could have a lot of fun with Kenzie. She was fun and pleasant to be with. "So, are you on your way to becoming a full-fledged medical examiner? I mean… I'm not sure what your training is or what your duties are now."

"I've still got a little way to go yet. It's like… an apprenticeship. I get to work with a brilliant doctor, get some practical experience while I'm doing my schooling. It works for me."

"And do you have family around here?" He was careful to phrase it as a casual question about her family and let her fill in the details, rather than putting her on the spot as she had done with him.

"My parents are about a three-hour drive away. Close enough to get there if they need me, or I need something from them. Far enough away to be independent. So that they don't call me about every little thing, and vice versa."

"Sounds good."

"I *am* an only child." She offered it up, knowing that he wasn't going to ask.

"Spoiled?"

"Not as much as you'd think."

Zachary's steak was gone. He sat back, having a sip of beer and thinking about his case.

"Parents don't always spoil their children, even if they only have one child."

"No, of course not."

"I don't think Declan was spoiled."

Kenzie nodded gravely. "Do you think they were strict with him?"

"Not strict..." Zachary made a face, trying to think of how to phrase it. "Well, maybe strict, but not big disciplinarians. They both have OCD, so there were probably a lot of rules. Things that they wouldn't let slide that a *normal* parent—"

"Neurotypical," Kenzie corrected.

"I think they were probably different than neurotypical parents. And I don't think they were that... *close* to him."

"Well..." She scraped at the gravy and mushrooms left on her plate. "Not all parents are as closely bonded to their children as you would expect. Though sometimes, it's just that they don't show it well. Not all parents are demonstrative."

"Maybe that's it. They act like they cared for him, but it feels funny. More removed."

"That's something you should probably consider."

He raised his eyes to hers. "You think..."

"I don't think anything, but if you're getting a funny feeling about it, you should follow your instincts. See if it leads anywhere."

"Yeah. Okay."

While Zachary was considering whether they should have coffee, or whether he should ask Kenzie if she wanted dessert— maybe they should share one—a group of men and women in fancy dress went to the front of the restaurant and gathered around a microphone. Zachary's heart sank.

"We should go," he suggested. "We're not going to be able to talk over that—"

"No, no," Kenzie protested as they started singing. "I love carolers! They always put me into such a Christmas spirit."

Zachary tried to signal to the waiter for the bill. He needed to get out of there. Kenzie watched the carolers, enthralled. She barely noticed Zachary getting the bill and paying it. Zachary tapped on her arm. "We can go now, Kenzie..."

She looked at him, startled. She took in the fact that he had paid the bill and was rising to his feet, eager to get out of there.

"What's your hurry, Zach? Relax for a few minutes and listen to the Christmas songs."

"I really... I really need to go, Kenzie."

"What's wrong? You didn't seem like you were in any hurry before. Where do you need to go?"

"Out of here." He knew his voice was angry, the words bitten off, but he couldn't explain it to her. He couldn't put it into words.

"The music isn't that bad," she laughed. Then she studied him more closely. "*Is* it the music? Is it some sensory thing?"

He made a gesture toward the door. Kenzie got up, and without any further protest, led the way to the coat check where they retrieved their winter gear.

Zachary breathed a sigh of relief. The door closed behind them, blocking out any residual sounds of the music. Kenzie took his hand, watching his face.

"Better?"

Zachary took a few more deep breaths and nodded.

"What was that? Sensory overload? Flashback? Can you explain it to me?"

"No... I just... don't like Christmas."

"You don't like Christmas."

"No."

"So, Christmas songs, decorations, movies, cookies, you avoid all of that?"

"Pretty much, yeah," Zachary gave a little grimace. "Sorry, I didn't know they did that here, or we could have gone somewhere else."

"Somewhere else where you might not accidentally hear Christmas music."

"Uh-huh." His face was hot, and he was sure it was bright red, but maybe she couldn't tell in the darkness.

"And where does this pathological fear of Christmas come from?"

"I'm not afraid of it. I just…"

"That was more than just not liking Christmas songs. I saw your face."

Zachary looked away from her, trying to put some distance between himself and the emotions. "Can I take you home? Or do you want to go somewhere for a coffee?"

Kenzie was staring at him, not ready to let it go.

"It's just a bad time of year for me," Zachary said. "I'm sorry. It doesn't have to ruin our night, does it? Let me take you for ice cream."

"Ice cream?"

He could see their breaths as they talked. The cold wind was cutting through his jacket and biting his cheeks.

"Uh—hot chocolate?" he amended.

Kenzie laughed, and after a moment of consideration took him by the arm.

6

Dave Halloran was the producer of *The Happy Artist*. He was a large man, balding, with a florid complexion, who always seemed to be panting and trying to keep up with some unseen race. Zachary had talked to him on the phone, and while Halloran seemed reluctant to meet with him, he eventually agreed when Zachary repeated that he had been hired by *The Happy Artist*'s family, and she wanted him to interview everyone.

In reality, he wasn't sure how Isabella would feel about him interviewing her coworkers. Zachary's employer was Isabella's mother, not Isabella, and the scope of his job was to investigate all avenues to help put Isabella's mind at ease and help her to avoid a breakdown.

He could justify it to Isabella. If any of her coworkers were jealous of her, they might want to harm her through her son. Therefore, he had to talk to them. But he didn't think that was really the case. She was their bread and butter, and if she had a breakdown, the show would be canceled. What he wanted was their take on Isabella herself. How she had behaved since her son's disappearance and death compared with how she had behaved before.

Zachary looked around the room as he sat down. A small

office, considering that the producer was the top man on the network's most popular show. It looked more like the size of an accounting student's office than a big-shot TV producer's. There was paper everywhere, reminding him vaguely of Isabella's studio. Binders lined up on top of filing cabinets, stacks of paper and scripts in piles on his desk, a colorful wall calendar so filled with symbols, arrows, and squiggles that it might as well have been written in Greek. There were framed pictures, certificates, and awards plastering the walls.

"We're all very sorry for what happened to Isabella," Halloran said tentatively.

"It's tragic," Zachary agreed. "And from what I understand from Isabella's mother, she has changed since her son's death."

Halloran's eyes were hooded. "I suppose."

"Is that not accurate?"

"I really don't feel comfortable talking about Isabella behind her back."

"This investigation is for her benefit."

"Still…"

"Isabella's mother is very concerned for her welfare. If something was to happen to her…"

Something changed in Halloran's face. "You don't think she would do anything… to harm herself… do you?"

"I've met Isabella once. You're the one who has known her for several years, who sees her almost on a daily basis. You tell me. What would happen to your viewership if you lost *The Happy Artist*?"

Halloran's ruddy complexion drained of color. When he spoke, his tone was flat, but that didn't fool Zachary, who was more interested in the nonverbal indicators. "Of course, that would be bad for the network, but we do have insurance in such cases, which would give us some protection while we changed our line-up…"

Zachary stared at the pictures and awards on Halloran's wall, considering his approach.

"Well then, I suppose there's no point in staying around here arguing. I'll let Molly and Isabella know that you were not comfortable in helping us. They'll have to look elsewhere for assistance." He printed in his notebook slowly and deliberately: *Halloran did it.*

Zachary was sure that Halloran was in no position to see what it was that Zachary was writing. It was the implication that Zachary had gained insight from the fact that Halloran wouldn't help him that was important. It was the pantomime that was meant to have an effect. He might just as well have written *The Cat in the Hat*, but there was a one in a million chance that Halloran's subconscious could tell what Zachary was writing from the movements of his pen or the sound of the scratches on the paper. Or there might be a reflection or surveillance camera of which Zachary was unaware. If there was any chance that Halloran could guess at what he had written, consciously or unconsciously, Zachary didn't want it to be nonsense. He wanted it to be an accusation.

"No, no, I didn't say I wouldn't help," Halloran protested quickly, taking the bait. "I'm just... having difficulty reconciling how any of this is going to help our Isabella."

"You leave that part to me. I've done my best to explain it to you, but I can't tell you everything I know."

Halloran vigorously scratched the top of his bald head, scowling.

"Isabella has always been a little... flighty. She has an artist's disposition. They're not always the easiest of people to work with. She takes offense or gets put off. Or something is wrong, and she gets preoccupied with it. Not because she's a prima donna, she just... gets stuck when things aren't right. The wrong kind of water. Someone gets the wrong shade of paint or the wrong shape of brush. She gets all bent out of shape over it. That's just the way it is when you're dealing with artistic temperaments. Actors are just as bad, or worse."

"Sure," Zachary nodded. "Just because she's brilliant and

comes off as happy and friendly on the screen, that doesn't mean that's how she is in private."

"That damn title," Halloran snapped. "Why did we have to call it *The Happy Artist*? Practically doomed it to failure."

"Because you can't exactly have your happy artist in mourning on screen."

He nodded. "And let me tell you, happy she is not."

"She just lost her only child. Who could expect her to be?"

"She didn't *just* lose him. It was months ago."

"And you expected her to be over it by now?"

"Not exactly... but she wasn't the motherly type. She didn't talk about him all the time and post his crayon drawings in her dressing room. She barely mentioned her family." At Zachary's look, he shook his head. "Maybe she was just the private type. Maybe she was all kisses and cuddles at home. I have no way of knowing, but we do have a contract. She's required to be here and to fulfill the terms of her contract. Even before this happened, I wouldn't say she was happy. Off screen. There was always some problem."

"Did she rub anyone the wrong way? Was there anyone in particular who was bothered by her moodiness?"

"*Was* there?" Halloran repeated. "You mean before her son died? You're asking if anyone had a motive to kill her child because they didn't like the way she behaved on set?"

"I'm just exploring the possibilities."

"You can put that one right out of your mind. She was annoying, but no one wanted to destroy her. No one would kill her child just to stop her from showing up for work."

Zachary nodded. He hadn't expected the line of questioning to lead anywhere. "Still, was there anyone who was particularly irritated by her? Or jealous of her success? What would you have done if she had been unable to continue her show?"

"We would have had to change the lineup. I can't be sure who we would have put in her place. We would have needed something new; we didn't have anything that would have the same success in that time slot as *The Happy Artist.*"

"Is there anyone who might have thought that they would get it?"

"I'm sure that all the other shows thought they were as good as she was or had the same draw, but one over another... no. Sorry."

"Do you have a list of the other shows...?"

"You can pull that online. There's nothing confidential about the line-up."

But that didn't stop him from being obstructive. Zachary leaned back in his chair, trying to give Halloran the impression that he was calm and relaxed, finished with the serious questioning.

"How has she been since her son's death? Any... unusual or concerning behavior?"

"She was always eccentric, but since then, things have gotten a little out of hand. That tattoo, all her memorial jewelry... I had a hell of a time talking her into taking off the jewelry when she is on screen. She can wear the ring and one of the necklaces. Not the one with the teeth!"

Zachary suppressed a snort of laughter. He could just see Isabella wearing that one during the show.

"She does not appreciate being told that she has to cover up her tattoo during the show. Can you imagine how distracting that would be? We have to show close-ups of her hands to show technique. Lots of zooming in, and that great big tattoo on her arm! The viewers wouldn't see anything else. Why couldn't she just do something small and tasteful in a part of her body that wouldn't be on the screen? Her ankle. We never show her ankles."

"Was there anything in her contract that said she couldn't get a tattoo?"

"No, but we have the right to make wardrobe and makeup choices, and covering up the tattoo falls into wardrobe, so she has to suck it up."

"And has she?"

"There was trouble over it the first few days, but she's gotten used to it now."

"I gather she can be pretty stubborn."

"Stubborn doesn't even begin to describe it. We've had to have her therapist on site a few times to figure out how to get past her emotional issues."

Zachary raised an eyebrow. "Before or after the accident?"

"Both. More often when we first started the show. Then things settled into a routine, and she does well if everything is routine. It's when something has to change that there's a problem."

"Right. That makes sense."

"Is that everything, then?" Halloran demanded. "I really do have to get back to work here." He made a gesture to take in all the piles of paperwork on his desk.

Zachary nodded. "I'll be in touch." He started to rise from his chair.

"She can't paint blue," Halloran said suddenly.

Zachary froze halfway out of his chair, then sat back down. "What?"

"Since her son died, she can't paint blue anymore. We've had her therapist in, and we're working on it, but it's damn inconvenient. What do you do with an artist who can't paint the color blue?"

"What *do* you do?"

"We can't put blue on her palette, but we can put purple or green. Each time we film, we put a little less red and yellow in those blends, trying to work back to pure blue. But the woman can't paint blue skies or water. When you've got an artist, who is famous for painting landscapes, and she can no longer paint blue skies or water..."

"But you can't fire her for that."

"No. Of course not. That would be discrimination against the mentally ill. We have to find landscapes that don't include blue. Sunrise and sunset. Trees inside a forest, with no view of the sky.

We've started throwing in some portraits and still lifes, even though that's not her thing."

"Nobody with blue eyes."

Halloran nodded. "Nobody with blue eyes. Combine that with trying to edit out her verbal tics…"

Zachary raised his brows. "Her tics…?"

"You've talked to her?"

"Yes."

"She didn't repeat a prayer when she was talking to you? For her son?"

"Oh." Zachary nodded. "May he hold you in the hollow of his hand."

"That's the one. We can't have her saying that every two minutes in the show. It has to be edited out. Every single time. She isn't even religious. I think she's an atheist!"

Zachary wrote a few notes in his notepad. "You would say that her behavior has changed since her son died and that you have concerns about her mental stability."

"That better not get out to the press."

"No, I'm not talking to anybody about it, just making an observation. I wondered whether you shared any of Molly's concerns, and it would appear that you do."

Halloran wrung his hands together briefly. "I hadn't realized how much we have been accommodating her the last few months. Yes, we're all concerned. If this show was to tank because of her mental instability…" He shook his head. "It would be very bad for the network."

Zachary pondered the information he had gleaned from Halloran and the few network employees he had managed to talk to as he scrolled through lengthy Facebook feeds and other social network sites, compiling background on his latest targets of interest.

Isabella's inability to paint the color blue was intriguing. The first thing that came to mind was that blue was the color to signify the birth of a baby boy. Even as they grew up, pink was for girls and blue was for boys. Neither color was exclusive, of course, and gender norms were changing too rapidly to keep track of it all, but in his mind, and in the minds of his generation and older, blue was for boys. Declan's room was decorated in shades of blue and Isabella had said that she would never redecorate or repurpose his room. She intended to keep it just as it was. She must have associated her son with the color blue, and that was what prevented her from painting with it.

He had observed the verbal tic without realizing what it was. While annoying, the repetition of the little prayer was appropriate. For someone who was religious, but for someone who was an atheist, or close to it, it was just one more indicator of how deeply she was suffering from the overwhelming pain and guilt at the death of her son.

Zachary's mind went to his own family, and suddenly he was no longer able to see the screen. He stopped scrolling. For a few seconds, or perhaps longer, all he could do was sit there, with old memories and impressions washing over him, holding him paralyzed. His heart thudded dully in his chest, each beat painful. Why, after all that had happened, was *he* still alive, still carrying on as if he were a normal person?

He remembered the word that Kenzie had suggested. Not normal, but neurotypical. He liked the flavor of the word. It pathologized people with normal brain patterns, the same way that people with normal brain patterns had been pathologizing the atypicals for hundreds of years.

Thinking this through helped to take him away from the memories. He was able to break out of the clutches of the past and look at his screen once more.

After checking through the feeds of his current subjects of investigation, he searched for Spencer's and Isabella's accounts. Unsurprisingly, Spencer's was sparse. Maybe Isabella had set it up for him, as he didn't seem the type who would normally use it himself. Facebook was too messy for someone as tidy and orderly as Spencer.

Isabella had a couple of accounts. She had a personal account. He could see Molly and Spencer on her friends list, but mostly, names and faces of people he didn't know, who had nothing to do with the case. She also had a fan page for *The Happy Artist*. He didn't know whether she had set it up and answered fan queries herself. Chances were, it had been set up by the network, and they were the ones managing it. There were fans sending their condolences, but mostly it was excitement and discussion over her latest shows. The accident had taken place months ago; it was no longer in the public's awareness.

Isabella's personal account, however, was another story. She tended to post Madonna-like woman and child pictures and memes about grief and loss. Zachary saw that Spencer had posted a number of these somber posts onto Isabella's timeline. No jokes and cute kittens for the couple. They were obviously still deep in the grieving process.

The phone rang, and Zachary picked it up without looking at the caller ID.

"Goldman Investigations."

"Mr. Goldman, this is Eugene Taft's assistant? We talked before? I told you I would call you?"

"Yes," Zachary agreed.

"If you would like to come down to the police station, you will be given access to the Bond accident investigation file. You won't be able to make any copies or take anything with you, but you can make notes for your case."

"Great. Will that be available today, or do I need to wait for it to be pulled from storage somewhere?"

"We've already pulled it for you. You can come down anytime."

"Perfect. I'll be down to see it soon."

"You'll need to sign a confidentiality agreement. The information on the files is only to be used in your own investigation, to verify the results of the accident investigation to the family. You are not, under any circumstances, to speak to the media or release any information to them. The police force always has to be sure to keep the details of a death out of the public eye, so that they can be sure of who has legitimate information and who might just be repeating information the police already have and trying to pass themselves off as knowing them first-hand."

Zachary turned this over in his mind. He took a sip of his cold, bitter coffee. "Does that mean the police force had doubts in this case? That there were details held back from the public that would only be known to someone who was there on the scene when it happened?"

"I don't know anything about the specifics of this case. I am speaking in general terms."

"You don't know if they had any suspicions about a third party being involved."

"No, I don't know anything about it," she repeated.

Zachary hung up the phone, still wondering whether she was telling the truth or trying to give him a heads-up.

Spencer looked surprised when he answered the door and found Zachary on his doorstep once again. He stood there looking at Zachary.

"I didn't know you were coming by again, Mr. Goldman."

"Zachary."

"Zachary. Did you find something out? Something of significance?"

Zachary thought back to poring over the police records. All the handwritten notes, pictures, and bits of scribbles. He wished that he could put his finger on one piece of evidence and say, 'here it is, this is what the police missed.' But so far, he was just seeing the same routine information pointing to an accident. No evidence of foul play. No one who wanted to hurt either Isabella or Spencer by hurting their child. There were lists of the registered sex offenders in the area with notations or brief interviews beside each name. Alibis. No one had seen any of them around the Bond home or near Declan. None of them had done any work there.

"No, I haven't found anything out. I just wanted to speak with you and Isabella again, now that I have a bit more information. Just a few additional questions."

Spencer didn't answer immediately, then gave a sigh and stepped back to allow Zachary in. They went back to Spencer's office as before and took their seats.

"I don't know what else I can tell you," Spencer warned. "I wasn't the one supervising Declan when he disappeared. I don't know anything except that he was in our yard, and then he drowned in the pond."

"I understand. How has Isabella been doing?"

Spencer shook his head. "You were here. You saw her."

"I did, but I don't think I'm getting the full picture. I think there is a lot more going on than I can see. Than anyone who doesn't live here would see."

"Of course... that's true of anyone."

"I talked to Isabella's producer and some of her coworkers."

"Yes...?"

"Were you aware that she can't or won't paint the color blue?"

"No. I don't have anything to do with her painting. Why, what does that have to do with anything?"

Zachary found it hard to believe that he wouldn't know even that little bit of information about his wife's painting. Wouldn't it have come up in conversation? "Does the color blue have any significance for Isabella that you are aware of?"

"Blue." Spencer looked at him blankly. "No. Why?"

"I'm just wondering if it has something to do with the case. Maybe she associates it with something. It could be a clue to what happened to Declan."

"No. Compulsions don't really work that way. They aren't logical or symbolic."

"Sometimes they can be traced back to a particular trigger," Zachary pointed out.

Spencer cocked his head, and his eyes narrowed at Zachary. "What would you know about that?"

"It's true, isn't it?"

"Sometimes... but not always; and as far as Isabella not being able to paint the color blue... no, I don't think it has any significance at all. It's just one of those bizarre things."

"What is it that concerns you the most about Isabella right now? Is there anything that worries you?"

"The praying gets on my nerves more than anything. I've gotten used to her... messiness... the way that she collects things... but that same prayer over and over again, it grates on my nerves."

Zachary nodded. "I can see how it would. She's doing it a lot, then?"

"Compulsions are something that you can suppress for a little while by exercising self-control. I can sit here and not clean my hands again, probably for the whole time you are here. Or if I have to go to an outside meeting; but eventually, the urge becomes overwhelming, and I have to act."

Zachary nodded. "And her praying?"

"She can stop while you are here. For a while. As soon as you are gone, she'll start up again."

"Her boss said that they were working with her therapist. Has he come here too? Does he make suggestions of things that you and she can do to address her issues?"

"He's never been here. That's the first I've heard of him going to her work. We are private people, Mr. Goldman. We don't like putting ourselves on display."

Spencer didn't, perhaps, but Isabella did. Every week.

"Is there anything that would help Isabella? Her mother hoped that if I found something, it would alleviate her guilt and help her to recover. What do you think?"

"I don't think this is doing her any good." Spencer shook his head. "I think she needs quiet. Not to be disturbed by people like you and by the network. Just give her some time by herself to sort it all through."

"I see."

"We have a couple of friends who are moving back to town. The Raymonds. I'm hoping that seeing them again, having a girl-friend she can talk to… maybe that will help. They moved to New York seven or eight years ago, and we haven't really seen them since. Maybe they can bring back memories of what it was like before we had Declan. We—she—was happier then."

"She doesn't have many friends that she can talk to?"

"No. It's not easy for someone like Isabella to make friends. She's so emotional, and she lets herself get caught up in her compulsions. People want you to be normal."

"Neurotypical," Zachary suggested.

"Normal," Spencer repeated.

"Okay. Is there anything else? Have you thought any more about what happened the day your son disappeared? Anything at all."

"I've told you all I know."

"Maybe you could outline what a typical day was like around here. For Declan."

Spencer made an irritated noise in the back of his throat and shook his head.

"He would get up in the morning on his own without being wakened. If Isabella was working, he would come find me, and we would have breakfast together. I would play with him, maybe read with him. Then he would play quietly until lunch. I would make sandwiches for us both. Turn on one of his cartoons, and he would fall asleep. When Isabella got home, she would wake him up and do something with him."

He stopped and looked at Zachary.

"And after that?"

"That's when he disappeared," Spencer said. "His day didn't go any further than that."

"But on a regular day, what would happen after Isabella played with him?"

"Our supper hour was pretty early. Then I would take Deck for his bath and get him ready for bed. We would read stories. Maybe watch a TV show. Then he would fall asleep around eight."

"That all sounds pretty... quiet. He didn't get rowdy and noisy? Get into things when he was supposed to be entertaining himself? Argue or cry?"

Spencer scowled, scratching the back of his neck. "Of course. Those are all normal child things. You asked what a typical schedule was. That's what I gave you. But he wasn't a trained dog; he had a mind of his own."

"So, he would disobey."

"Yes."

"Did he ever leave the yard before when he knew he wasn't supposed to?"

"No, never."

"I want you to think about it," Zachary insisted. "He never tried to reach the latch? Never climbed the fence to get a ball that he threw out of the yard?"

Spencer considered these scenarios, actually thinking instead of just answering defensively. "He was a pretty quiet child. Not like some of the little demons you see around here. He usually tried to do what he was told."

Zachary waited for him to work through his answer.

"There was one day when I couldn't see him in the yard. When I went out to look and see what he was doing, he was talking to a woman over the gate. Not the back gate, the one to the front." Spencer made a motion to the side of the house where it could be found, out of sight of his windows.

"Ah. So how did you react to that? What did you tell him?"

"First, I told the woman off for talking to him. Kids may not know better than to talk to strangers, but adults should know better than to approach children who don't know them."

"How did she react?"

"She was angry and defensive. She said he talked to her, and she just stopped to answer him because he was so cute."

"And then you told Declan…?"

"I told him he had to stay in the back where I could see him. Not out of sight of the windows. And that he wasn't supposed to talk to adults who came up to the house. If someone came up to him, he should come inside and get one of us."

"How long was that before his disappearance?"

Spencer rubbed the center of his forehead, thinking about it. "It's hard to say. I don't remember that clearly. Maybe it was a few weeks or a couple of months."

"Did you ever see the woman again?"

"No. Not someone I ever saw again."

"Did you tell Isabella about it?"

"Hm… Yes, I think I did. Just so she would be aware that part of the yard was out of view of the windows, and she should make sure Deck didn't go over there… if he was out of sight, she should check there and make sure someone wasn't trying to talk to him."

"And did she do that the day he disappeared? Did she go outside and check that part of the yard?"

"Yes, of course. So did I. We both checked every inch of the back yard. It was obvious he wasn't there."

"The police didn't find any helpful footprints."

"No. They didn't find much of anything," Spencer agreed.

"Did it surprise you that there wasn't a clear trail to follow?"

"No. Conditions that day… it was pretty dry. It had been for a while. The ground was hard and dusty. Declan wasn't heavy enough to leave a trail to follow."

"And there were no footprints from a third party. No one who shouldn't have been there."

"No." Spencer shook his head. "He just wandered off, Mr.—Zachary. Maybe somebody had been in the yard and left the gate open. Somebody looking for bottles or something worth stealing. Or the woman who talked to him that day, to get back at us for being such rotten parents, in her eyes. Or maybe it didn't latch securely when I took the garbage out because the wind caught it and kept it open. But he just wandered out. He wandered out, and he drowned, just like a hundred other kids."

"Is that what you hope happened?"

"Yes. I'd rather not think there was someone out there who took him to hurt us. Or intending to hurt him. The police didn't think there was anyone else involved. I just want to let him rest."

Zachary thought about Isabella's jewelry, all the parts of Declan that she wore on her body and her skin. She hadn't been able to lay her child to rest. Zachary couldn't think of anything less restful than dangling in Isabella's constantly moving layers of jewelry.

"Okay." Zachary nodded. "Thank you for your time. I'll let you know if I have any other questions. Feel free to call me if anything occurs to you."

"I'd rather you called before showing up here."

Zachary didn't apologize for the surprise visit. Sometimes, it was helpful to catch people off-balance. He stood.

"And, Zachary..."

He raised an eyebrow at Spencer and waited.

"I do worry about my wife. Quite a bit. I'm hopeful that having the Raymonds back in town will have a positive effect... distract her from her grief and give her someone to talk to. Because..." His lips pressed together. "I don't know how much longer she can go on like this."

7

Zachary recognized the phone number that popped up on his call display and smiled.

"Hi, Kenzie."

"Hey, just thought I'd call and check in on my new PI buddy."

"I'm glad you called. I wouldn't mind having someone to discuss this case with…"

Zachary didn't need someone to talk it over with, but it was the first thing that came to mind. And he wasn't lying; he wouldn't mind discussing it with her.

"Oh, yeah?" Kenzie asked brightly. "How about I treat you to a sandwich at *It's a Wrap*. I love their artisan breads."

He hesitated. It wasn't that he didn't like them too, but it was Bridget's favorite sandwich shop, and he didn't want to risk running into any of her friends there. What were the odds that any of them would approach him? They would all be on her side and wouldn't have anything to say to him.

"Yeah, sure. That sounds great," he agreed. "We could get a booth for a little privacy…"

"Perfect. We should probably hit it early, before the lunch crowd. Do you mind meeting at eleven?"

"Works for me. You're not working today?"

"No, I have a doctor's appointment today and just took the full day off. I'm free until two-thirty."

"Doctor's appointment? Anything wrong?"

"No, it's nothing. I'll see you there? At eleven?"

"I'll be there."

Zachary hung up his phone and decided he'd better shower and shave to make himself presentable. No point in showing up looking like some homeless guy. The look might help him blend in with a crowd while on a job since people didn't want to look at the less fortunate, but it wouldn't work for a date.

He again made sure he was at the restaurant before Kenzie, cornering a booth for them. She wasn't far behind him. They gave the server their orders and exchanged some pleasantries.

"Did you really have some questions about the case?" Kenzie asked, raising one brow mischievously.

"Well... not so much that I had questions, I just thought it would be nice to talk through some of the details."

She nodded. "Sure."

"You said that one of the signs of drowning is bruising. From holding the victim down."

"Right."

"The boy did have bruises."

She shook her head. "Not that were typical of drowning. Did you bring it with you?"

Zachary dug the report out of his bag and slid it across to her. She turned quickly to the appropriate page. "Shins and knees, elbows. All typical of little boys—and girls—in their regular play. He had several bruises, and they were different ages. Fell down one day. Walked into a coffee table another. Skinned elbows on a trampoline a couple of days later. All kids have those kinds of bruises. If he had been drowned, we would expect to see bruises on his neck or back. Those are the kind of bruises a drowning victim gets."

"Ah." Zachary nodded. He hadn't been too concerned about the bruises. He had thought that they looked pretty innocuous, but he wouldn't know without asking. There could have been something atypical there that he simply hadn't been able to see.

"Now what about the nail scrapings?" he asked. "We didn't get time to talk about those before. Why did they do nail scrapings? Are they looking for DNA? Seeing if he tried to fight back against an attacker?"

"Sure. That's part of it. Skin under the nails is always a big red flag. Sometimes you can find other evidence as well. It's like a mini archeological dig." She flipped through the pages and worked her way down the list of what they found under Declan's nails. "The victim had soil under his nails, consistent with what was in his yard, not around the pond. He had no foreign DNA under his nails, so, no, he didn't fight off an attacker. He had a mixture of oil and mineral pigments... oh!" She laughed. "Paint, of course. An oil-based paint. Mostly green."

"Paint." Zachary mulled it over, wondering if it was significant. "I guess as the child of a painter, that shouldn't come as any great shock. He must have been around his mother's work. Probably instructed by her and encouraged to produce his own paintings as well."

"I would think so."

Kenzie continued to flip aimlessly through the medical examiner's report, looking for anything else of interest. "Was he autistic?"

"No. Not that anyone has said. Why? What's in there that would make you think—"

"Don't get excited. It's not anything I saw. I just wondered because a lot of the children who are attracted to water and drown have autism. I don't know any real stats. Just that it seems like a high percentage."

"No, he wasn't autistic. From what the family tells me, he didn't even like the water. He'd avoid it when he could. I wondered whether there were steep or crumbling banks, and he fell in by accident before he even saw it, but I saw the police photos yesterday, and it had pretty shallow banks. To drown in it, he would have had to walk right into it."

Kenzie frowned. "Pretty unlikely if he was afraid of water."

"It's the only argument against it being an accident that I've come across yet. I know that kids can drown in a very small amount of water... but to drown in the pond, he had to actually be in it. A kid doesn't just lie down on the shore and stick his face into two inches of water. And his body was found floating in the pond. He had to walk out into it."

He hadn't put the thought into words before. Kenzie frowned, and Zachary felt a chill. Was Molly right? *Had* a third party drowned the child?

The server brought them their sandwiches, and for a few minutes, they both just ate, enjoying the fresh, crusty bread and thinking over the problem.

"Maybe there was a dog or something else that attracted his attention," Zachary said. "His father said he loves dogs. If he saw one swimming in the pond and thought it was in trouble, or just wanted to see it or pat it... who knows? He could have been trying to retrieve a ball or a Frisbee."

"None were found at the crime scene. Could have been an animal, even a fish near the surface and he thought he could grab it. If he was afraid of water, then presumably he couldn't swim."

"I would guess not."

Zachary's eyes caught on a man walking toward him. A big, broad man with the physique of a halfback. His face broke into a smile when he recognized Zachary.

"Look who's here! Zach, my man! It's been too long! How the hell are you?" He reached out his hand to take Zachary's, but Zachary's attention was caught by the thin blonde woman behind him. He froze, not taking Joseph Reichler's hand, not saying anything, his brain seizing up in his panic at seeing her there.

His own reaction was mirrored by Bridget. She swore when she saw him.

"What are you doing here?" she demanded. As if it was obviously her place and Zachary had no right to be there.

Joseph was turning to look at Bridget with dawning comprehension, realizing belatedly that she and Zachary had a history and might not want to run into each other in such a public place. "Oh, ah, Bridge..."

Kenzie stared from one of them to the other, waiting for someone to explain to her what was going on. A server came over, and blithely blind to their expressions and body language, asked whether they would like to be seated together.

"Maybe we should go somewhere else," Joseph said weakly. "I didn't mean to..."

"I'm not going anywhere else," Bridget insisted as if she owned the place. Like she got her favorite sandwich shop in the divorce. Like she had the right to demand that he vacate immediately. Zachary looked down at his half-eaten sandwich, no longer hungry. The first half sat in his stomach like a bowling ball. He looked at Kenzie, wanting to suggest that they leave.

Instead, Kenzie stuck out her hand toward Bridget and introduced herself. "Kenzie Kirsch. You must be..."

Bridget looked down at Kenzie, her face flushing pink. She was practically quivering with indignation. "Don't you be taken in by him," she warned. "Don't be taken in by the whole hurt-puppy, tragic past act. He's impossible to live with, and not fixable. Move on and find one that's whole, instead of wasting your time on this loser. Do you hear me? Do you understand what I'm saying?"

"I hear you." Kenzie's voice was low and clear, unflustered. "And I think maybe you'd better move on."

"*I* should move on?" Bridget was outraged. "Why the hell should I move on? This is..." It seemed to occur to her for the first time that she didn't have an excuse for her behavior. She didn't own the place or have a restraining order on Zachary. He had the right to eat wherever he wanted, with whomever he wanted. "You're a nice-looking girl," she said to Kenzie in a quieter voice. "He always did have a good eye for beauty. Believe me; you do not want to be roped into a relationship with this man. You will do nothing but suffer."

"Thank you for your advice," Kenzie said coolly, as if it happened every day.

Joseph was making apologetic gestures to Zachary, trying to get Bridget to move on and leave him alone. Just to keep walking. They could find another restaurant. There was no reason it had to be the same one as Zachary.

"My old friend," he said to Zachary apologetically. "I'm so sorry. I never meant…"

Zachary jerked his head at Joseph to just go. No apology necessary. If he left, hopefully, Bridget would follow. Joseph backed away, and after a moment of mulishness, Bridget followed him, whispering imprecations the whole way.

Zachary closed his eyes and let out a long sigh. He was afraid to look back at Kenzie, his ears burning. He felt like rushing out the door, but he couldn't end a second date like that or she'd wonder what the heck was wrong with him.

"Your ex, I assume," Kenzie said in amusement.

Zachary gave a hollow laugh and opened his eyes to look at her. "That was only slightly awkward, right?"

"That was classic. I don't think we could have designed a better scene if it had been planned and directed. Congratulations."

"On creating the perfect scene?"

"On getting out of that relationship. Are you telling me you would still want to be together with her?"

Zachary shook his head, but more in confusion than denial. He still loved Bridget, no matter how badly she had treated him. He would have gone back to her if he had thought there were any hope of reconciliation, but there simply wasn't. She was lost to him forever.

"Were you actually married? Or just dating or living together?"

"We were married," he admitted.

"I thought so. That kind of anger doesn't come from just dating. It had to be marriage."

"I don't know what you must think of me. If you want, I can just pay for this now, and we can get out of here..."

"No need for that. I'm perfectly fine where I am. She's gone away, so you can relax. I don't think she'll be coming back. In fact, I don't know if she'll ever be coming back here again. It's always going to remind her of you and how she made a fool of herself now."

"That won't stop her." It wasn't their first scene. It wouldn't be their last. Sooner or later, one of them was going to have to leave town. The only way Zachary was leaving town permanently was in a coffin.

"Relax. Honestly, I'm fine. It was all very entertaining. Tell me all about her and what a witch she is."

"She was the love of my life," Zachary said hopelessly. "We were once so happy. I don't even know where to start. We lived and breathed for each other, but over time... things happened. Feelings were hurt. We had to weather some storms that... most marriages just don't survive. Ours didn't."

"I'm sorry." She lowered the eyes that had been dancing with amusement just a moment before. "Here I am making light of something that was really tragic to you. I didn't mean to make you feel bad."

"You didn't. There's not much that could make me feel worse than that. When I think about how much in love we used to be, and how it could turn into *that*..."

"She's jealous."

"What? She's not jealous. She's angry. She thinks that I... we disagreed on a very important subject... and I think she blames me for what happened to her. She's not jealous of me. She doesn't want anything to do with me."

"I beg to differ." Kenzie reached across the table and put her warm, smooth fingers over his. "I saw her face. She was shocked to see you here, but she didn't get *really* angry until she saw me."

"She can't be jealous. She hates me."

"No, she doesn't. She's angry with you, but she doesn't hate you."

Zachary shook his head. "You only saw her for a few seconds. I've lived with her. I'm the one who has had to live through this disastrous divorce. I know."

"Okay. You know. Let me just say that she has no right to treat you that way, and I'm sorry you had to put up with that crap. You deserve better."

Zachary shook his head. If Kenzie knew all about everything, he was sure she wouldn't say that.

"Don't let her get to you," Kenzie advised.

"Yeah."

"Let's go across the street for dessert. They have these fantastic, chocolate-mousse-filled croissants. They are just to die for. I don't think I can eat a whole one myself, so even if you're not in the mood to eat the rest of your sandwich, you still have to help me with dessert."

Zachary couldn't help but smile at this. Chocolate-mousse-filled croissants sounded like a pretty good solution to his troubles.

Zachary's next step was to develop a map of the area surrounding Isabella's house. The police had done plenty of sketches of the crime scene and the route from the back yard to the pond, but Zachary had something different in mind.

He started with the list of sex offenders that the police had identified and spoken to and pinned each address on a digital map. Then he went to a few other sites to track down houses that had been reported as marijuana growing operations, where violent crimes had been committed, or which had been condemned by the Board of Health. The pins on the map became thicker.

Zachary knew that any other neighborhood would look the same. No one could escape all the sickos.

Once he had his map finished, he would take a drive around the neighborhood, checking out each of the houses in question. Chances were, everything would be quiet, and nothing would seem off. But maybe... maybe someone would object to his surveillance, or a face would be familiar, or someone would act in a way that identified them as a suspect. The police should already have visited most of the houses, just as they had the sex offenders, but there were no notes on the file he had reviewed saying that they had. It was always possible that he would turn up something more.

Checking out all the pinned locations on his map had turned out to be an all-day affair. Zachary had only expected it to take a couple of hours, but he had obviously made his canvassing area too big. He had gone according to the area the police had used for the sex offender canvass, but they had plenty of cops to run them down, and Zachary had only his two feet. At least he didn't need to interview everyone, just to snoop around.

He did end up talking to a few people when he was confronted by homeowners or neighbors who didn't like him sneaking around, but mostly his reconnaissance was ignored. People who wanted to know what he was doing backed off pretty quickly when he explained he was investigating Declan Bond's death. Most of them.

He was footsore and spirit-weary when he got back to his apartment at the end of the day. Second-guessing why he was still investigating the case. Everything pointed toward an accident. There was no malevolent force behind young Declan's death. Just a child who had wandered out of an enclosed yard while his mother's back was turned. Tragic, but there was no one to blame.

Zachary could see from the end of the hall that there was

something taped to his door. His stomach tightened. A notice from the landlord that his rent was going up or they'd had to access his apartment because of a burst pipe? A neighbor who had some complaint about him? He drew up to the door and looked at it.

Drop the investigation.

He stared at the note.

It wasn't the first time he'd been told to back out of a case, but it was usually face-to-face with a lover who had caught on to his surveillance and was furious about it. A couple of times by the police, who felt like he was interfering with one of their cases with an accident reconstruction or interviews with the victims. A note on his door; that was a first.

Zachary tried the handle and found, to his relief, that it was still locked. He had envisioned the scene from a bad TV drama; finding the door unlocked and walking into his apartment to find that it had been tossed, maybe a dead body left in the bathtub or something equally sinister.

He unlocked the door and opened it slowly. It was dark. He turned on the light and scanned the room. He realized he had still been expecting it to be a mess. He was still expecting threats and a body or frame. But the room appeared just as he had left it. A little messy, but nothing seemed to have been touched.

Still, Zachary was nervous as he checked each of the other rooms. Including the bathtub. No body. No planted cocaine. No lipsticked threats on the mirror. No dead rat or horse's head in the bed. His heart thudded. He knew he was letting his imagination get the better of him. It was just a note. There were no threats, no profanity; no letters clipped out of a magazine to form the words.

He went back to lock and bolt the apartment door before searching the fridge for something to eat.

8

Zachary slept restlessly. He woke up several times during the night, listening to the noises of his apartment and the surrounding apartments, worried there was someone there.

But even if the person who had left the note were someone who would consider harming him, they would at least have to wait until the next day to see whether he had dropped the case; whichever case it was. He was irritated that they hadn't said which case he was supposed to drop. Did they think that he only had one case at a time? At least the previous threats had been made in person, so he knew which case they were talking about. It was incredibly annoying to be warned off without knowing what he was being warned off of.

Of course, there had been no threat. Only an instruction. That in itself left him feeling unsettled. Drop the investigation—or what? A threat to his life? To his welfare? Perhaps to the case itself? Or maybe nothing would happen. Maybe the most that the note writer could bring himself to do was to leave the note, and that would be it.

The next morning, Zachary downed two cups of coffee before leaving the apartment. Not something that he would usually do before going on surveillance. He would end up having to make a rest stop by midmorning. He didn't know how long he was going to have to wait before he got his opportunity. Maybe it would be quick.

The familiar yellow VW was parked outside the coffee shop, where he expected it to be, but he didn't dare get out and approach it yet. She would spend only a few minutes inside, depending on how long the line-up was. Then she'd be back out with her to-go mug, heading to work or wherever else she had to go. He found a parking space down the block and watched for her.

It was ten minutes before he saw her blond head bob out of the door, and disappear as she got into the car. He shifted into drive and waited for her to pull out. He envisioned her taking a small sip of her hot coffee and then settling it into the cup holder. Maybe changing the station on the radio before she headed out. Buckling her seatbelt. Turning the key in the ignition. Finally, she was pulling out into traffic.

Zachary let a couple of cars pass him before pulling out, putting a cushion between them so she wouldn't spot him.

She didn't go to work, but made an unexpected turn on Main. Zachary followed, lagging behind as much as possible. He didn't know where she was going until she pulled up to the big, square, brick building. The doctor's office.

It was perfect. She would be gone for a long time. There would be no danger of her walking back out and catching him in the act. Even after she went in, he waited another ten minutes to make sure she hadn't forgotten anything in the car.

As he worked, he thought about Kenzie. She had said that she had a medical appointment. That was why she had taken the day off and met with him for lunch. Was she sick? Of course, it could just be an annual physical. Or an eye check-up or dental visit. It could be a hundred innocuous little things.

After looking around the parking lot for surveillance cameras or anyone watching, Zachary felt under the bumper of the car, looking for a good place.

He hated the thought that Kenzie could be sick. She looked well enough. Pretty and in the peak of health. But then, so had Bridget. Neither of them would have guessed that there was anything wrong. She'd had no symptoms. No weight loss or pallor. She hadn't been tired or nauseated. It was disconcerting to find that someone could be so sick without even realizing it.

There was a smooth, clean ledge under the bumper. Perfect for Zachary's purposes. He used a rag to wipe it down blindly, making sure that there was no layer of dirt and debris that would prevent a good mount.

Kenzie had said that the doctor's appointment was nothing. He was going to have to believe her on that count. There was no way to tell what was going on in her life unless he put her under surveillance too.

Zachary pulled out the small black box. He switched it on and made sure that the green LED lit. Then, resting it on his fingertips, he put his hand under the bumper again and bent his fingers to attached the tracking unit to the ledge. It clinked softly. He nudged it with his fingers, seeing if it would slide or shift. It stayed solidly in place.

He stood up and wiped his hands on the rag. He looked around again to make sure that no one had shown up who might be watching him, wondering what the hell he was up to. There was a mother with a child walking from her car into the building, but she didn't look in his direction. He wondered vaguely if she were sick. Surely there were other kinds of doctors in the professional building as well. A gynecologist or pediatrician. He hoped that neither she nor the child was seriously ill. He hoped that she simply had a routine appointment or checkup.

He went back to his car and sat down before checking the tracking app on his phone to make sure that the GPS tracker was transmitting properly. Now he would have a reliable log of every place she went.

Having taken care of the various surveillance and routine background work that had been languishing on his list, Zachary returned to the medical examiner's report. He had just about decided he was ready to close the case and give Molly his final report. He would confirm that it had, in fact, been an accident and there was no indication of any outside involvement. He hoped that, as Kenzie had suggested, Molly and the family would feel better knowing that there had been no holes in the police investigation and that everything had been properly handled and could be put to bed. Then they could lay Declan to rest. Figuratively speaking, since his remains were still dangling and swaying restlessly in Isabella's numerous necklaces and injected into her skin.

Kenzie had said everything in the blood tests had been within normal parameters, but as Zachary read every line of fine print, he could feel his brows coming down. How could anyone who had read the blood test results have come to that conclusion?

Without looking up from the report, Zachary felt for his phone. It went sliding across the table away from his fingers, and he looked up to corral it and to call Kenzie Kirsch.

There was no answer. The call went to voicemail. Zachary ground his teeth. She was probably just helping someone to fill out a form. Or maybe she was in a conference with the medical examiner. Or she had another doctor's appointment.

Thinking about doctor's appointments, he switched quickly to the GPS tracker app and found the latest tracker broadcasting its coordinates. A street map and satellite picture were layered over the latitude and longitude grid, and a quick squint at the street showed that she was back home. Zachary wondered briefly if everything was okay, or if she had gone home to cry or compose herself.

As Zachary was looking at the map, a call rang through to his phone, making him jump at the sudden vibration and the call information flashing up on the screen. He answered the call. "Kenzie, hi."

"Sorry, I was on another call. What's up?"

"Just looking at the blood test results on Declan Bond's report."

"Yes?"

"You said that everything was within normal parameters."

"That's right. No red flags."

"Then why do I see numbers beside alcohol and amphetamines? Surely there's no 'normal range' for alcohol and amphetamines in a child?"

Kenzie laughed. "If you look at the further testing done after that, you'll see that the amphetamine is actually pseudoephedrine."

"And what is pseudoephedrine?"

"It is a decongestant. You probably have it in your medicine cabinet."

"I do?"

"It's in most popular brands of cough medicine."

"Oh… he was given cough medicine?"

"Yes."

Zachary thought about this. "They put alcohol in children's cough medicines?"

"Some of them. They used to contain cocaine! Or they might have given him a smaller dose of an adult cough medicine. People don't want to run out to the drugstore in the middle of the night, so they adjust an adult dose for a child. Not recommended."

"But it wasn't the middle of the night. It was the afternoon. Can you tell how much he was given?"

"I don't think they would have worked back to an exact dosage. No need to do that. Probably just checked to make sure it was within normal parameters. There are lookup tables for that sort of thing."

Cough medicine.

Zachary thought back to the interviews with Spencer and

Isabella. Neither one had mentioned Declan being sick. When Zachary had run them through the events of that final day, neither of them had mentioned Declan having a cold or a cough.

"What are you thinking?" Kenzie asked.

"I'm thinking that people give their children cough medicine to make them sleep."

"If they have a cold, yes. It's hard for a child to sleep while they're coughing their heads off or can't breathe properly. It's important for them to be able to get enough rest to get over the virus."

Zachary shook his head, even though she had no way of seeing it. "Not just when they have colds. Some parents do it every night. Or any time they want to go out on the town. Give the kids a dose of cough medicine, and they sleep right through. No danger of them waking up and making trouble while the parents are out."

"People don't do that!" Kenzie sounded shocked.

"More people than you think."

"Really?"

"Really."

"You don't have kids, though, do you?" Kenzie asked.

"No. Why?"

"I'm just wondering how you know that. Has it come up in one of your cases before?"

"No, but I was a kid once."

"And your parents gave you cough medicine to make you sleep?"

He had to smile at the outrage in her voice. "I lost my parents when I was young," he reminded her. "I was that kid who was always getting up at odd hours and getting into trouble. Or staying up all night unable to get to sleep. If I wasn't on sleep meds, more than one home gave me cough medicine."

"That's unconscionable! You don't give children cough medicine to make them sleep. That's completely wrong."

"What would a doctor have prescribed?"

There was a hesitation on the line. "Well, probably an antihistamine or Ambien."

"Have they been studied for use as sleep agents in children?"

"No," she admitted. "It's off-label, but that doesn't make it right to give kids cough medicine to make them sleep."

Zachary shrugged. "I'm not recommending it, just saying it happens. What if that's what happened to Declan?"

"He was drugged?" Kenzie asked, suddenly getting it. "He was drugged and then drowned?"

"That would take care of the bruises, wouldn't it? No need to hold him down."

"His body would still fight back, struggle, even unconscious."

"But it wouldn't be the same. He wouldn't be trying to push himself up and escape, he'd just be flailing, right?"

"I… don't know."

"And all the person drowning him would have to do was make sure his mouth and nose stayed below the surface of the water."

Kenzie swore, not answering.

"How much cough medicine would it take to knock a kid out? Would it be outside the 'normal parameters' table?"

"I don't know. I imagine it would be different for different children. Depending on age, body weight, metabolism, and the way they reacted to the ingredients. Some kids get hyper. Some fall asleep. Some don't show any particular reaction."

Zachary realized he wasn't going to be able to close the case.

Not yet.

———

Despite Spencer's previous request, Zachary didn't call to set up another interview. He timed his visit for when Isabella would hopefully be home from work, and he'd be able to talk to both of them. Separately, not together.

It was Spencer who answered the door again. He looked Zachary over with distaste.

"Mr. Goldman. Again?"

"I have some important questions to ask you and your wife. I found something the medical examiner's report."

Spencer blinked, his complexion turning ashen. "What do you mean, you found something? The medical examiner determined it was accidental drowning."

"It may be nothing. On the other hand, it might show *modus operandi*."

"Modus operandi?" Spencer repeated. "What are you, a British detective novel? This isn't murder; this is an accident."

"We'll see," Zachary said flatly. "I'd like to talk to Isabella first. Is she in her studio?"

"Of course." Spencer didn't move out of the doorway, blocking Zachary's way.

"I'd like to go talk to her, please."

Spencer stood there for a few more seconds, considering his options. He eventually decided there was no point in slamming the door in Zachary's face, and stepped back to let him in.

"Thank you."

Of course, if Spencer had shut him out, he could have just called Isabella to get her to let him in. Or Molly. She probably had a key too.

He hadn't asked who had keys to the house or if the doors were left unlocked during the day. How many people would have had access to Declan while he was inside the house? Not that it mattered, when there was no key needed to access him while he was out playing in the yard.

If that was really what he had been doing before he disappeared. Zachary was no longer sure that was even what had happened.

What if Declan had been rendered unconscious by a dose of cough medicine, his breathing and heartbeat so depressed that they couldn't be detected? What if they took him out to the pond and left him floating face down, thinking that he was already dead?

Spencer stood there for a moment, then walked away briskly, back to his office, not offering to walk Zachary to Isabella's studio. That was not a problem; he knew the way on his own.

He stood in the doorway watching Isabella for a few minutes unobserved. She was painting, engrossed in her work. There was no blue on her canvas. Her palette was resting on a high table instead of in her hand, and her free hand ran up and down the necklaces, touching and fiddling with the pendants. She released the necklaces and brushed her fingers over the tattoo on her right forearm.

"Until we meet again, may God hold you in the palm of His hand."

Even with no one in the room with her, she was still repeating it. Spencer had suggested she could suppress the tic with an effort of will, but that it would return once she let go. And he was right.

Was it grief or was it guilt? He knew the stats. Most child homicide victims were murdered by their parents. Had her mental decline started before Declan's death, and his drowning 'accident' was only another symptom of how sick she had become? Or had he gotten in her way too often, disrupting the life that she had tried to build for herself, and she had simply had too much? Motherhood wasn't for everyone, Zachary had learned that lesson the hard way. More than once.

Or maybe it had just been a tragic accident that they—or she —had clumsily tried to cover up after the fact.

Zachary tapped on the door before he entered, alerting her to his presence. "Isabella?"

Isabella looked in his direction with a vague expression. It was a moment before she focused on him and realized who he was.

"Oh... Mr. Goldman. I didn't know we were expecting you."

"I have some new questions for you."

She shook her head, looking back at her painting again. She stroked her tattoo, and then her left hand dropped to the necklaces again as she continued to paint. "I've already answered all of your questions. I don't know what else you could possibly have to ask."

Zachary moved farther into the room. He made space on a chair and sat so that he wouldn't be looking down at her or be perceived as being confrontational. Nice and low-key. See if he could get the information out of her without her becoming defensive.

"Tell me again about the day that Declan disappeared."

"I've already told you everything. I've told the police. I've told you. It's still the same. Nothing has changed."

"There is nothing that stands out about his behavior that day before he disappeared?"

"No, nothing at all. It was just a normal day. He was playing outside; I was watching him through the window while I was painting. And then... he was just gone. He wasn't there anymore."

"How as Declan feeling that day?"

"Feeling?"

"Was he well? Happy?"

"Yes, just like normal."

"He wasn't sick?"

"No."

"He didn't have a cold?"

"No."

"Was he a pretty active child? Did he get into things a lot?"

Isabella looked away from the painting to Zachary. "No... he was a normal boy, perfectly normal. He got into things sometimes, but kids do. That's just the way they are."

"He wasn't diagnosed with ADHD? Anything like that?"

"No!" Her mouth formed a thin, straight line. There were a couple of angry lines like exclamation marks between her eyebrows. "He wasn't diagnosed with anything. He was perfectly normal. Perfectly healthy."

She acted as if Zachary had accused Declan of being a serial killer. With her own mental illness issues, was it that awful to suggest that Declan might have a diagnosis as well? ADHD diagnoses were so common; there wasn't *that* much of a stigma attached anymore. Isabella clearly did not like this line of questioning.

Perfectly normal. Perfectly healthy.

"Then why was he given cough medicine?"

"Cough medicine." Isabella stared at him. "He wasn't given cough medicine. What are you talking about?"

"When Declan died, he had cough medicine in his body. In his bloodstream. So why was he given cough medicine, if he was perfectly healthy?"

"He wasn't. I would never give him that poison. It's very bad for children."

"Do you have cough medicine in the house?"

"Of course." She fluttered a hand in the direction of the master bedroom and bath. "Everyone has cough medicine."

"But you didn't have anything for Declan? What would you do if he got sick? Surely you'd give him a decongestant if he was having trouble sleeping."

"No." Her voice was firm. "I wouldn't. There's no proof that any of those medicines are good for children. They've only been tested on adults, and then the results extrapolated. Children's bodies don't work the same way as adults' bodies. You can never be sure what effect they will have."

"You've never given cough medicine to Declan?"

She shook her head. "When he was younger... I don't know, two or three, he had a bad cold, and I gave him some baby cold medicine. Not the liquid, one of those instant dissolve tablets. I didn't know how bad they could be for children, but the way he reacted to it... he was practically comatose for the next few hours. I never gave him cold medicine again."

Zachary's heart sped. "Do you know what kind of medicine it was? What was in it?"

"No... I don't remember. I don't know what brand it was or what the active ingredients were. I've never used one again."

"Would you still have the package around somewhere? It was

only a year or two ago; people keep medications around for much longer than that."

"You can check. It would be in the medicine cabinet, down the hall."

Zachary sped out of the room and looked both ways down the hallway, paranoid that Spencer might have been listening at the door and might reach the bathroom to destroy the evidence ahead of him. But there was no sign of Spencer. Zachary found the bathroom and opened the medicine cabinet. He had known before he had a chance to itemize the contents that the children's medicine would not be there. The bathroom, including the cabinet, was pristine. Nothing leaking or out of date. The bottles and sundries in the cabinet stood in rigid rows, equidistant apart. He checked each label anyway. There was, as Isabella had indicated, adult cough medicine. None of the children's cold tablets that she had referred to. She had probably said that she was never going to use them again, and Spencer had taken her at her word and thrown them out.

Zachary took out the cough medicine, wondering even as he took it out if he should have put on gloves first. Surely the police had looked at it already when they determined Declan had cough medicine in his system. Zachary tried to keep his fingers to the edges where they wouldn't smear any other fingerprints anyway and checked the ingredients.

Pseudoephedrine was listed under the active ingredients and alcohol in the inactive ingredients.

Had Declan been given cough medicine from that bottle? Or had someone else, a third party, given him cough medicine to keep him quiet and compliant? Maybe panicking when he became 'almost comatose.' Certainly, using cough medicine to sedate a child was a widely-known practice, as Zachary himself could attest.

He set the bottle down on the sink and took pictures of the brand name on the front and the ingredients on the back. He put it back in the medicine cabinet where he had gotten it and took another picture. Just in case it happened to disappear before he could get the police to look at it.

If the police looked at it.

Zachary returned to the studio, where Isabella was still painting, running her fingers over the memorial objects, and whispering her never-ending prayer.

"You're right," he told her. "There is a bottle of cough medicine in the cabinet, but not the medicine you gave to Declan when he was younger."

She gave a little shrug of unconcern. "I don't know what would make you think we would give him that. There's no way I would let anyone give Deck cough medicine."

"Maybe he wasn't feeling well, and Spencer gave him cough medicine," Zachary suggested.

"He wasn't sick. I told you that. Spencer knows I wouldn't let him give Declan cough medicine. He would never have done that."

"Maybe he thought he'd just give it a try. Just to see if it would help. He never expressed any concerns to you?"

"No. He didn't say anything was wrong or that he had given Deck medicine. Declan was happy and playing. If he'd had that stuff, he would have been asleep. He wouldn't have been able to walk around. He wouldn't have been playing." When Zachary opened his mouth, she rushed to fill the space. "I was watching him. I would have known if he had been drugged."

"But you weren't watching him the whole time. You were only checking occasionally to make sure he was okay."

"I was watching. I never looked away for long."

"How long? Five minutes?"

She shook her head in irritation. "No, I don't think it was that long. Two or three. I was keeping track of him."

"But then you couldn't see him anymore."

"I know that."

"And you didn't go out the first time you looked and couldn't see him. You waited to see if he came back into view again."

"Only for a few minutes."

Zachary knew how that was. If she said she hadn't seen him for five minutes, it was probably at least ten. From what he'd seen, she got pretty wrapped up in her work, and she could have gone half an hour without thinking any time had passed. It was only five minutes at the most to get from the back yard to the pond. It only took two or three minutes for a child to drown. In fifteen minutes, either of them could have done the deed, without the other realizing they'd been out of the house.

"Could Spencer have left the house without you realizing it?"

Isabella looked away from her painting and studied him, looking confused. "Of course not, he was here the whole afternoon. I don't understand why you're asking that."

"He could have left for five minutes without you noticing, just like Declan could wander off for five minutes. You weren't watching Spencer."

"No... but I was watching his coat."

"What do you mean, you were watching his coat?"

Isabella laughed at Zachary's consternation. "I wasn't painting in here. I was in the bedroom."

"Right. We established that."

"And I was standing in front of the closet. Just a few feet away from Spencer's coat. It was right there in front of my eyes. He wouldn't leave the house without it."

"He could have."

"No! It was a cool day. Spencer would never have left the house without it. He's *very* rigid about it."

OCD as an alibi?

"Do you know what Spencer was doing during that time? Is there any way we can check his alibi?"

"His computer," Isabella said vaguely. "I imagine he left a digital trail somewhere."

"And what about you? Is there any way we can verify that you were in the bedroom like you say you were?"

"Where would I go? I was painting. Watching Deck. I couldn't go anywhere."

"Would Spencer have known if you left the house?"

"You will have to ask him," Isabella snapped. "He has a view of the back yard too. We both had a view of the back yard, and neither of us saw anything."

"You alibi each other."

"Unless you think that we both colluded to murder our son, that's going to have to be good enough for you."

Could they have conspired to kill their son? Zachary couldn't see it, no matter how he tried to mold the picture in his mind. While they were not demonstrative, he believed they loved Declan. One of them could have hurt him in a moment of anger or frustration, or by accident, but he didn't see how either of them could have hurt him intentionally.

And that meant he was back at the beginning again. To a mysterious stranger coming into the yard, or up to the gate, luring Declan out, drugging him with cough syrup, and then abandoning his body in the pond. If the time of death was five o'clock, they would only have had, at most, an hour with the boy. It didn't make any sense.

There was a knock at the studio door. Zachary and Isabella looked up. Spencer hovered in the doorway. He held a cordless phone toward Isabella.

"It's Melissa Raymond," he explained. "I thought you would like to talk to her... set something up, maybe?"

Isabella looked at him for a moment, not excited by the suggestion. Eventually, she laid aside her paintbrush and walked to the door of the studio to take the phone from him.

"You're done here?" Spencer asked, looking at Zachary. "Give them some privacy to talk."

Zachary conceded, leaving the studio so that Isabella could talk privately with her friend. Spencer led him back toward the front door.

"Melissa will be good for her," he said. "She always used to be able to draw Isabella out before. She needs someone to talk with. Someone who isn't a cop or a therapist or a private investigator." He considered. "Or her husband."

Zachary glanced sideways at him. "Marriage isn't for cowards."

"You're right about that," Spencer agreed fervently. "You're married?"

"Divorced."

"Sorry."

Zachary nodded. "Yours has lasted longer than mine did. I hope things improve."

"Neither of us is good with change; we'll avoid it as long as we can."

At the door, Zachary offered his hand. "Thanks for your help. One thing before I leave. Did you give Declan cough medicine? That last day?"

Spencer raised his brows. He pursed his lips and shook his head. "No. He wasn't sick, and I know how Isabella would feel about that."

"When Declan was playing in the back yard, did Isabella leave the house?"

Spencer scowled as he shook his head. "No, I can't imagine she would."

"I'm not asking if she *would*. I'm asking if she *did*. Was there any time that you might have heard or seen her leave? Or when you were away from the windows and wouldn't have seen her leave?"

"But why would she do that?"

"Could she have?"

"No… maybe when I was in the kitchen, but then she would have had to sneak out the front door instead of the back. Or when I was in the bathroom; but I'm sure she was here the whole time. Neither of us left the house. Just Declan."

"How long was Declan playing outside before Isabella said he was missing?"

"An hour… maybe an hour and twenty…?"

"And in your experience... how closely did she supervise him? How often would she have looked out at him?"

"I've never sat down and timed the intervals. I don't know how you could expect me to know. I suppose it depends on how involved she is with her painting."

"And does she tend to get distracted and lost in her work?"

Spencer's hand was on the door, eager for Zachary to be gone. Wanting just to shut the door and be done with him.

"I don't know."

"You don't know if she gets distracted by what she's doing? So involved that she isn't paying attention to what's going on around her?"

"I suppose she does. Anyone does."

"Has there been any time when Declan has gotten hurt or upset while he was in the back yard and Isabella was supposed to be supervising him? Or another time when he was her responsibility, and you got angry at her for not watching him closely enough?"

Spencer's face got red. "I don't appreciate your implications. Declan's death is not Isabella's fault."

"I didn't say it was. I'm trying to establish how long it was between the last time Isabella checked on him and the time that he died. What is the longest possible length of time he could have been missing from your yard?"

"It's impossible to know that."

"Unless you know what time it was that Isabella checked on him last, or have a pretty good guess. Did she look in on him every five minutes? Every ten? Every half hour? Maybe she only checked when he came near the window, or she heard him crying."

Zachary stared at Spencer, waiting for his answer. Spencer was a man who liked an ordered, predictable experience. He must have had certain expectations of his wife, and must have known when she broke what he considered to be the house rules. If she didn't do a good job supervising Declan or she left the house unexpectedly, he would have had some idea.

Spencer wiped his hand down his face in a tired gesture.

"I can't tell you how often she checked on him or how long he was missing from the yard. I know she was in the house and I know that she was supervising Declan playing outside. That's all I can tell you."

Zachary stared into Spencer's face, looking for any sign of deception. He nodded. "Okay. Thanks for your help. Good luck."

He had started to turn away to leave when Spencer's voice recalled him.

"Zachary…?"

"Yes?"

"Your investigation… it will be done soon? It's causing a lot of stress on the family."

"I'll do my best."

9

Looking down at his phone, Zachary realized that he had a voicemail message. Swiping over to the screen, he saw a message had been left by 'unknown caller.' Probably a telemarketer, but some of his legitimate contacts had blocked caller IDs as well. The police department, for one. He tapped the message and held the phone to his ear.

You've been warned to drop the case. This is your last warning.

He pulled the phone back away from his ear and stared at it. A voice changer had been used, which made the voice of the caller impossible to recognize. Which, of course, meant that if he were to hear the caller's voice unaltered, he would have recognized it. Zachary closed his eyes, drumming his fingers on his steering wheel and considering.

The Antonelli insurance fraud case was rumored to involve the mob, but he suspected that any threat that came to him from organized crime would have more finesse, and they would leave no doubt as to which case it was they wanted him to drop. He had a couple of infidelity cases that he hadn't reported on yet, but he had most of the information he needed to finish them off, so there wasn't any point in dropping those cases. The Senator's background checks weren't likely to cause him any trouble. They were all routine, and none of the subjects had any reason to threaten him.

It bothered him that there was no real threat. His 'last warning' was not even a legitimate warning. There was a possibility that the warnings were about the Declan Bond case. It was the kind of case that made people emotional. The police or medical examiner might not like him reinvestigating the case. Isabella and Spencer were tired of his questions, and maybe one of them just wanted him off the case. Or Halloran, worried that word would leak out that his star was being investigated. Even Molly, afraid that the expenses were adding up, but too timid to call him off.

Zachary's address and phone number weren't that hard to find. Everyone had his phone number. His home address was more difficult to find, but only slightly. He wasn't a big name. He wasn't like the private detectives on TV, solving a murder a week. He was a nobody, and there was no need to hide from the public or discontented clients or police. He received threats from time to time. The one on his door had been a little disturbing. He tried to tell himself it was nothing, but whoever had left it wanted him to know that they could reach him. They knew where he lived. That was the message.

He didn't delete the voicemail. If the caller did escalate from half-threats to action, Zachary might need something that the police could trace.

Kenzie had come to Zachary's apartment when he called her, but she seemed cautious and reserved. She didn't have her usual bright eyes and quick smile. They sat in the living room, and he told her about the latest developments in the Bond case, the responses from Isabella and Spencer to his questions on whether either of them had given him cough medicine, and exactly how long he might have been missing from the yard before his death. Kenzie didn't seem to be as interested in the case as she had previously. She stared away from him, her brows down slightly.

"Maybe it's time to let it go," she said finally. "You're not getting anywhere with it. There's no indication that there was foul play involved. So why not let it go? Tell them you've looked into everything you can, and everything seems to be kosher. No need to pursue it any further."

"Not now, when I finally have some actual evidence that there might have been foul play!"

"You haven't found anything new. Nothing that the police haven't already investigated."

"It might not be enough to make any arrests, but I think it's enough for them to investigate it further. The boy was afraid of water. He wouldn't have walked into the pond to drown. He had cough medicine in his system when his parents deny having given him any. He has a previous history of being knocked out by a single dose of cold medicine. Don't you think those things add up to suspicion of foul play?"

"It's nothing *new*. The police knew all that and closed their file. They believe that he did walk or fall into the pond. They already know there was cough medicine in his system. It's in the medical examiner's report."

"You don't think I should bring my suspicions to anybody. I should just tell the family that I agree it was an accident and let it go."

She looked at him steadily. "Yes, because that's what happened. Look, Zachary... you're going to have unanswered questions in any case, right? There are always going to be a few things that just don't fit. That's what happens when we try to reconstruct every detail of a person's life. People are variable creatures, and we can never predict everything. If you look at any death, trying to pull apart every single detail, you can convince yourself that there was foul play, or a conspiracy, or something malevolent. Just because you're looking for it. There will always be clues that don't fit anywhere because they're not really clues.

They're just random bits of information. It's never going to fit like a lock and key. Real life isn't *Murder She Wrote*."

Zachary listened to her as he poured some munchie mix out of a box into a bowl and placed it on the coffee table between them. They each had a cold can of beer, but Kenzie hadn't yet touched hers. He shook his head.

"Why don't you want me to continue with the case?"

"Me? I don't care. You can waste your time if that's what you want to do. I thought you wanted my advice as to what to do next." She sat back, moving a couple of inches farther from him and keeping her back straight instead of relaxing into the couch. "And that's my advice. Wrap it up and tell them you're done."

"Is Dr. Wiltshire upset that I'm reviewing the case? Is that what this is about?"

"Dr. Wiltshire couldn't care less if you're looking over his report. It's not like he has anything to hide. He's always very conscientious in his investigations and reports."

"And you just think I should give up and let it go."

She gave a little shrug. "Yes."

He wasn't sure she was telling him the full truth, but he wasn't going to get it out of her with direct questioning. Maybe they'd get around to it from another direction. Zachary picked a pretzel out of the mix and popped it into his mouth.

"So how was your doctor appointment the other day?"

Her eyes widened a little bit. "My doctor…? How did you know about that?"

"You mentioned it to me when we set up lunch. You said you had a medical appointment to get to in the afternoon. I just wondered how it went."

"It isn't any of your business, is it?" She bristled at his intrusion. "That's private."

"Okay…" Zachary held up his hands defensively. "I didn't mean to overstep my bounds. I'm sorry. It's just that with my wife's history—my ex-wife's history—I get worried. Things can come out of the blue… serious things."

Kenzie popped the top of her beer and took a little sip, looking at him. "What happened between the two of you?"

He shifted uncomfortably, not so happy with having personal questions thrown back his way. He tried to avoid it.

"You know how it is between married couples."

"I know something happened that left the two of you pretty bitter."

Zachary nodded.

"Mario Bowman, he said that the two of you were lovebirds, very close, like you had the best relationship in the world. Then everything fell apart. He wouldn't give me any details. Or maybe he didn't know them. Either way, he protected your privacy. I just can't help wondering... what it was that left the two of you both so hurt and bitter."

Zachary swallowed. "It's private," he said. "It's not just my privacy... it's more about Bridget's. She's the one... with the most to lose."

As if on cue, Zachary's phone started to ring. They both looked down at the display on the coffee table between them and saw her name. Bridget.

"How did she know we were talking about her?" Kenzie said in a stage whisper. She covered her mouth, giggling, while Zachary picked up the phone. He didn't laugh. If Bridget was calling him, it was serious. Despite his efforts to move on, he wanted to be there for Bridget if she needed him. He answered the call.

"Bridget? What is it?"

"You just shut up," she snapped. "I didn't call to hear your excuses."

Zachary closed his mouth. He looked over at Kenzie, who could obviously hear Bridget's strident voice, in spite of his attempt to turn down the volume of the call.

"You've been following me!" Bridget accused. "What a low-down, creepy thing to do!" He tried to respond, but she cut him off mercilessly. "I told you not to talk. You stop stalking me, or I'm going to take out a restraining order! I'll get your butt thrown in jail! This is the most despicable thing—if I see your car near me again, I don't care what your excuse is, I am going to have you slammed in jail so fast you won't know what happened. Understand?"

Zachary didn't say anything.

Bridget's voice had risen to a screech. "I said, do you understand?"

"Am I allowed to talk now?"

"Don't get smart with me, you jerk! You stay the hell away from me, you understand? I don't want to see your car in my rear-view mirror! I don't want to see you at any of the restaurants we went to together. I don't want to see or hear about you anywhere I go! You got it?"

Zachary tried to answer, but she hung up. He pulled the phone away from his ear and looked at the screen to confirm that she had terminated the call.

Zachary looked back at Kenzie, his face hot. "You still don't think she hates me?"

She shifted uncomfortably. "No, I don't, but… what's up with that? *Have* you been following her?"

"You're the one who suggested *It's a Wrap*," Zachary reminded her.

"And you're the one who didn't object and say that you didn't want to run into your ex there. You didn't answer my question. *Are* you following her?"

"It's a small world. We still have friends in common. We both still live in town. We're going to run into each other."

She stared at him, waiting for a straight answer. Zachary struggled to come up with something she would understand.

"That's not how it is."

She used silence as a weapon. Zachary shifted and picked a few M&Ms out of the snack mix. He chewed on his lip.

"I might have… driven past her house a time or two, making sure she was okay. Or I might have seen her car downtown. I miss her." He shook his head and blinked to prevent tears from forming in his hot, prickling eyes. "I loved her very much. The break-up was such a shock. It was so traumatic."

"What happened?"

He tried to think of how to tell it without getting cut up over it all over again. The silence gathered around them.

"She was pregnant," he said finally.

Kenzie nodded slowly. "And you weren't ready for a baby?"

"I *was*. I was over the moon about it, but she didn't want it. We were using birth control. She didn't want a baby. I wanted a family of my own, but she... she wouldn't budge."

"That's tough," Kenzie sympathized.

"Yeah. That was the beginning. She said I didn't have any right to dictate... that I had no rights over the pregnancy... over her... It was her body, her choice..."

"And legally, she's right."

"But we were in a relationship. That kind of thing... it's supposed to be something you decide together. You talk about it. You come to some kind of decision together. It was my baby too."

Kenzie just nodded. Her dark eyes were intense, drinking him in. Zachary's heart pounded painfully in his chest as if it were happening all over again.

"She decided it didn't matter what I wanted. She was going to get an abortion. As soon as possible."

Kenzie continued to watch him. Zachary popped another pretzel in his mouth, but it was as dry as chalk. He couldn't even taste it, and it turned to glue in his mouth. With difficulty, he washed it down with a large amount of beer.

"The doctor said that the good news was, she wasn't pregnant. It was one of those point-one percent of cases where the pregnancy test was wrong. A false positive."

Kenzie gave a little intake of breath that Zachary knew meant that with her medical background, she had an idea what was coming next.

"The bad news was that she had cancer. An HCG-producing

tumor in her ovary. That was what triggered the false positive on the pregnancy test."

They both sat in silence.

"So that's it," Zachary said finally. "There was no pregnancy. No baby. No need for an abortion. Instead, she had to have the ovary removed, and chemotherapy."

"And a big elephant in the room."

"Oh, we talked about it," Zachary said. "We talked about it constantly. How I wasn't ready to be a father but thought I was. How she was the responsible one, the one who had to make the hard choices. How she would kill a baby to avoid responsibility. How I was trying to make her feel guilty while she was going through chemotherapy and should only be having positive thoughts. I tried to help her through her treatments, but she didn't even want me in the room. She didn't want anything to do with me."

He sat there in silence.

"What a mess," Kenzie said finally. "I understand what you mean about it being a traumatic break-up."

Zachary nodded. Sweat dribbled down his back. He tried to wash away the lump in his throat with a few more swallows of beer.

"But you have to move on," Kenzie said. "You can't be hanging around her house or following her around. She's right; that is creepy. You could end up in jail if you keep it up."

"I know."

"Then stop it."

He didn't tell her that it wasn't that easy. Not for him. It was so hard for him to maintain a relationship in the first place; letting go of what had been a successful one was more than he could handle.

The evening with Kenzie had ended unsatisfactorily. As much as they had tried to move on to more natural topics, neither one could seem to maintain a conversation that didn't lead either to the Bond case or Zachary's relationship with Bridget. They turned on a movie on the TV and cuddled on the couch, but in the end, neither could focus on the show, and they didn't even finish it. Kenzie looked at her watch and announced the need to go home, and Zachary didn't have the energy to argue with her about it. She tried to brush him off at the door, but he walked her down to her car like a gentleman, patting the top of her trunk.

"Sweet ride."

She patted the little red sports car. "It's my one indulgence," she said with a laugh. She bent closer to give him a quick peck on the cheek, but was turned around and sliding into the vehicle before he could reciprocate.

Without making any plans to get together again, or even so much as a 'see you later,' she shut the door and pulled away. Zachary watched the car until it drove out of sight, then made his way up to his apartment.

One of the good things about being a private detective was

that on nights he knew he wouldn't be able to sleep, he could work. There was always some surveillance that he could do, following a straying spouse, or else he could stay in and run backgrounds and do other computer work.

He was too restless to sit at the computer, so he donned dark clothing, grabbed his cameras, and headed out. He had a new case, an executive who believed that his wife, a high school principal, was out fooling around when she claimed to be out with her girl friends or working late.

Zachary had her cell phone number, to which he'd previously texted a video file. The video file had a GPS app embedded in it, and provided she was curious enough to see what video an anonymous sender had texted her; he would be able to pinpoint her exact location. He opened the tracker app on his phone and noted the locations of his most recent targets. He noted with satisfaction that the principal now showed up as a virtual pin on the satellite map. A zoom-in suggested she was probably in Rancheros, a rowdy cowboy bar, rather than stuck at her desk grading papers or doing whatever it was principals did.

Once at the bar, he scanned the faces of the patrons, looking for her. He had a good head for faces and didn't need to pull up her picture on his phone to refresh his memory. The bar was busy, the lighting dim with strobing dance lights, and had some private booths that it wasn't easy to see into unless a person were right beside them. He worked his way around the dining area and eventually spotted her at a booth, sitting across from a younger woman, a heavily made-up brunette.

The principal was a blond. Not with bright, shining locks like Bridget's pre-chemo hair, but a dirty blond with short, messy curls. She was comfortably overweight, with the middle-age spread of many fifty-year-old women. Zachary looked for somewhere he could sit to observe them unobtrusively. He found a booth that hadn't yet been cleared of its dirty dishes and sat down, pushing them aside and pretending to be intently interested in something on his phone. He didn't look at the two women. If they glanced at him, they would see nothing but a man occupied with his phone, like any other man who was waiting for his date, or whose wife had abandoned him to go to the bathroom.

"Uh…" a skimpily-clad cowboy waitress hovered over Zachary. "I'm sorry, this table isn't ready yet, maybe I could…"

"It's fine," Zachary said, "just clear it. I'm waiting for a friend, and she wanted somewhere… private. This is perfect. Thanks."

"But…" She stood there for a minute, then shrugged. "All right. If that's what you want."

She cleared away the dishes. "I'll be back to wipe the table down in two shakes."

"Thank you. Much appreciated."

She gave him a nod and a strained smile and took the dishes back toward the kitchen.

Zachary snuck a glance at the ladies at the other table. The younger one was looking his way, and he tried a friendly smile and raised eyebrow. She looked quickly away from him and back at her friend, Principal Montgomery.

Zachary again pretended to be busy with his phone, watching them covertly. He tried to pick up on their vibes. Two coworkers out for an after-work drink? An assignation? Parent-teacher conference?

The dim lights made it difficult to make out more than general features, but a couple of times, dance lights flashed over the ladies' faces. Zachary frowned, studying the second woman's features.

She was young. Younger than he had first thought. Certainly, not the parent of a student. Maybe a student teacher or office aide. Or a therapist who came in to work with the students. He had seen baby-faced professionals before.

Teachers who could almost be mistaken for their students.

The girl's makeup was heavy and had contributed to the impression that she was older. Which was, he assumed, the reason she was wearing it. She was trying to hide the fact that she wasn't old enough to be in the bar, even if it was just soda in her tall glass.

Rather that pull out his full-size camera, Zachary brought up the low-light photography app on his phone. He braced his elbows on the table to minimize any camera shake, and aimed his camera lens at the two ladies, with their heads close together. He looked around casually, keeping his body language relaxed, so it only looked like he was reading or looking something up on his phone instead of taking a picture. He snapped several stills, and then a short video of the two women. While he had the video running, the younger woman reached across the table and held the principal's hand.

Bingo!

The waitress returned, wiped down the table, and pulled out her order pad. "What can I getcha? Or are you waiting for your friend?"

"How about two coffees, to start?" he suggested.

Her face relaxed a bit, and she nodded. "Sure. Nothing else? Desserts? Drinks?"

"We might have to get one of those hot fudge brownie deals. I'll wait and make sure the lady approves first, because I don't want to eat it alone."

She flashed him a genuine smile. "That may or may not be a good idea. No self-respecting woman would order such a high-calorie treat. You know, everyone's on a diet, but if someone happened to order one before she had a chance to say no…"

"Ah," Zachary nodded agreeably, "then why don't you bring me one, and we'll see if I can get her to share it?"

She wrote it down on her order form. "Anything else?"

Zachary leaned forward. "This is a sort of unusual question. I don't usually do things like this…"

"What?" Her eyes narrowed, but she continued to smile pleasantly.

"Don't turn around too fast, but the two ladies at the table behind you. Are you sure they're both legal?"

Her smile dimmed. She obeyed his advice and didn't whirl around to stare. She looked over her shoulder toward the dance floor, scoping the two women out peripherally without being obvious about it.

She swore and looked back at Zachary. "The brunette, right? Doesn't look a day over seventeen." She sighed and shook her head. "I don't know how they let her in without carding her. I'll have the manager come over and check them out. Thanks for letting me know."

He nodded. She walked back away. Zachary continued to watch the couple, a knot of anger growing in his stomach. The waitress returned with his coffees and a brownie with two forks and placed them down without a word. It was some time before the manager came over to talk to the two ladies. Zachary had taken several pictures in the interim, as the two became decidedly more cozy.

The manager, dressed in worn blue jeans and a big cowboy hat, leaned over the table to talk to them, his voice too low for Zachary to catch his words. There were exaggerated movements from the two women, feigning shock and amusement at his questions. He was firm, insisting on proof that the younger woman was legal drinking age. Eventually, they both rose, expressing their outrage, and stormed out of the bar. Zachary watched them go, wondering if he should follow them and pursue the matter further. The manager watched to make sure that they left. He noticed that Zachary was watching them too.

"You're the one who pointed them out to the wait staff?" he asked Zachary.

"Yes. I don't normally go out of my way to ruin someone's date, but..."

The other man scratched his two-day-old whiskers and shook his head. "Can't be allowing underage drinkers in here or we'll get shut down. I appreciate you pointing them out." His eyes went over Zachary's coffee mugs, one full and one empty, and the half-eaten brownie. "Please don't worry about the bill, we'll pick it up."

"Oh, you don't need to do that." Zachary would bill it to the client anyway. "They left without paying theirs, didn't they?"

"Yep."

"Then let me pay mine and tip the waitress."

The cowboy shrugged at him. "If you insist. Again, thanks for helping us out."

After the manager had again withdrawn, the waitress came back to see if Zachary needed anything. "I guess they couldn't prove she was of age," she observed.

"No, I guess not. She didn't bother trying to show a fake ID, at least."

"Can I get you anything else?"

"Just the bill, if you could."

"Sure." Her eyes went to the remains of his dessert. "Your friend never showed up?"

"She had an emergency." Zachary gave an exaggerated shrug. "What can you do?"

"Sorry about that."

"It's fine. Next time."

"Okay. I'll bring you your bill."

After he had settled up, Zachary went out to his car. He sat there with his guts in a knot, trying to decide what to do. He pulled up his tracker to see where Principal Montgomery had gone after leaving the bar. Her phone showed her at a shopping center, which eased his anxiety. Maybe they were going to look at clothes. Try on shoes.

Still, he went to the police station and approached the duty officer. He was pleasantly surprised to see that it was Joshua Campbell, who was normally too high-ranking to do desk duty, but must have had to fill in for a sick officer until they could find someone else to do the job. That meant that Zachary at least didn't have to introduce himself and explain why he would be following someone around and taking pictures.

Joshua finished dealing with the gray-haired lady in front of Zachary. It was a quiet night. Still early, the crazies not yet out. Joshua motioned Zachary forward, giving him a big grin.

"Zach, my friend! What brings you by today? Somebody key your car? Run you off the road?"

He hadn't been run off the road before, but he'd certainly been keyed or had a window smashed. People tended not to like it when he pried into their private lives.

"No, not this time," he said. He hesitated about how to approach the issue.

Joshua raised an eyebrow and waited.

"Normally when misbehavior comes across my radar, it just gets reported to the client, and then it's up to them whether they are going to report a crime or not."

"Yeah. Normally."

"But in cases that involve minors..."

Joshua's smile quickly disappeared. "You got an abuse or neglect case to report?"

"Something like that." Zachary placed his phone on the counter between them and opened his photo app. He swiped through a few pictures and found the one that showed the minor's face most clearly. "This girl. They were at Rancheros. I had management card them, and she wouldn't show any ID. The two of them took off in a huff."

"Could be something. Do you know the identity of either one?"

"The older woman is Principal Dana Montgomery."

Joshua's eyes snapped up to Zachary's face. "Principal?"

"She's a high school principal."

Joshua swore. "Tell me they just like the food at Rancheros."

Zachary flipped to further photos. Joshua looked ready to leap over the desk and go after the woman on foot all by himself.

"You didn't follow them when they left the bar? Any way of knowing where they went?"

"They did go over to the shopping center." Zachary picked up his phone and held it so that Joshua could no longer see the screen. "You won't ask how I know, right?"

"No. You tell me where they are and I'll send someone over there to have a word."

Zachary looked down at the map to make sure they were still at the shopping center, looking at shoes or lip gloss. But the pin had moved in the time that it had taken him to get to the police station and to make his report. He swore and looked at Joshua, feeling sick.

"Motel."

Joshua echoed his sentiment. He clicked on a handheld radio and started giving directions. When he paused for the name and address of the motel, Zachary turned the phone around for him to see.

"I'll get a picture of the two of them to your phone," Joshua told the officer who had answered his call.

He looked at Zachary after clicking off. "Email all the pictures to me," he instructed. He gave the duty officer email address, and Zachary got to work on it.

"I'll have to batch them; it won't send that many at once. And there are two videos."

"Great. Get me the best facial pictures first so that I can distribute them, and then send me the rest."

Zachary nodded.

Joshua was going through the forms under his counter, rattling papers. "I'll need to get your signed statement on what went on over at the bar. Did you get any other names? The manager's?"

"No... some guy dressed as a cowboy."

"Don't they all dress as cowboys over there?"

"I imagine so."

Joshua rolled his eyes. "Then that's not exactly helpful, is it? I'll send some officers over there to find out what they can before anyone finishes their shifts."

He shoved a stack of forms at Zachary. "If you want to move down the counter here while you fill those out, I'd better deal with some of these people waiting behind you. Okay?"

Zachary did as he was told, filling the forms out in his neatest printing, trying to make sure that he got all the pertinent details. It took a good length of time to go through all of them. He sidled closer to Joshua as he finished up with another citizen.

"Done?"

"Here you go."

"Everything signed?" Joshua thumbed through them to make sure that Zachary had signed in all of the appropriate places. He picked up his radio again and made an inquiry. Zachary couldn't make out the staticky response and code talk and waited for Joshua to fill him in.

"They got her," Joshua said with a satisfied nod. "The two of them together in the hotel room, just getting friendly."

Zachary sighed. Things didn't usually move so quickly. He felt like he had run a race when all he'd done was stand at the counter.

"And she is one of the students at Montgomery's school," Joshua informed him.

"I can't believe it. How did she think she was going to get away with it?"

"In my experience, we never catch them the first time. They've always gotten away with it before. Sometimes dozens of times. Predators don't just hunt once."

"Well... thank you for getting right on it. I feel like I did something good today."

Joshua offered a handshake, and they clasped tightly. "You *did* do something good today. That girl's parents are going to be indebted to you." He released Zachary's hand. "Who was your client? Montgomery's husband?"

"I can't discuss private client matters with you... but that would be a good guess."

"Take care, my friend. You should sleep well tonight. The sleep of the just."

Zachary could only wish.

His eyes were puffy and bloodshot in the morning, and it wasn't because of a couple of beers with Kenzie. Far from being able to sleep soundly because he had done something good, Zachary hadn't even been able to lie down to try to sleep. He was too wired. His head whirled with anxiety over how many other students Montgomery had preyed upon, what he was going to tell Mr. Montgomery about his wife's activities, and how he was going to explain going to the police with the information.

But he'd had to. He couldn't stand by while a minor was in danger. He might not be a mandatory reporter, but he couldn't ignore it and leave it up to the client, who might be too embarrassed to do anything.

In the small hours of the morning, he had gone through as much of his busy work as he could, preparing final reports and invoices, finalizing the Senatorial background checks, and for a while just browsing through the various Facebook accounts he was keeping track of. Socially acceptable cyberstalking.

He was just trying to rev his engine with a second cup of coffee when the phone rang. Looking at the screen, Zachary saw that it was Isabella. The idea that she would have any reason to call him made him feel unaccountably worried. She hadn't exactly approved of Molly hiring him in the first place. She had answered questions but hadn't been particularly cooperative. Had something happened? Maybe to Molly or Spencer? He was pretty sure she wouldn't be calling him to tell him she had remembered something new from Declan's last day. Or maybe that she'd found the box of cold pills so he could see what their active ingredients were.

Zachary swallowed hard and answered the call. "Goldman Investigations."

"Is this Zachary?"

"Yes. Isabella. Hi. What can I help you with?"

"It's nothing, really. Nothing that will be of any help to your case. I just thought… I wanted someone to share it with."

Zachary breathed slowly and evenly, wishing it would calm the wild pounding of his heart.

"Sure. What is it?"

"Mittens. He came back."

"What?" Zachary couldn't find the words.

"Mittens. My cat. Remember I told you about him? Well, the cat came back."

"Your cat... that disappeared eight years ago."

"Yes, that's right."

"He came back."

"Yes." She sounded pleased; happy and relaxed like she hadn't ever sounded before. "The cat came back."

"Are you sure it's the same cat?" Zachary demanded, unable to wrap his mind around it. A cat disappears for eight years and then comes back? Was she imagining that a stray she saw was her old cat, Mittens? Maybe she'd even tempted one into the house with a bowl of kibble?

"Of course, do you think I wouldn't know my own cat? He came to the door. He was yowling and scratching to get in. When I let him in, he went straight for his bowl." For eight years, she had emptied and refilled that bowl, and she sounded triumphant. Nobody had believed the cat would ever return, but she had continued to feed it, and she had been right.

"That's pretty amazing. What did... what did your husband have to say about it? He *saw* the cat?"

"What, do you think it's my imagination? Am I that deranged?"

She could be. Zachary didn't know. Maybe she had finally snapped and gone over the edge. Having lost too much, she had decided to resurrect her old pet. She did sound manic.

"Of course, Spencer saw it. He was surprised. But it's Mittens. He knows it's Mittens." Isabella's voice dropped to a conspiratorial tone. "Spencer doesn't exactly like cats. They shed, you know, and their litter tracks. It's just so amazing. I'm so happy. And I think... it must be a good omen for the case. I think that since Mittens came back, that must mean... that you are going to find something in Declan's case. You're going to figure it all out."

"Yes," Zachary agreed. "Maybe I will."

Zachary had called Kenzie several times, but she wasn't returning his calls. He took a quick look at her social networks to confirm that she was not sick or out of town, but she was posting the same type of stuff as usual. He gave her a couple of days. If she had been put off by Bridget's call, she would need a couple of days to cool off. She'd found out a lot about him all at once, and she was apparently the type who needed to think about it for a while before she felt comfortable talking to him again.

It was a painful couple of days. He also called Molly and told her that he would be preparing his final report shortly, wishing that he could have uncovered something new like Isabella had suggested.

"What did you find?" Molly demanded.

"That will all be in my report."

"But you can tell me what you found. Tell me whether you found anything to indicate that it wasn't just an accident. I'll wait for your report, but you can tell me that, can't you?"

"I... I really can't. My investigation was... inconclusive. I didn't uncover anything that the police didn't already know, but there were a few facts that... I think could lead in other directions."

"So, there was someone else involved? Someone took him?"

Zachary didn't like being forced into a corner, especially before he had a chance to write his report. Once he laid it all out in a report, he could just reference the appropriate paragraphs and say, 'it's all there.' He didn't ad lib well.

"It's possible, but I didn't find anything that could be used to persuade the police to look into it further. I don't know what help that is."

"But at least... we would know. Maybe something would

come up later on down the line that would let us pursue it. For now… at least we'd know that it wasn't just… negligence."

The way that she said the word made Zachary flash back to his own childhood. Missed meals, ratty clothes that didn't fit, absent caregivers, institutions with thin, hard mattresses and exploitative staff. He held tightly to his phone, and breathed in the smell of stale coffee, trying to ground himself in the present. Declan hadn't been neglected. He'd had two parents who loved and cared for him. He'd been well-fed and clothed. They might not have been perfect, but they were there for him.

The way Molly said it made him wonder what had happened in her past. Had she been the neglected child? Or was she the negligent parent? Or both? Did she hire Zachary because she wanted to assuage her own guilt rather than Isabella's? Maybe she needed to believe that she had raised Isabella to be a good, caring mother, not an emotional wreck who couldn't care for herself, let alone a child. Or a cat.

"I'll write up my report," Zachary promised. He looked at the calendar. "I'll try to get it to you by Friday."

"That's Christmas Eve."

It was, but Zachary didn't understand why that made it a bad day for him to finish his report. Wasn't it good to have it settled before Christmas so that they could be at peace during the season of peace and goodwill blah, blah, blah?

"Right. Christmas Eve," he agreed. "I'll have it to you by then."

But Zachary hadn't written it yet. He had scribbled down some notes. He had made an outline. He had tried to summarize his thoughts, but he couldn't do it without putting down the words of the report first, to get everything laid out and itemized.

He found himself avoiding his computer, knowing that the work was waiting for him there.

Instead, he decided to go to the medical examiner's office to see if Kenzie were around. If she weren't busy, they could chat for a few minutes. Hopefully, things would be pretty quiet with the

Christmas season approaching. People would be going on vacation. Just a skeleton staff at the police station.

Down in the basement, a few red garlands had been strung along the top of the wall, but it didn't make it look festive. It just made it look like a bare, clinical hallway with a tattered red garland running along the top. Like when Zachary had pulled discarded garlands from his neighbor's garbage and tied them to his tricycle. In his mind, he was going to make it into something fabulous, like Santa's sleigh; but it had just been a beat-up old tricycle with streamers tied to the handlebars. He'd gotten in big trouble for stealing from the neighbor's garbage.

Kenzie was at her desk. She hadn't gone on vacation. She had reports stacked up, but it didn't look like she was so busy she couldn't even return a phone call. She looked up at him with an expectant smile, and then some of it dribbled away, leaving her looking serious and questioning. Like he wasn't supposed to be there.

"Happy holidays," Zachary told her. He hadn't brought her a gift. It hadn't occurred to him until then that he might need a little something to break the ice. She was looking awfully cold.

"Merry Christmas, Zachary," she returned, face like stone.

"You decorated. It's very pretty."

"It wasn't me. I think it looks pathetic."

"Yeah... it does."

"Then why did you tell me it was pretty? I don't want you telling me stuff that's not true, just because you think it sounds good or is what I want to hear. I can't stand you lying to me."

Zachary licked his lips. "I'm not lying." His voice was barely above a whisper.

"I don't think you're very good at telling the truth, are you?"

"What do you mean?"

"Just what I said. You haven't had much practice with it. You'd rather tell stories than actually figure out the truth and say that."

"I don't know what you're talking about. I didn't lie to you."

"I don't think you even know what the truth is."

Zachary shifted his feet anxiously. "Who told you I lied? I can't think of anyone who would tell you that, except Bridget. Why would you talk to Bridget?"

She just looked at him, and Zachary knew he'd hit the nail on the head. She *had* been talking to Bridget. Why, he didn't know. Had she approached Bridget? Had Bridget approached Kenzie? He couldn't understand why either one of them would want to talk to the other.

"She said she told you right from the beginning that she didn't want kids. It shouldn't have been any great shock that she wanted to terminate an unplanned, unexpected pregnancy."

"I… didn't say it was a surprise… but I was still hurt. Do you know how it hurts, to have someone tell you they don't want your baby? A part of you? A child would have really made us into a family."

"She says that you were always pushing having children, right from the start, even though she said she wasn't ready. When she felt like you were forcing a pregnancy on her…"

Zachary winced. It was a slap in the face. She made it sound like he had assaulted Bridget. That he had impregnated her against her will. They had always used birth control. He had been willing to wait until she was ready.

"I never forced anything on her. She might 'feel like' I did, but we're talking facts here, not feelings. I never forced her to do anything. Sure, I wanted kids. I still want kids. I want a family of my own." He shook his head, unable to find strong enough words.

"I'm not ready for kids either," Kenzie said. "I want you to know that. I thought you were a guy I'd like to get to know, have a little fun with, but I'm not looking for a serious relationship. Everything about you is serious."

Zachary couldn't think of what to say. He thought he should crack a joke. Make her see that there was more to him, that he did have a fun side. But down there by the morgue, with the sad Christmas garlands, and Kenzie spouting the Gospel According to

Bridget, there was nothing he could say that would come out funny or lighthearted.

He swallowed and shook his head. "We're not serious enough to be discussing kids," he said tersely. "That's not why I wanted to see you."

Kenzie stared at him for a minute; then she gave a little laugh. Not laughing at him, just a little cough to break the tension.

"I guess I got ahead of myself, then, didn't I?"

"It's going to be a while before I can talk to anyone about having kids again."

As much as he longed for that missing family, he knew it was the truth. The talk of abortion, the phantom pregnancy, the traumatic breakup with Bridget; it was all too much. Too fresh.

"Yeah." Kenzie looked sorry that she had brought it all up. At least she wasn't calling him a liar anymore. "What was it, then? Why did you come down here? You're done with the Bond case, aren't you?"

"Yes... just trying to put together the final report. It's hard... because I don't really believe it."

"You have to put what you believe in the report. Otherwise, it's just another lie, isn't it?"

"But just like you said... I didn't find anything the police didn't already know. There are no grounds to reinvestigate it. It was... just an accident. A tragic accident."

"So that's what you put down."

"But I don't believe that. I think someone drugged him and drowned him."

"You don't know that."

"How could I *know* it, unless I was there? There's evidence to back it up."

"There isn't."

"He had cough medicine. Both parents said they didn't give him cough medicine."

"Maybe they forgot. Did it absentmindedly. Or they thought they'd be in trouble for it. Maybe they figure he drowned because he wandered into the pond while under the influence of the cough medicine, so they're afraid to admit it. Maybe somebody else had taken cough medicine, and he decided to take a drink out of the little dosing cup without anyone knowing about it. There are a hundred different scenarios, Zachary. There's no evidence of a third party. Just put *that* in your report."

"I suppose."

He knew he was going to have to, but he hated to do it. He didn't want to stir things up between the family and the police. He didn't want it getting into the news again. He didn't want people getting hurt because of him.

"So..." Kenzie gave a forced smile. "What other cases have you been working on? Tell me something interesting about another case. One that doesn't involve a death."

Zachary considered, and told her about the other case that was top of mind. There had been some press coverage, even though the school had tried to keep it quiet. They had tried to distance themselves from the charges against Principal Montgomery, which wasn't possible, when she was dating one of her students.

"I heard about that! That was one of your cases? How did you end up investigating child sex crimes?"

"It didn't start out that way. Just surveillance on a party to see what she was up to. Like dozens of others I've done. This is the first time I've turned up a teacher-student relationship."

"The principal's husband hired you?"

"I can't say who hired me. I'm not at liberty to say."

"But that's who it was."

Zachary shrugged and didn't say one way or another.

"Wow. I'm really impressed. That was a really big bust."

"It was unexpected, but once I knew what was going on, I had to protect the minor."

"You did the right thing. Boy, did you ever. That's amazing."

Zachary was finally able to smile at Kenzie, and she smiled back.

11

It was the day before Christmas, and Zachary knew he was supposed to have the final report ready for Molly. But maybe it was bad timing. She wouldn't want to get that news right before Christmas. He still hadn't managed to work out the language to his satisfaction. He wanted to be able to clearly state that Declan had been given cough medicine, but that nothing had been overlooked in the police investigation. He couldn't say both of those things. Not when the cough medicine seemed so significant to him.

But more than the writing of the final report, the season weighed heavily on him. The last few years he had gotten through Christmas only because of Bridget. His hope for a new life with her. With that whole life shattered, he didn't know how he was going to struggle through one more. It was a crushing weight.

He ignored the calls. He could see by the caller ID that the caller was Molly, and he knew what she was looking for. She wanted his report. She wanted to put the case to bed once and for all and to have a Christmas without guilt for Declan's death hanging over their heads.

As the evening drew on, there was one call from Mr. Peterson, one of Zachary's former foster fathers. The only one that he had kept in touch with over the years. Mr. Peterson had given him his first camera and had been the only one to encourage Zachary in his photography. Mr. Peterson left a stilted voicemail, his tone concerned.

"Zach... just calling to see how you are. To... wish you a Merry Christmas and make sure you're okay. Okay? Call me back and let me know you're all right... Okay? Pat says 'hi'... Talk to you soon."

There were no other calls. No friends, no family, no special person in his life. When people had asked him what he was doing for Christmas, he'd brushed them off, saying he had plans but remaining vague about what they were. He didn't want pity invitations. He didn't need people trying to fit him in at their Christmas tables just because of how miserable he was.

He found himself in the bathroom, with the medicine cabinet hanging open. Spencer would have been horrified by the mess. Zachary started pulling medications from the shelf. A cough medicine with codeine. Painkillers. Sleeping pills, some of them over-the-counter and some of them prescription. Pills for anxiety. For ADHD. Risperdal. Cold tablets in various daytime and night-time formulations.

Overdoses were a risky business. Not as certain as a gun or slashed wrists. Not that those were guaranteed either. But with pills, a person might throw them up again. Or wake up three days later with a headache. Or do permanent liver or kidney damage without that last, final sleep they were seeking.

The phone was ringing again. Zachary wearily dragged himself out of the bathroom to the bedroom, where his phone sat on the bedside table, vibrating noisily. He looked down at the screen.

Molly.

Again.

The least he could do was tell her he wasn't going to be able to get the final report to her until after Christmas. Sometimes, things just didn't work out as planned.

He picked up the phone and answered the call.

When he reached the hospital, Zachary looked around the emergency room for Molly. He saw Spencer first, pacing back and forth near the windows. He probably couldn't sit down for fear of catching a hospital infection.

Molly was sitting in one of the uncomfortable, slippery plastic chairs, her elbows on her knees and hands over her face. Zachary sat beside her.

"Molly?" He put his hand lightly on her back. While he wasn't one for touching strangers, she needed some comfort, and it was all he could manage.

Molly raised her face to look at him, and then put it back down in her hands again.

"I called you and called you," she said in a flat, stony voice. "I've been trying to get you for hours."

"Yes. I'm sorry. It hasn't been a good day for me."

It was a stupid thing to say. Once the words were out of his mouth and he heard them, he knew. *He* was having a bad day? Isabella had just attempted suicide and Molly didn't know if her daughter was going to make it.

"I'm sorry," he said quickly. "I didn't mean that. At least, I didn't mean it to sound like that. I'm sorry I didn't answer your earlier calls."

"I know." She sniffled. "It's not like any of this is your responsibility. I just didn't know who else to call."

"You hired me in the first place because you wanted to avoid this. I'm sorry. I failed you."

"You didn't fail me. It was going to happen with or without you. I knew it was. We all saw it coming, but we couldn't watch her twenty-four hours a day. Even if we tried to put her in an institution for her own safety, they'd only do a seventy-two-hour evaluation. If she didn't want to stay and they didn't think she was a danger to herself, they would let her right back out."

"They wouldn't have let her out, would they?"

"They would," Molly said with certainty. "I know they would. We've been here before."

"I'm sorry. I didn't know that. I guess I should have done a little more background on the case."

Molly wrung her hands.

Spencer hovered nearby, pausing from his pacing.

"Like she said, it wouldn't have made any difference. You couldn't have done anything to change it. We were doing our best to keep an eye on her, but… it was bound to happen anyway."

Zachary studied Spencer, shaking his head. "It wasn't inevitable. You can't know that."

"She was getting more and more depressed, slipping further and further into unreality."

Zachary remembered Isabella's bizarre call. "She phoned me. She said that her lost cat Mittens came back. I thought it sounded strange; I wondered if it was a psychotic break… was it?"

Molly raised her head, and she and Spencer looked at each other.

"The cat did come back," Molly said, her voice distant. "I swear, I never thought there was a snowball's chance in hell. Did you, Spencer?"

"No. Of course not."

"I thought it was just crazy talk. I thought it was just Isabella…being Isabella. She would get stuck on things. For years at a time. I don't know how many bags of that damn cat food she went through. Putting food out for it every single day it was gone. It was crazy."

"But now, the cat is back," Spencer said.

He started pacing again.

Zachary sat with Molly. There wasn't much to say to her. She told him about Isabella and Declan, little stories about them. The things that become legends in families. *Remember when...*

Zachary couldn't help thinking about his own history while she talked about her child and grandchild. What would it have been like for him if he had still been part of a family? Would he still have been teetering on the edge like he was? It didn't seem to have helped Isabella to have a loving, interested parent. She had still attempted suicide.

Or maybe Zachary was looking at it all wrong. Maybe he wasn't paying any attention to the dysfunction in the family, and that was the key to Isabella's instability. Maybe the mother who was outwardly loving and kind actually wasn't. Maybe the fact that she was still trying to control her adult daughter's life and to manipulate her mental state was part of the problem. Maybe she was too involved. Too ready to take the reins and control a family that was no longer hers.

Molly had told Zachary on the phone that Isabella had taken pills. The very method Zachary had been considering when he finally decided to answer the phone. Was it a coincidence? Or were they both influenced by some outside factor? Maybe it was the fact that Declan had cough medicine in his system when he died. Zachary's focus on it had directed both of their thoughts to the medicine cabinet.

Was it his fault that Isabella had been impelled to attempt suicide?

"Why do you think she did it?" Zachary asked Molly, in the midst of a retelling of one of her cute stories. "Was it because of my investigation?"

Molly stopped and looked at him, mouth open. "What?"

"Something made her decide to take action. Was it me? Because I was asking her questions?"

"No." Molly shook her head. Her face was chalk white. "No, I really think your investigation was helping. Giving her something positive to focus on. That maybe you would be able to find out the truth."

Unless the truth were that Isabella had given Declan the cough medicine, knowing the reaction he would have to it.

"Then why?" Zachary demanded. "Why now, without even waiting to see what my report said? Was she afraid of what it was going to say?"

"I told her that you were going to give it to us before Christmas. That maybe it would help her to see that it wasn't her fault."

Zachary shook his head.

It was past midnight. Christmas Day. He'd missed his deadline. It was Christmas Day, and he was sitting in the hospital waiting room, trying to comfort the mother of the woman he might have pushed toward suicide.

"It's a bad time of year for suicides," Molly said.

Zachary raised his head to look at her. Unaware that he had been covering his face, in much the same position Molly had been when he first came into the waiting room.

"Christmas is a bad time of year for people who are depressed," Molly said. "There are lots of suicides around this season. It's not your fault."

"I wish I could believe that."

"I don't know why Christmas," Molly went on. "Maybe because people expect to be happy for Christmas, and then when they're not... the expectations make it worse... seeing other people who appear to be happy."

"Isabella bought presents for Declan," Spencer said, his pacing bringing him closer to them again. "I couldn't understand why she would do that. She knew he was dead. She knew he wouldn't be opening presents and spending Christmas with us."

Just like she had fed the missing cat. How many years would she continue to buy her dead child Christmas presents?

Molly looked at Spencer, nodding sadly. "Isabella always loved

Christmas. I was hoping maybe she'd perk up a bit for it. That it would be good for her."

"What could be good about Christmas without your child?" Zachary demanded, his throat aching. "How could she look forward to that? How could she celebrate when her arms were so empty?"

Molly and Spencer both stared at Zachary. His reaction was over the top. It was too much. They were wondering what was wrong with him, how he could be so emotional over someone he barely knew. What did he know or care what she felt?

Zachary dropped his head into his hands again. "I hate Christmas."

There was silence. Spencer started to pace again.

"When Isabella was a little girl…" Molly started in on another Isabella story. Then she faded out and gave a sigh. "You must have somewhere to be today. I shouldn't have called you down here when there's nothing for any of us to do. What did you have planned for today?"

If Zachary had used a day planner, there would have been a big, black hole for Christmas Day. He couldn't see anything past it. Just like so many years in the past, he'd been unable to see how his life would continue after Christmas Eve. It was the black beast that swallowed everything else up.

"Nothing. Just taking a break. Staying at home."

"It's different when you're on your own, isn't it? Sitting around in your pajamas watching Christmas specials on TV, because there's nowhere else to go? You don't have any family around here?"

Zachary sat back the best he could in the slippery plastic chair. He massaged his forehead, immensely tired. "I don't have any family."

"You don't? I'm sorry."

He shrugged. "I haven't had for a long time. Not since I was ten. The last couple of years, I had my wife. This year…"

"You're not together anymore?"

"We had a pretty ugly break-up. Yeah."

"You could come over and spend it with us," Molly suggested. Then she seemed to realize what she had just said. "I mean... I guess this is it, isn't it? This is how we're spending our Christmas. Here. Waiting for word."

Zachary nodded. "Might just as well be here as anywhere else."

In fact, it was probably the safest place for him to be on Christmas Day.

Y ou are recently divorced?" Spencer asked, drifting closer to Zachary when Molly took a break to find a bathroom and more coffee. He'd obviously overheard at least part of the conversation with Molly.

"Yes," Zachary admitted. "Just this year."

"What was that like? The whole process?"

"It was... devastating," Zachary admitted. His face grew warm, and he looked far off into the distance, away from Spencer.

Spencer eased back and forth on his legs, looking tired. If he'd been pacing ever since they discovered Isabella, he had to be exhausted.

"Things haven't been good between Isabella and me," he said in a low voice. Even though Zachary had already sensed that, it was difficult for Spencer to get it out in the open. "We've never really been compatible. We thought we were, but we didn't know anything. I told you about the plate."

"The one you threw out," Zachary confirmed.

"Yeah. That's just one example out of many. We've tried to make it work. Set up boundaries, so that she can be comfortable in her studio and know that I won't touch anything, and I know her things will be confined to certain areas. We've set up our timetables and parenting duties…" Spencer paused for a moment, getting past the fact that he no longer had any parenting duties. He swallowed hard, his Adam's apple straining. "So that really, it's just like we're two single people sharing a house, and up until this summer, sharing custody of a child. It's not any kind of partnership."

"And you want to know if you should get divorced."

"I know we should. I've known that for a long time. Since Deck died…"

Zachary waited for a moment to see if he would pick up his broken thought. Zachary and Bridget had only the idea of a child standing between them. A phantom pregnancy that would never be. For Spencer and Isabella, it wasn't academic. It wasn't just an idea. They had shared a child for almost five years. It had, perhaps, been the only thing left holding them together. Having Declan torn from their lives had ravaged both of them. It had damaged them, and maybe their relationship was beyond repair.

"You have to do what's best for you," Zachary said finally, aware of how inadequate the advice was. He didn't know what was best for himself; how was he supposed to give marriage advice to someone else? "For you and Isabella."

"But what if the same thing isn't best for both of us?"

Zachary scratched at a spot on his pants and found that it was a snag. He tried to smooth the pulled fibers back down. Bridget had insisted on the separation and divorce. Zachary had been more than prepared to fight for the marriage. To find a way to make it work again. He had known that if they just worked together, they could heal the rift.

Spencer was on the other side. It was Spencer who had decided his marriage was unsalvageable and that he couldn't move on until he was free. Zachary was supposed to tell him to leave, while his wife was fighting for her life a few rooms away.

Zachary was silent.

"Am I supposed to stay because Isabella needs me?"

Zachary took a deep breath. "For now," he said, telling

Spencer what he already knew. "I don't know for how long... but you need to wait and make sure she's going to be okay. Then you two need to have a long talk, and decide how to make the split as pain-free as possible."

Spencer nodded, staring off into the distance. Molly was returning with a tray of coffees for all of them.

"Is that what you did?" Spencer asked.

Zachary shook his head. "No. It's not."

It was almost noon before a doctor came to talk to Molly and Spencer about Isabella's condition and prognosis. He looked at Zachary but wasn't rude enough to ask who he was and why he was there.

"We lost her a couple of times," he said. "But she's finally stable. We've done everything we could to clean her blood and minimize the damage to her liver and kidneys. We won't know what level of functioning they have for a while. There will be a lot of testing to do over the next few days."

"What about brain damage?" Spencer asked.

"We are hopeful that there will be no perceptible brain damage. Only time will tell. For now, she's sleeping, and we want to keep her asleep for the next day or two."

Molly was nodding along. "Can we see her?"

"Yes." He glanced over the three of them. "Family only."

Molly looked like she was going to object to this, but Zachary shook his head. "That's fine. You don't need me in there."

She clutched at his arm. "Are you going to be here when we come back out?"

"No. I think I'll head home now. I haven't had much sleep the last few days. It will be good if I can get some rest."

She held his arm tighter. "We need to know what happened to Declan," she pleaded. "You can see that, can't you?"

He nodded, defeated, unable to answer aloud. Molly let his arm go.

Zachary put his key in the lock and turned it. Nothing happened. There was no resistance or snick as the bolt slid back. He turned the key the opposite way and heard and felt the bolt slide. Then he unlocked it again.

Was it possible that he had been in such a hurry when he rushed from the apartment to the hospital that he had forgotten to lock the door behind him? He stood there for a moment, frozen, listening for any movement. He tried to replay his departure in his mind, but locking the door behind him was so routine he couldn't remember it.

There was no note on his door this time, nothing that hinted at the presence of an intruder.

He slowly turned the handle and pushed the door open, ears pricked for any sound.

There was a noise. He couldn't identify it at first. Someone rifling through the contents of his bedroom drawers?

He didn't have a gun. It had never seemed like a good idea to have a lethal weapon that convenient. Zachary pulled the door shut again, as quietly as possible, and took out his phone.

The police were there in five minutes. No one had left the apartment by the door, and there was no fire escape or way to leave by the window.

"He's still in there," Zachary said in a low voice, which he hoped would not carry as easily as a whisper.

"You know who it is?"

"No. I've had a few threats lately, but I don't know who from. I didn't see."

"I'd like you to go down the hall." The policeman gestured the way they had come. "Don't want you right outside the door. Just wait over there."

"Okay."

He retreated and watched the operation as the policemen pushed the door quietly open and looked around before entering.

If Zachary were a TV detective, he would have had two guns, at least, and would have rushed the apartment all by himself, guns blazing. It wouldn't have mattered whether the apartment was filled with a dozen ninjas with sharp blades, he would somehow be able to overcome them all. Or maybe he'd be the ninja himself and go up against a dozen armed men with his bare hands.

But it wasn't TV.

He heard the shouts of the police as they confronted the intruder. There were no shots fired. In a few minutes, one of the other policemen came sauntering out of the apartment and down the hall. He had a grin on his face.

"You got him?" Zachary asked. "He wasn't armed?"

"We got *her*," the officer said, smiling wider. "And no, she wasn't armed."

Zachary's stomach flipped. Her? She? It didn't make any sense.

If Principal Montgomery had been granted bail, then maybe she had gone to his apartment to try to find any evidence he had of her affair and destroy it. But the lock hadn't been tampered with. He couldn't think of any other woman who would invade his apartment. Kenzie? Even if she had come by to wish him a Merry Christmas, she couldn't have let herself in.

There was only one person who might still have a key.

In his bedroom, Bridget was on her feet. If the police had taken her to the ground and handcuffed her, they had released her again after a short discussion.

"Your intruder was in the bathroom," the policeman said. "Apparently inventorying your medications."

Zachary looked around the room. His drawers had obviously been opened, no longer all closed flush. A tie was sticking out of one of them. He looked over at the bathroom and saw a garbage bag on the floor. There were still some items on the counter where he had left them the day before, but most had been put back in the cabinet or tossed in the garbage bag. Zachary finally looked back at Bridget, baffled.

"What's going on? What are you doing here?"

Her face was bright pink. She tried to look cool and casual but was obviously embarrassed by the scene she had caused. "I couldn't get ahold of you," she explained. "Your phone was going straight to voicemail like it was turned off." She shifted uncomfortably, arms crossed in front of her, ears turning a deep scarlet. "I was worried about you."

Zachary looked at her, at the bathroom, and at his drawers.

"I know it's a bad time of year for you." Bridget's voice faltered. "I called to make sure you were okay. I came over because… I had to make sure you hadn't done something." She glanced toward the bathroom. "When I saw everything out on the counter… I was getting rid of it. Before you could…"

He was so stunned by her actions he didn't know what to do or say. In spite of the way she had screamed at him every time she had seen him, she had reached out to him on Christmas Day, worried about his state of mind. She had abandoned whatever other plans she had for the day to go to his apartment and check on him. To dispose of the pills that might be too much of a temptation for him.

"Do you want to press charges?" one of the cops asked, humor in his tone.

"No. No, I'm sorry I got you all out here… I just heard someone… I wasn't expecting visitors…"

"Better than getting shot or cracked over the head by a burglar. We discourage people from rushing in if they think there's someone in the house."

They prepared to leave, finishing their various notes and calls and whatever else had to be done to document the incident before leaving. They all wished Zachary and Bridget a Merry Christmas and headed out.

And then it was just Zachary and Bridget. Standing there looking at each other, not sure what to say or do.

"I'm sorry," Bridget apologized. "I didn't mean to scare you. I was really worried."

"It's okay. I was at the hospital." He held up a hand before she could rush in, demanding to know if he was okay. "I had a client attempt suicide last night."

She gave a laugh of disbelief. "I'll bet *that* was a shock."

"It was, and it wasn't. The timing was… fortuitous… if a suicide attempt can be fortuitous."

She looked back toward the bathroom. "Because you were considering it yourself." She said it baldly. There was no beating around the bush with Bridget.

"More than considering," Zachary admitted.

"I'll finish going through this stuff." Bridget went back into the bathroom and continued to examine the pill bottles. "Do you want me to stay with you today?"

"No. You go on back, have dinner with Gordon and his family."

She turned and looked at him through the doorway, her eyebrows shooting up. "What? How do you know my plans?"

"I just assumed…"

"You just assumed what? I've never even told you who I'm seeing!"

"It's a small world. I still hear from friends."

She threw a couple of pill bottles away with a scowl and quick, angry movements.

"I told you before; you stay out of my business. Just quit it!"

Zachary leaned against his bureau, watching her. "You're the one breaking into my house," he reminded her.

"I didn't break in. I have a key."

"And you called Kenzie to warn her off?"

Bridget paused, and he saw her biting the inside of her cheek as she thought up a response.

"I felt like it was my duty to let her know... how things are."

"Why didn't you call her when you couldn't find me? I might have been having Christmas with her."

"I did," she admitted.

"But *I'm* the one interfering in *your* life."

"I'm sorry if you think I'm sticking my nose where it doesn't belong, Zachary, but it's for your own safety. Just because things didn't work out between us, that doesn't mean that I don't still care about you. I don't want you to... I don't want you to be unhappy."

Zachary sighed, watching her clear away the last few bottles of pills. Her instincts had been absolutely correct. She knew from experience how difficult the season was for him.

She lifted the garbage bag and tied the top.

"Did you leave me with anything?" he asked.

"A few Tylenol. A few Ambien and Xanax." She shrugged. "If you need something... call me."

What he needed was the life that they had had together.

But she had ripped that away from him, and she wouldn't be giving it back.

A few days after Christmas, while Zachary knew that Isabella was still in the hospital, he made arrangements to see Spencer. He called ahead like Spencer had asked him to, as if he were making an appointment with a lawyer or dentist. As far as he knew, Spencer's days were filled with testing and reviewing products on the computer. He didn't have meetings or a school or studio schedule to coordinate. Just sitting in his home office, doing his work there. Zachary wanted Spencer to be in a cooperative mood, not in a hurry to kick him out of the house because he hadn't been prepared to receive a visitor.

He arrived on time, and Spencer opened the door for him before he even had a chance to knock.

Spencer looked as though he had aged ten years. His face was creased and pale. His Christmas obviously hadn't been any better than Zachary's. Maybe even worse. He nodded a polite greeting and took Zachary back to his office and had him sit in the chair. Zachary sat staring at the stuffed dog still perched on top of the printer.

"I want to have a serious discussion with you about Isabella."

Spencer rubbed the bridge of his nose. "What about Isabella? You know everything there is to know."

"Why do you think she tried to kill herself?"

Spencer looked surprised. "Because she is depressed. Grieving."

"But why would she want to kill herself? Lots of people are depressed or grieving. They go to the doctor. They get antidepressants. Therapy. Why wouldn't Isabella do any of that?"

"She did. She went to her therapist. Support group. She didn't want any medications, because of the side effects. She called Molly and had her stay over sometimes. She painted."

"Why wouldn't she take meds?"

"Because they can cause worsening of symptoms. An increase in suicidal thoughts. She didn't want to risk it. She's had meds before. They never seemed to work out well for her."

"It takes some fiddling around sometimes," Zachary said. "Trying different medications and different dosages."

"She didn't have the patience for it. If the first prescription didn't work... she didn't want to try anything else. That was it; she'd had enough."

Zachary doodled in his notepad. He had sympathy for Isabella. He'd been there himself. He knew what it was like to be broken, and none of the things that were supposed to help would.

"Are you sure it wasn't guilt that drove Isabella to suicide?"

"Guilt? I suppose." Spencer gave a shrug. "She felt guilty about Declan getting out of the yard without her realizing it. That she was too late. We all feel guilty for being too late."

"I wonder if it went deeper than that. What if she was the one who gave him the cough medicine?"

Spencer grimaced and shook his head. "She wouldn't do that. She wouldn't give him cold medicine because it might knock him out. It scared her."

"Maybe she *wanted* to knock him out."

"Why?"

Zachary couldn't bring himself to say, 'so that she could drown him.' Not to her husband. Not to Declan's father. "Maybe he was getting underfoot too much, and she wanted him to be quiet and leave her alone. Maybe she wanted to paint in peace."

"Isabella wouldn't do that."

"I know plenty of women who would. Who have done exactly that."

"You do *not* know Isabella!" Spencer snapped. He slammed his palm down on the desk. "Isabella wouldn't dream of doing that!"

He was breathing hard. He coughed, clutching his side. Pain lightninged across his face. Zachary watched him closely, frowning. Spencer swore and felt his ribcage tenderly. Sweat was gathering around his temples.

"Are you okay?" Zachary asked.

"Yeah. I'm fine. Picked up a bug at the hospital, and all of the coughing and sneezing… you know how sore it can make you."

Zachary didn't believe it. "Take a deep breath," he suggested.

Spencer obeyed, and instead of coughing, winced heavily and protected his side. Zachary got up and went around the desk to him.

"Hold still." Without asking or giving Spencer a chance to object, he tugged Spencer's shirt out of his pants and pulled it up. Spencer was too busy guarding his side to stop him.

Spencer's hand covered much of the area, but Zachary could still see black and blue bruises. He tried to nudge Spencer's hand away and caught a glimpse of the dark bruises under his hand.

"You've got broken ribs."

Spencer shook his head. "It's just like I said. From coughing."

"You don't get broken ribs from coughing."

"You can," Spencer argued. "I've done it before." He stopped talking and just breathed for a few minutes, pain etched on his face. "Isabella got rid of all of the cough medicine in the house after you asked if we gave it to Declan. She will freak out if I bring any more into the house. What am I supposed to do? How am I supposed to stop coughing? Maybe honey and lemon. Honey and lemon don't work for a cough so bad it breaks your ribs!" Anger and pain made his voice thin and strained.

"Who's hitting you? Isabella? Or is it someone else you've gotten on the wrong side of."

"No. No one is hitting me. It's just the coughing."

He started coughing as if to demonstrate, and for a few minutes was so racked with choking coughs that Zachary could feel the pain of it himself.

"You should go to the doctor. Maybe you've got pneumonia or bronchitis."

Spencer nodded. He didn't attempt to answer. Sweat and tears streamed down his face. Zachary sat on the edge of the desk, watching him.

"Do you want me to drive you to the doctor?"

Spencer shook his head. He held up one finger, and after a moment managed to get enough breath to answer, without bursting into another fit of coughs. "At the hospital. When I go to see Isabella."

"You'll see a doctor? In the ER?"

Spencer nodded his agreement.

Zachary just watched him for a few minutes, trying to think of what else to say to him, how he could help the man.

"A lot of men are abused," he said. "It isn't just women who are abused by their spouses, but men are afraid to speak up. Afraid that they'll be made fun of. That it makes them less manly and people will look down on them."

Spencer shook his head. "I don't care about machismo, Zachary. Look at me. I'm as geeky as they come. I don't have a reputation to protect." He rubbed his chest and side. "It's not Isabella. It's just from coughing."

It was a crisp, cold day, and Zachary had to keep moving to keep his toes from freezing. Moving around constantly wasn't a very good way of keeping surveillance. People tended to notice a grown man bobbing and pacing as if he badly needed to pee.

He held his camera up and took some random tree shots. He zoomed the telephoto in on a squirrel and tracked it is it busily gathered nuts or pinecones and went up and down the tree. He looked back toward his subject to make sure he hadn't gone anywhere or met anyone and went back to taking pictures of the squirrel.

Maybe if he ever retired, he'd take up wildlife photography. At least he wouldn't have to write up surveillance reports. Retirement was a long way away. If he lived that long.

Glancing back, he saw the subject was on the move again, and swung his telephoto lens the other direction, pretending he was focusing on the waterfowl near the pond that hadn't completely iced over.

As he watched, the subject handed a thick catalog envelope to a man in a long, black overcoat. Mae Gordon's insurance agent. He was given a smaller envelope in return. An envelope that, while thinner, could still contain a pretty nice wad of cash. Zachary clicked away, recording all the details he could.

Kenzie answered the phone after four rings. Zachary had almost decided it was going to go to voicemail, and then there she was.

"I wasn't sure I'd find you at work," he told her. Though, of course, he knew that was exactly where she would be. "I thought maybe you would take off a few extra days for Christmas."

"No, it's a pretty busy time of year down here. Christmas is hard for some people."

"Yeah." Zachary kept his voice carefully unemotional.

"Your ex called me Christmas Day looking for you. She sounded pretty upset. I gather she found you?"

"Yes. Eventually."

"What did she want?"

"Just to wish me a Happy Christmas. Make sure I was okay."

"See, I told you she doesn't hate you." There was reserve in Kenzie's voice. A tinge of jealousy? "That was nice of her."

"You don't have anything to worry about. We didn't get together. She just wanted to make sure I got through Christmas okay."

"I'm not worried," she said breezily. "So… when are you going to tell me about it?"

"About Bridget?" Zachary asked blankly.

"No, not about Bridget! What your deal is with Christmas. It must be one helluva story."

"Oh… well, it's not a fun story. Nothing you want to hear."

"I do, though. You've got me curious."

Zachary hummed. "Not yet," he said. "It's not a story I tell casual acquaintances. Maybe later… when we know each other a bit better."

"You're very secretive."

"I'm just… a private person. There are a lot of things in my past that I'd rather forget. If I have to keep telling the story, I can't leave it behind."

"I don't like secrets."

"It's not a secret. Just private," Zachary repeated.

"Huh. Does it apply to New Year's too? Do you have bad feelings about New Year's?"

"Not specifically."

"Good. Why don't we do something, then?"

Zachary's spirits perked. "I'd like that," he said. "What did you have in mind?"

"I haven't decided yet. Maybe you can help me with that. I don't want a big party. Maybe a smaller gathering, or maybe just watching TV with a big bowl of popcorn."

Either way, the last strike of midnight signaled not only the playing of Auld Lang Syne, but also a kiss. So far, his dates with Kenzie had not been very intimate, and he looked forward to the possibility of that changing.

"I like the popcorn idea," he said. "But I'm open to whatever you want to do."

"Great! I'll put together some options and run them by you, but I'd better be getting back to work here."

"I did have one more thing," Zachary inserted before she could cut him off. She didn't hang up the call.

"Oh. Sorry! What was it you called about?"

"I didn't call just to ask you, but I did want to know…"

"Fire away."

"I wanted to know if it's possible to break a rib coughing."

"Well!" She giggled at that. "That's a funny question. The answer is yes, it is possible. Not real common, but possible. You can break a rib coughing or sneezing. Or blow a blood vessel in your face or eye and end up looking like someone battered you. Or you could have an accident because of coughing or sneezing, banging your head on something in front of you with the force, or tripping, or breaking a tooth or a filling. Or crashing your car. You could do an internet search. There are lots of bizarre injuries that can be attributed to coughing or sneezing."

"Huh."

"Is this a case, or just random trivia?"

"It is a case, actually. A case involving spousal battery… or maybe just a cold."

"That's a tough one. She could be telling the truth. Or it could just be a more creative version of 'I walked into a door.'"

"Any way to tell?"

"No. Not really. Just watch for patterns. A broken rib from coughing isn't something that should reoccur with any regularity. Especially in the absence of a cold or pneumonia. Keep an eye on her."

Kenzie had suggested they begin with a nice dinner at the local inn, which was renowned for the on-site chef and his expensive creations. Zachary's pocketbook would certainly take a hit, but he imagined that the dress Kenzie would pick out for such a fancy restaurant on New Year's Eve would be well worth it.

"Are you sure it's okay?" Kenzie had checked. "We're not going to run into your ex there?"

"No. Bridget has other plans for New Year's."

"You know her plans?"

"She told me over Christmas," Zachary assured her. "Besides, I know the kind of things she likes to do New Year's Eve, and quiet little restaurants in out-of-the-way places are not on the list."

"Okay. I just want to make sure. I feel like we always end up running into her or getting a call from her, and I want this one to be just you and me."

"No one else," Zachary promised. "She's going to be with her new boyfriend. They aren't going to be anywhere near the inn."

After dinner at the inn, they would return to Zachary's apartment and have popcorn in front of the TV, if they still had enough room for it. Zach knew that fancy gourmet meals tended to be smaller than the typical burger or prime rib dinner, so he figured he'd still have room for popcorn. He'd been craving it ever since Kenzie suggested it.

He would have the perfect evening with Kenzie, with no interference by Bridget or anyone else.

14

The inn's reputation was well-deserved. Zachary had been a little nervous about trying anything gourmet, which made him think of caviar and escargot and other kinds of raw fish and meats. He wasn't sure he'd be able to stomach anything too unusual. He usually returned to meat and potatoes as his comfort food.

But the restaurant's New Year's menu had been excellent. A whole series of small courses, with tastes from all around the world. Even if a diner didn't like one item, there were so many to choose from that skipping over one or two courses along the way was not a problem. Zachary left the inn with Kenzie, feeling satisfied but not overstuffed. He'd still be able to eat some popcorn while they watched old movies on TV, or whatever Kenzie felt like watching. He didn't care what it was, as long as he got to cuddle up with her on the couch. She had on a daring red dress, and he was looking forward to the chime of midnight, if not earlier.

He helped Kenzie with her coat as they stepped outside and were assaulted by a biting cold wind. At least she'd had the presence of mind to bring more than just a filmy wrap to cover her up while she was outside. A smart woman dressed for the weather in spite of fashion, prepared for any car trouble rather than relying on the car heater for the evening.

"What's that?" Kenzie asked, pointing.

Zachary held the car door for her, then went around to the driver's side to pick up the flyer pinned under the windshield wiper. He got into the car and started it up, making sure everything was set to warm before dropping his eyes to the flyer.

You were told to drop the case. I warned you.

"What is it?" Kenzie repeated.

Zachary's first instinct was to crumple it into a ball and insist that it was nothing, but she was a grown woman and had made it clear she didn't want to be lied to and protected. He handed it to her.

Kenzie's eyes went over the page. A crease appeared between her eyes. She turned it over, examining the blank back as well.

"That's kind of disturbing," she said. "How often do you get these?"

"Third one from this idiot." Zachary checked the controls for the heater again, not wanting to look at her. "Trouble is, they're all as half-baked as that one."

"What do you mean?"

"I mean, he doesn't say which case it is!"

She looked back down at the note and gave a little laugh.

"Oh! Well, that's an ego problem, I guess. He—or she—thinks his case is the biggest and most important, and you should know right away which one it is."

"Exactly. He also never actually makes a threat. Or what? Drop the case, or he'll do what?" Zachary shook his head.

"And you don't know which case it is?"

"I can narrow it down, just because of the timeframe. There are only three or four cases that started before I got the first note that I'm still working on now."

"And which of them would fit the profile of this note?" She squinted at it, considering. "Something personal, I would think, where someone's reputation is at stake. With a... less-than-brilliant target."

"I'm not sure about that. He's smart enough to find my house and my car. It might just be ego, like you said, not lack of intelligence."

"I suppose that's a little more difficult... especially the car, when you're out and about like tonight. How did he know you'd be here? Who did you tell your dinner plans to?"

"No one." He didn't tell her that he didn't really have any friends close enough to care where he was going or what he was doing New Year's Eve. That just sounded pathetic. "It's possible he just happened to see my car in the lot and thought he'd use the opportunity." Zachary shook his head. That didn't sit right. He didn't think it was a viable theory. "You stay here for a minute."

Leaving Kenzie to enjoy the warmth of the heater, he climbed back out into the biting wind. He took a walk around the car, turning on his phone flashlight app to look for markings in the packed-down snow around the car. He couldn't find anything suspicious. He crouched down by the bumper first at the front of the car, then the back, and took off his glove to feel under the bumper. That's where he would have put a tracker. But it could be anywhere on the underside of the car, and he wouldn't be able to do a thorough search until he could get underneath and examine every inch with a good light.

Zachary got back into the car.

"Anything?"

"No. Not that I could find. I'll have to get it up on a lift later to see."

He clenched and unclenched his fingers a few times to get the blood flowing again, and used numb fingers to turn on his GPS tracking app. The chances were not great, but it was worth a try. He searched to see if there were any transmitters nearby that he could pair with. No luck. He skimmed over the map, checking whether any of the subjects he was tracking were close by.

"What's that?"

Kenzie was looking at his phone screen. Zachary shut it off and slid it into his pocket.

"Just a GPS app."

"You don't know how to get home from here?"

"I'm just checking who might live or work nearby, who might happen to drive by and see my car here."

Kenzie put on her seatbelt. "Your car isn't that distinctive," she observed. "It looks like a hundred other cars in the city. Who is going to drive by and know that it's yours?"

She was right about that. They would have to know his license plate or be following or tracking him. It wasn't just serendipity that they had seen Zachary's car parked at the inn.

He sighed and put the car into gear to back out, and then pulled onto the highway.

"Is it just like the other notes?"

"I… don't know. It's pretty generic. Why?"

"I'm just wondering if maybe it isn't about a case. Maybe it's your ex, and she's trying to disrupt our date."

"No." Zachary was certain Bridget was nowhere close to the inn. "It's not Bridget."

"How can you be sure? Like you said, the note doesn't say which case. It doesn't actually specify any threat. Maybe that's because she's trying to disrupt your date, not get you off of any particular investigation. When did you start getting them? Or maybe this one is a copycat. Does Bridget know about the other two?"

"Uh… no. She doesn't know anything about them. I'm the only one who does. Me and the person sending them."

"And you're one hundred percent sure that's not Bridget."

"One hundred percent," Zachary agreed. His skin prickled with goosebumps at the suggestion. Zachary readjusted the direction of the heating vents, trying to get warmed up. "It's not Bridget. You can be sure of that."

"Okay… because you know she's jealous about you seeing me, right?"

Zachary blew his breath out his nose. "I don't know whether it's because she's jealous, or just because she's mad at me."

"She's jealous."

"Why? She's been dating other men almost since the day we broke up. Why would she care if I start seeing someone?"

"People are rarely logical."

There was a period of missing time.

Zachary was aware of a haze of pain. Of someone crying and shouting beside him. He couldn't move. There were lights and voices, the chaos around him making it too difficult to focus on one thing, to figure out what was happening.

"It will be okay," a voice told him. "Help is on its way."

He felt as if everything were upside down. He couldn't make heads or tails of the shapes around him.

"Zachary? Are you okay?" A woman's voice. Not Bridget's. He couldn't figure out whose voice it was.

"What happened?" he asked. But the words didn't come out properly, and all he could hear was moaning.

He drifted in and out, sometimes trying to pinpoint the source of his pain and sometimes trying to turn the world back the right way around again. People kept fading in and out, telling him not to worry. Telling him everything was going to be okay.

Lights strobed in his eyes, so bright he had to screw his eyes shut to avoid their assault. He wanted to put his hand over his eyes because it was still too bright, even through his eyelids.

"Sir! Sir, can you hear me?"

The new voice was loud and insistent. Zachary tried to block it out. His body was cold, and he had an overwhelming feeling of sleepiness. He decided that he must be home in bed. Maybe someone had left the window open. That was why he was having such strange dreams. He was cold, and his body was trying to wake him up. If he just snuggled under the blanket and waited, the furnace would kick in, and he'd be able to go back to sleep.

"Sir! I need you to stay awake. Can you talk to me? Can you tell me where you're hurt?"

Zachary tried to shake his head, but it felt wobbly and weak. The world did a couple of somersaults.

"Sir, can you tell me your name?"

Zachary tried to form the words. Only a moan came out.

"Zachary," a woman's voice said. "His name is Zachary."

"Zachary?" The loud, insistent voice burrowed into his head. "Are you in pain? Can you squeeze my hand?"

The world spun. The loud voice stopped for a while. Zachary tried to process some of the words that whirled around him.

Jaws of life.

Backboard.

Inside his belly, he started to shake. Where was his blanket? Why wasn't he warm enough?

He wished he could get out of the dream he was trapped inside. Maybe he needed to go to the bathroom. Sometimes he had bad dreams when his body was trying to wake him up to go relieve himself. Zachary tried to focus on his body's signals. Did he have a full bladder? Was that why he needed to wake up?

He was just floating in mid-air and couldn't read his body's signals. Maybe he had left his body in the dream. Maybe he was experiencing an astral projection. He was really somewhere else. Maybe in his bed, maybe sitting in a hypnotist's chair somewhere. He'd had out-of-body experiences before. He'd never told anybody about them, but he'd experienced that removed feeling before.

"We're going to lose him. Zachary. Zachary!"

He tried to rouse himself. The voice was just so damn loud! Why couldn't they just leave him alone? He wanted to fall deeper into the dream. Into the part where he could do things he couldn't do in his physical body. Fly. Breathe under water. Project himself into another plane of existence.

"Zachary! Stay with me, buddy. Focus on my voice. Can you count? Backward from one hundred. Ninety-nine, ninety-eight..."

Zachary wanted to wake up enough to tell the idiot that that was what you did to go to sleep, not to stay awake, but he couldn't rouse himself. His lips moved like he was counting too, but there were still no words, just animal moans.

"Finally here."

Zachary didn't know what was finally there. Maybe he was ready to wake up. He thought maybe he'd fallen asleep riding the bus, and he had reached his destination.

"Cold as a witch's backside," someone complained.

There was laughter and some joking around, but the mood was mostly somber. Zachary wasn't cold anymore. He had finally warmed up. Maybe he had pulled the blanket on, or maybe the furnace had kicked in.

There were more lights in his eyes, so bright that they cut into his brain even through his closed eyelids. He tried to tell Bridget to turn off the light. Just because she couldn't sleep, that didn't mean she had to keep him awake too. He wanted to sink deeper into sleep, to find that peaceful, restful place.

The noise was even worse. Like the building was going to fall on top of him. Zachary tried to reach out to steady himself, to keep the world from falling down around him or to keep himself from falling into the world. More moans came out of his mouth.

"It's okay. Just a few more minutes."

Zachary's head spun. He waited for it to all settle down. How much had he had to drink at supper? He couldn't remember what he had eaten. Or what day it was. He thought it might be Christmas. He'd had too much to drink and he needed to throw up, but he had to wake up and get to the bathroom. He didn't want to barf in his shoes. Doing that once was enough.

There were tearing, rending noises around him. More light. More noise. It was overwhelming. Zachary felt his jaw clench. There was an explosion in his brain. All the sights and sounds were gone, and he was stuck inside his brain, in blackness, with no way to get out.

He didn't know how long it lasted. A second or an eternity. With no external stimuli, there was no way to gauge it.

A moan woke him.

"He's coming back."

The world tipped this way and that, trying to reestablish a horizon. Zachary realized his eyes were open again and he couldn't command them to shut.

There were hands on him. Moving him, then strapping him down. His head felt like a watermelon. He tried to speak to one of the figures moving around him, dark silhouettes against the bright lights.

It's going to be okay. Everything will be all right.

We need warming blankets.

Shock and hypothermia.

Zachary thought the world was right-side-up again. He tried to look around, but he was still in the grip of the nightmare and couldn't move.

"You've been in an accident," a new voice told him.

There were blankets around him, but he didn't feel warm. His body started to shake again. He tried to speak but still couldn't form the words.

"Try to relax. We're going to take care of you. Everything is going to be okay."

Then he was driving again. Or maybe he wasn't driving, but he was in a moving vehicle. He didn't seem to be able to control it or to anticipate the curves and the forces that pulled him to one side or the other. There were unfamiliar noises around him. Beeping and pumping and the whooshing of air. People spoke to him from time to time, but he seemed to be losing his ability to understand them.

15

Z achary woke from the nightmare with a start. He was in bed. He was warm and not shivering.

But there was still beeping, and other unfamiliar sounds, and the light around him was a flat, uninspiring white. Zachary tried to move. They had him strapped down. He couldn't move a muscle.

Had he attempted suicide? So they had put him in restraints to prevent him from harming himself?

"Wha—what happened?"

"You were in an accident." The voice was soft, female. Reassuring but unfamiliar.

"Drinking and driving," someone farther away said.

Zachary tried to counter this. He would never drink and drive. He might be a screw-up, but he would never put someone else's life in danger.

Or maybe the driver of the other vehicle had been drinking and driving. Maybe that was what the other voice meant.

He was there. Or somewhere else. There was one long shadow across the ceiling he couldn't remember being there before. That must mean that he was somewhere else. He tried to move but again was unable. His previous awakening, or one of them, at least, came back to him.

"An accident," he murmured.

"Yes, you were in an accident," a voice confirmed. Familiar this time.

"Bridget?"

"No. Bridget's not here."

Zachary's head was still spinning. He felt nauseated. But he couldn't move if he needed to throw up. If he threw up when he was flat on his back, unable to turn his head, he'd drown in his own vomit. Zachary tried to keep this thought in his head to convince himself that he couldn't throw up and to push it out of his mind because it was so disgusting and frightening.

"Colder than a witch's behind."

Who had said that earlier?

"Are you cold? I'll get you another blanket."

Zachary wasn't cold, but he didn't object as she unfurled another blanket over him and tugged it this way and that to cover him.

There was a hand on his arm, shaking him. "Mr. Goldman. Mr. Goldman, can you wake up for me?"

Zachary tried to pry his eyes open. It took some work. He finally opened them and blinked a few times, trying to focus and to clear the stickiness from them. He wanted to rub his eyes but he still couldn't move. If it was an accident, why had they strapped him down?

It was a man. A doctor or nurse. He nodded encouragingly. "That's right. How are you feeling today, Mr. Goldman?"

Zachary tried to lick his dry lips with a sore tongue. "An accident."

"Yes. You were in an accident." The doctor waited for him to say more. "Do you remember it?"

"No."

"How do you feel this morning?"

Zachary blinked some more. He tried to turn his head to look around, but that didn't work.

"Are you in pain?"

Zachary considered the question, trying to evaluate his body's signals. "Some."

"That's not surprising. It's actually a good sign." The doctor shone his light in Zachary's eyes. He took Zachary's hand. "Can you squeeze my fingers?"

Zachary wasn't sure whether he succeeded or not. The doctor continued to move around his body, testing reflexes and giving him instructions. He ended up at the head of Zachary's bed, opposite to the side he had started on.

"It was a pretty serious accident. I understand your vehicle is a total write-off. They needed the jaws of life to get you out. There is some spinal cord trauma, but it looks like it is just bruising. We believe that as the swelling goes down, you'll regain full mobility."

Zachary tried to comprehend this. "There was an accident."

"Yes. You don't remember it?"

"No."

"You feeling warmed up now? Your body temperature is back up to normal, but you keep complaining about being cold."

"Cold," Zachary repeated.

The doctor used a thermometer that beeped in Zachary's ear. He took his pulse. He smiled down at Zachary.

"Okay. I'll let you go back to sleep. That's probably what your body needs the most."

Zachary closed his eyes and opened them again, listening.

"Bridget?" he asked.

"The young lady has gone for something to eat. I'm sure she'll be back before long."

Zachary closed his eyes again.

———

"Hey. How are you doing?"

Zachary opened his eyes and tried to turn his head.

"Bridget?"

"Bridget has been in to see you, but you were asleep."

"She was in an accident."

"No. *We* were in an accident. Not Bridget."

"She was hurt."

"No, Zachary. I was in the car with you, not Bridget. You're mixed up."

"Are you sure?"

"Yes. I'm pretty sure." There was a laugh in her voice. "All I have to do is look in the mirror."

"Oh."

She leaned over him so he could see her. Kenzie. Not Bridget. He had taken Kenzie to the inn for New Year's dinner. She had two black eyes and a number of cuts on her face.

"Kenzie."

"That's right."

"You're hurt."

"Superficial."

"Oh."

"You were hurt worse than me, but the doctor says you'll be fine."

Zachary drifted for a while, on the edge of sleep, but not quite able to fall asleep again.

"It was cold."

"Yes," Kenzie leaned closer to him. "It was really cold. They couldn't cover you up because you were upside down."

"I was?"

"Yes."

Zachary's brain worked in slow motion, making it difficult to work through each thought.

"Why?"

"Because the car was upside down. I got out, but we couldn't get you out."

"Colder than a witch's behind."

She laughed. "That's what the fire chief said."

"Oh." He closed his eyes. They were aching from the light. He was close to sleep. "Do you remember what happened?"

The room was darker, or maybe it was a different room. He could still hear the machines, and the PA system, and the people walking around and talking to each other. It was night. Zachary strained to turn his head and look around, but it wouldn't move.

He was still awake when a nurse came in. A black, overweight, middle-aged woman. She smiled down at his face. "Well, look who's awake. How are you feeling, sugar?"

"Okay."

"Good. I just need to check all your vitals and the machine. Can I get you anything? Are you comfortable?"

Zachary licked his lips. "Water?"

She retrieved a cup and held the straw to his lips. The water was tepid but felt good in his mouth and throat.

"Tongue hurts," he noted.

"Yes, it's a little cut up. You had a seizure at the accident scene before they brought you in. I guess you bit your tongue then."

"I did?"

"Or maybe you bit it during the accident. That can certainly happen when the car is rolling over and crashing into a ditch."

Zachary couldn't remember the accident happening, but when she described it so matter-of-factly, panic took over. He could suddenly feel the car rolling, the suspended feeling of not knowing which way was up. Debris was flying around the car, the windows shattering, Kenzie was screaming beside him.

"Whoa, there," the nurse said, laying a hand on his arm. "Calm down. Deep breaths." The beeps and noises of the machines had sped up, complaining loudly. "You're okay, sugar. You're safe here."

She put two fingers over his carotid pulse, even though she could surely hear his racing heartbeat on the machine next to her. Her touch was soothing.

"There, hon'. It's okay. Deep breaths. Blow it all out. Deep breath in... blow it all out... no gasping, you're fine. Just breathe it all out again. It's okay."

She stroked his hair, speaking soothingly, and the panic attack gradually passed. She waited for a while.

"Okay now?"

"Yeah. Okay."

"You've got nothing to worry about. You're safe, and your girlfriend is safe, and we're going to make sure you're all fixed up. Okay?"

"Okay."

"That's a boy. You want another sip of water?"

"Yes."

She gave him the straw again, and Zachary drank a few sips.

"I'm going to go on and do my rounds now, but I'll check back on you again. Don't worry. Even though you can't reach the call button, the machines will let me know if you're in trouble. You can just rest."

Zachary blew out a breath. "Okay."

16

He slept and woke restlessly, never sure how long he had been unconscious or what time of day it would be when he awoke again. Kenzie was often there. Sometimes a doctor or nurse talked to him and tested his reflexes and other signs.

Then there were a couple of policemen beside his bed. Not ones he knew. A department or precinct he hadn't worked with before.

"How are you feeling today, Mr. Goldman?" asked the big, hearty one. His name tag said Farrell.

"Been better," Zachary said, trying weakly for a smile.

"Yes, I imagine you have been. You're pretty bruised up today. You'd make a good addition to a zombie walk."

Zachary tried to think of a clever comeback, but his brain still wasn't operating at full speed.

"I wonder if you can tell me what you remember of the accident?"

"Not much. Just after... them cutting me out of the car."

"What do you remember of that evening? Do you remember going out to eat?"

Zachary tried to replay it in his mind. "Yes… Kenzie. At the inn."

"That's right. You have a nice meal?"

"Yeah. Really good. But I wasn't drunk. I wouldn't drive drunk."

"No. Your blood tests are back, and we know you weren't drunk."

"I wouldn't do that."

"Do you remember going back out to your car?"

"Yes. Was there…" Zachary focused, trying to pin down the ephemeral images. "Was there a flyer on the car?"

"Was there?" Farrell prompted.

"There was… a paper."

"An advertisement for a local bar or band?" Farrell suggested.

"No… no, it was another note." It formed in Zachary's mind. "A threat… because I hadn't quit a case."

"What case?"

"I… don't know which one. They never said."

"They?"

"Whoever was leaving the notes. They didn't say which case I was supposed to stop investigating."

"Do you have any idea?"

"A few… but I don't know for sure."

"You had received other notes?"

"One other note taped to my apartment door; and… a voicemail. It's still on my phone, but they used a voice changer."

"We'll requisition it from your phone company. Since your phone was… not recoverable."

Zachary hadn't thought about his phone until that point. He hadn't thought about whether any of his possessions had survived the accident. He got out of there with his life, and that was as much as he could hope.

"You have an idea of who might be sending the notes?" Farrell pressed.

"Maybe. I'll have to think about it."

"We'll need to question anyone who might be a suspect."

Zachary tried to process this. "Why?"

The other policeman moved. Farrell scribbled something down in his notepad, saying nothing, but keeping an eye on his partner.

"Rick Savois," he told Zachary, who couldn't shake his hand. Savois leaned in close to him, dropping his voice. It wasn't like there was anyone there to overhear him. Who did he think was going to hear? One of the nurses out in the hallway? His partner? "It would appear that your car was tampered with."

"Tampered..." Zachary echoed. He knew he should be angry or frightened, but he was just blank. The idea of someone tampering with his car was unthinkable. "I... I checked the bumpers. For a tracking device."

"A tracking device wouldn't cause an accident," Farrell pointed out.

"Oh... but... if there was an explosive... it wasn't under the bumper."

"No," Savois agreed. "It wasn't a bomb. It was your brake lines."

"The brakes were cut?"

"Looks like it. That fits Miss Kirshe's recollection of the accident. She said that you tried to hit the brake rounding a curve, but nothing happened. It was going too fast to make the curve, went off the side of the road, started to roll..."

The heart monitor started beating faster. Zachary drew in his breath and couldn't get enough oxygen. He gasped harder, trying to drag it in. The two officers looked at him with wide eyes. Farrell grabbed the call button for the nurse, clicking it repeatedly.

"Mr. Goldman, are you okay?" Savois asked, leaning right over Zachary's face, competing for his oxygen. Zachary tried to object, but couldn't speak while he was trying to breathe.

"What's going on here?" A nurse came in. Skinny. With an accent that Zachary would have associated with blacks. Caribbean. Rastafarian. Something like that. But she was white, with big blue eyes and blond hair. "You said you wouldn't be upsettin' my patient. Go on, back up, get out of my way."

The two officers quickly backed away from the small woman. The nurse looked over the equipment and laid a hand on Zachary's arm.

"There," she soothed. "None of that. Your machines are just telling me you're a bit upset. Nothing serious. You just take a few breaths. Nice and slow and easy."

"Can't breathe," Zachary gasped.

"You are breathing. Doin' a fine job of it. In fact, if you don't slow down, you're going to make yourself pass out. Long breaths. Slow down."

She picked up the chart hung on the wall, her eyes scanning it.

"You had a panic attack last night. Is this something you do a lot of? Are you on medication?"

"No—I can usually—control—it." Zachary gasped between the words. His chest was hurting. Maybe it had been damaged in the accident. Maybe his heart had been damaged during the crash, and they didn't know it. He was having a heart attack, and they thought it was nothing to worry about because he had a history of panic attacks. "I'm going—to—die!"

"You're not gonna die, sweetie. Not on my shift."

She went to the doorway and called for one of the other nurses to fetch her something.

"Just calm yourself, Mr. Goldman. It will all be all right. Keep breathing. Out with all the bad air. The problem is carbon dioxide, not oxygen."

Tears started to track down Zachary's face, but he was in too much of a panic to be embarrassed by his childish display.

Another nurse hurried into the room and handed the first a needle and a vial. The Caribbean nurse stood beside Zachary's bed. It seemed like she was moving at glacial speed, waiting for him to pass out, before she stabbed the needle into the access hole on the vial and drew out a dose.

"I can give you a sedative, or you can relax and calm yourself down," she advised him. "Do you really want the needle?"

Zachary breathed heavily, each intake burning all the way down his throat, chest, and side. Did he have broken ribs from the car accident too? Was that what Spencer felt like when he tried to breathe?

The nurse injected the contents of the needle into the IV tube that already fed into Zachary's arm. He hadn't been aware of it up until then. A coldness started to work its way up Zachary's arm, and then it spread to the rest of his body. He could feel his muscles start to relax. The soreness in his lungs faded. The machines slowed their beeping. Zachary started to drift.

"You can't talk to him any more tonight," the nurse told the cops firmly. "You will have to come by tomorrow and try again." She put her hands on her narrow hips. "And next time, try not to upset him."

"Happy New Year."

Kenzie looked surprised at Zachary's greeting. She stopped and looked at him for a moment, looking confused. Then she smiled.

"Happy New Year," she told him back. Her bruises were starting to fade. Or maybe she was masking them with makeup. Either way, he suspected she looked a lot better than he did.

"I guess I missed out on that kiss," Zachary joked.

"What kiss?"

"New Year's. The countdown. The kiss."

"Oh." Kenzie leaned over him and kissed him softly on the lips. Short, fleeting, and gentle. She didn't linger, but gave him a silly sort of smile, then sat down in the visitor chair, where he couldn't see her.

Zachary tried to turn his head to look at her and thought that maybe he made a small movement. The doctor had said that as the swelling went down, he'd be able to do more. Maybe it was starting to heal.

"You're in a good mood today," Kenzie suggested.

"I'm feeling pretty good. I'd like to get out of here soon…"

"I don't think you're going to be waltzing out of here for a while yet. Let's wait until you're mobile."

"Soon," Zachary insisted. "I'm getting better."

"Okay, buddy boy. If you say so."

Zachary sighed, staring up at the ceiling. "Do you remember the crash?"

"Vividly. Still a blank for you?"

"Yeah, mostly. I vaguely remember you being there, talking to me. Being upside down. Cold."

"Yeah."

"But not the actual crash."

"It was freaking scary, so be glad you don't have to. I don't think I've ever been so terrified in my life. I was sure we were both going to die."

"I'm sorry."

"It's not your fault."

"I know… but I feel responsible. If someone cut the brakes because they wanted me off a case… that comes back to me."

"Someone cut your brakes?" Kenzie repeated in disbelief.

"Didn't the police tell you?"

"No! I knew they didn't work… that you hit the brakes and they didn't slow us down. I thought… it was a malfunction."

"Apparently not."

"The letter! Do they think that whoever left the note on the windshield cut your brake lines? Tried to kill us? Or to kill you, at least?"

"Yeah."

She swore softly and was quiet. Zachary couldn't see her expression. Couldn't reach his hand out to touch her and comfort her. "Are you okay?" he asked after a few minutes had passed.

"Sure. I'm fine. No worries." She swore again, in a hard, flinty tone. "I guess New Year's can now take the place of Christmas as your least favorite holiday."

Zachary closed his eyes. She had no idea. Nothing would ever take the place of Christmas as his least favorite holiday. His least favorite season. His least favorite day every year. He had once thought that he could replace those memories. Supplant the bad ones with new, positive, happy family memories. But that was never going to happen. Even if he did someday get married again and have a family, he was never going to be able to root out the memories of the past.

"Zachary?" Kenzie persisted. "Maybe Christmas isn't so bad after all?"

"No. Christmas is still worse."

Kenzie was quiet, considering this. He could see her furled brows in his mind's eye. Trying to imagine what could be worse than being almost killed and paralyzed, at least temporarily, and spending the special day in the emergency room and ICU.

"You're going to have to tell me," she said. "What exactly happened to make Christmas so awful?"

Zachary took long, slow breaths. His heart rate didn't pick up, and the machines stayed quiet and calm beside him.

"It was a long time ago. When I was ten."

"Ten? What happened, you didn't get the toy or the puppy you wanted?"

"No. I was ten... my folks were fighting. It was Christmas Eve, and we all had to go to bed early because of a big fight. They wanted us out of the way while they screamed at each other. Like we couldn't hear them in our bedrooms."

"That sucks."

"I waited until they went to bed, which wasn't until hours later. They fought... not just arguing, but physical. I remember hiding under my covers, scared to death and trying to keep my little brother calm, pretending it was really nothing. I just huddled there, holding him, while they screamed up and down the house, hitting and slapping and throwing things. Then… they finally went to bed."

"Zachary… I'm so sorry." Her voice was much more tender than it had been. He wished he could see her. That she would hold his hand and look at him while he told the story, so he didn't have to see it all in his mind, to feel that terror and anxiety again. But his heart stayed calm. Whatever meds they had started running into his IV were obviously doing their job, keeping him from feeling the worst of the emotions of that day.

"I got up when they finally went to bed. I waited until I was sure they were down and asleep and weren't going to get up again."

"Why? To call for help?"

"No. I cleaned up… picked up everything they had thrown. Straightened all the furniture. I got out the ornaments for the tree. They had gotten a tree, but kept fighting whenever we were supposed to decorate it, so it was just standing there in the corner of the living room, all bare branches. I spent hours decorating it. I needed a chair to get the upper branches, had to keep moving it around the tree to put the garlands on. I untangled and tested the lights, picked out all the best ornaments. The ones with happy memories and special occasions associated with them. Baby's first Christmas. I Saw Mommy Kissing Santa Claus. All the silly ornaments that we made for school projects. Everything. I spent all night getting it all perfect."

"What a sweet thing to do. I'm sure they appreciated it, even if it didn't make things better."

"I got out the special Christmas candles. Beeswax ones that my grandma had brought back from Germany. Set them out. Lit them. Laid down on the couch to stare at all the beautiful Christmas decorations and imagine how everyone would feel when they came out in the morning, and Christmas had arrived. It would be magical. It would bring them all back together. We'd have Christmas together without any fighting."

"But that didn't happen," Kenzie guessed.

"I woke up to a room full of smoke. I couldn't see. Couldn't breathe. Couldn't get out of the room. We didn't have any smoke alarms. Not any that were working, anyway. I was screaming, trying to wake everyone up and get them out of the house, but I couldn't even walk across the living room to find the bedrooms, I was so disoriented."

Despite whatever they were putting in his IV, Zachary choked up. He couldn't help reliving it. The acrid smoke burned his lungs. The terror. Knowing that everybody in the house was going to die and it would be his fault.

"A neighbor's son who had come home for Christmas in the early morning saw the smoke and called 9-1-1. They got my parents and my brothers and sisters out of their bedrooms through the windows. The firemen had to break down the door and search the house for me. Room by room, because no one knew where I was."

"Thank goodness they saved you."

Zachary swore. "No. I wish I'd died. I wish they saved everyone else, and let the house burn down around me. That would have been better."

"You can't say that. No. It's not true."

"You don't know! You have no idea!"

"You must feel terribly guilty," Kenzie said. "But you were only a little boy, trying to do something nice for your family. It wasn't your fault."

"It *was* my fault."

"You can't say that."

"They split the family up."

Kenzie's voice was hesitant. "What…?"

"My parents separated. They put all the kids into foster care. They said we could never be a family again. We didn't deserve to be a family."

"Who said that?" Kenzie was horrified. She stood and leaned over the bed, grasping for Zachary's hand. "What a horrible thing to say! You can't believe it."

"My mother. My parents. They said I was incorrigible. A criminal. They didn't want Social Services to put me into foster care; they wanted to put me in prison. I spent a lot of my teenage years in institutions. All kinds of 'secure' facilities for kids with behavioral problems. Prisons for kids who had never been convicted of anything."

Kenzie stroked Zachary's hair, tears in her eyes. "No. How could they do that? You weren't being bad."

"I did awful things. Not as bad as some of the kids. Some of those kids... they *should* have been in prisons. Or insane asylums. Sadistic, psychotic kids. The kind of adults they could get to work places like that... most of them just as eager to torture you as any of the psychotic little—"

"Shh," Kenzie tried to stem the flow of Zachary's rising rage. He normally did better at controlling himself. The medications must have lowered his inhibitions. Made it easier for him to flap his gums about things he should just keep quiet about. A girl didn't want to hear that kind of thing. Nobody wanted to hear that kind of thing. They would rather deny such places even existed.

"You had to be really bad to be put in a place like that," Zachary asserted feeling hollow and empty.

"You weren't bad," Kenzie whispered, still trying to calm and quiet him. "You were hurt and traumatized. What a horrible thing to do to a child."

H i there."

Zachary turned his eyes toward the door and saw Bridget hovering there. Her glance darted around the room, and then back to him. Kenzie was still at work, Bridget didn't need to worry that they would run into each other at Zachary's bedside.

"Come on in," Zachary invited.

She entered the room, walking up to him, but staying just out of arm's reach of the bed. Like he might reach out and shake her hand or something equally as threatening.

"You're looking better," she observed.

He was finally able to sit up instead of lying flat on his back. Able to turn his head and make use of his arms. In a day or two, they would start him on physio for his legs, getting him up onto his feet for the first time since the accident.

"Yeah, glad to be able to move again," Zachary agreed, rolling his shoulders.

Bridget looked over at the visitor chair, considering. What was there to think about? Did she plan to just stand there beside him, exchange a few words, and then leave again?

"Sit, relax," Zachary encouraged.

She lowered herself to the seat. She held her purse in her lap, clutching it like she might have to leave suddenly and had to have it in her grasp.

"Did you have a nice Christmas?" Zachary inquired politely. "New Year's?"

"Better than yours, apparently."

"You visit what's-his-name's family?"

She narrowed her eyes at him. "You knew Gordon's name at Christmas, so there's no point in playing games with me now."

Zachary shrugged.

"Yes, we went to see his family for Christmas. They live on a little farm that's been in their family for generations. White board house. Red barn. Very picturesque in the snow."

"That sounds nice."

"It was very nice. Get away from the rat race. From all the stresses. Just enjoy a Christmas dinner with the family…"

"I hope I didn't make you too late for it."

Bridget's mouth quirked. "We did have to rearrange things a little, but it all worked out in the end."

"Thanks for… looking out for me."

She got a little bit pink. Zachary didn't like things being awkward between them, but it was better than being yelled at. At least there was some sign that they might be able to have a normal, amicable relationship someday. She still had bitter feelings, he knew. Feelings that she had never shared with him, but had shared with Kenzie about how he had tried to force the pregnancy upon her. The word *force* still made him furious at the implications. That somehow, he had done something violent or dishonest, when all he had done was express an opinion.

"I still care about what happens to you, Zachary," Bridget said carefully. "Even though we're not together anymore, I don't want you to…" she chickened out and didn't say, 'commit suicide' or any euphemism, but, "be unhappy."

She yelled at him for being at a restaurant and called his date to warn her off, but she didn't want him to be unhappy? Her words and her actions didn't correlate.

She *had* called him at Christmas and gone to his apartment to make sure he hadn't done himself harm.

"I care about you too. I never wanted you to be unhappy," Zachary told her. "I just wanted us to be happy together."

"Don't go over that old ground. We were never compatible."

Never. Getting married had been a mistake. It wasn't that they had been compatible and then he had screwed everything up. They had never been compatible in the first place.

She meant it as a consolation, but if anything, it made him feel worse. How would he ever know if someone was compatible? He'd thought they had fit together well. He'd thought she was someone he could spend the rest of his life with. Start a family with. But she'd never been compatible.

Was anyone? Was there some secret combination? Some code that he had to recognize when he dated? This one fits, but this one doesn't…

He had a feeling that nobody would fit Bridget's definition of compatibility. No one would ever be compatible with Zachary. He didn't know of anyone else who shared the kind of background he had come from.

"How are you feeling," Zachary asked Bridget, moving away from the dangerous ground, "now that you are finished your chemo?"

"So much better. Still tired, but I'm gradually getting my energy back. Knowing I have more than a few months to live… that's a comfort."

"I'm glad too."

She touched her wig self-consciously. She didn't need to be embarrassed about it. It looked perfectly natural. Just as soft and shining as her own hair. "And I'll be able to grow my hair back."

"You look amazing."

"All things considered," she temporized for him.

"No. You just look amazing. For anything."

"Oh." She played with the fringe of her hair with the very tips of her fingers. "Well, thank you, Zachary." She looked him over. "When do you think you'll be back out of here?"

"It depends on how long it takes to get back on my feet. How long it takes for the inflammation to go down. I hope… not too long."

"You gave us all quite a scare."

"It wasn't intentional, trust me." Zachary attempted a smile.

"You need to be more careful. Had you been drinking?"

Zachary opened his mouth, and at first, no words came out. He just stared at her. She should have known better. Even if no one had told her it was attempted murder, she should know that he didn't drink and drive. He didn't drink irresponsibly. In all the time she had known him, he had never once been drunk.

He found his voice. "No. I wasn't drunk. Somebody cut my brake lines."

"Cut your brake lines?" her voice was derisive. "What makes you think that? *Somebody's* been watching too many Phillip Marlowe movies."

"I'm not imagining things. I'm not being paranoid—"

"You're always paranoid. Your distrust is what drove us apart."

Not the way he remembered it. Yes, he had sometimes had occasion to question her about her activities, but what did she expect from someone who spent half his time trailing unfaithful spouses?

"The police told me my brake lines were cut," he informed her, instead of attacking her faulty memory. "They wanted to know who would have motive to kill me."

She stared back at him. "That obviously wouldn't be me, since I was trying to save your life just days earlier!"

Zachary felt an uncomfortable chill. He hadn't accused her of being the one trying to kill him. Was her defensiveness evidence that her anger toward him ran much deeper than he wanted to admit? She claimed she still had friendly feelings toward him but had she already regretted reaching out to him at Christmas? Or had her presence in his bathroom, messing around with his meds, been more sinister than it appeared? It was easy to cover it up with the explanation that she was just trying to keep him from killing himself. But maybe she had been looking for a way to conveniently get rid of him, knowing how he handled the Christmas season.

He shook off the thought. Bridget was right; he did have a deep-seated paranoia surrounding his relationships. A paranoia engendered by repeated abandonment and his inability to form a long-term relationship. What else did she expect from him, given his past?

"I know it wasn't you," he said. "It was something to do with work. With one of the cases I'm working on."

"Oh." She nodded. Her face softened. "Which one?"

"I don't know." Zachary rolled his eyes and forced out a breath, frustrated. "It would be nice if people who left threatening notes would be more specific."

Unless it wasn't anything to do with a case. If someone had a personal grudge against him, they wouldn't have any idea what his current cases were. The threats pointing toward his investigations might just be misdirection. An effort to keep Zachary and the police looking at his current cases instead of his personal connections. That opened up the possibilities to a lot more people.

What about Gordon, Bridget's new boyfriend? He probably didn't appreciate having his carefully-arranged Christmas plans disrupted by Bridget running off to her ex's house to make sure he hadn't offed himself. Zachary knew little about the man. He had done only very basic background on Gordon; little more than his vital statistics and resume. If Zachary dug deeper, what would he find? A history of violence? Connections with organized crime? A propensity to start fistfights in bars? An auto mechanics course?

"Maybe you should consider a change in career," Bridget suggested. Not for the first time. It had been a recurring theme during their doomed marriage. Private investigations work was too dangerous. It reflected poorly on her. She was always full of suggestions of things he could do instead, things that held absolutely no interest to him.

Zachary wasn't looking for a desk job. He liked the ability to leave his computer and head out to the field. He liked the flexibility of working for himself. Having something legitimate to do when he couldn't sleep. If he were really to be honest, he even liked skirting the law. The minor, not-so-legal things he did to dig out the truth and get justice for his clients. Even that was alluring.

"You need to remove me as your emergency contact."

Zachary looked at Bridget.

"You can't have them calling me whenever you get into an accident," she expanded. "We're not together anymore, Zachary. I'm not the person they should be calling."

"Oh."

He considered this. On the surface, it made sense, of course. But who would he put in her place? He didn't have any family. No close friends. He couldn't make every new girlfriend an emergency contact. Someone he barely knew. Besides, what if, like Kenzie, they were in the same car with him when something happened?

"Yeah. Okay."

Zachary couldn't drive and hadn't replaced his car yet, so he took the bus to Molly's house. He was conscious of his legs and feet as he walked from the bus stop to her door. Walking was not yet automatic. He felt like he did when someone was watching him critically. Awkward, like he didn't know where to put his feet. He had to think out every step and was sure he must look jerky and robotic to anyone watching him. He had rejected the idea of a cane for stability but was starting to regret it. If nothing else, it would at least signal to anyone watching him that he had a condition, that he wasn't drunk or impaired but had a good reason for wobbling and hesitating like he did.

Molly answered the door. She looked Zachary over, her eyes bright and curious.

"Come in, come in," she invited, and opened the door the rest of the way, directing him in.

Zachary's toe caught on the edge of the carpet at its transition from the floor, and he skittered a bit but managed to avoid flailing or landing on his face. Molly walked to his right and slightly behind him, holding her hands out a bit like she wanted to catch him or guide him to his seat. He got into the chair and shifted, settling himself in.

"How are you feeling?" Molly asked. "It looks like you're healing."

Zachary nodded a little jerkily. "Yes. I'm doing well. Everything will be back to normal soon. My doctors are happy with the rate of my progress."

"I couldn't believe it when I heard about your accident. They said it was very bad. That you had a spinal cord injury and were paralyzed." She shook her head solemnly. "I certainly didn't expect to see you walking around so soon."

The police must have interviewed her, as one of his clients, to find out her alibis for the times he had received the threats or when the brake lines had been cut. He knew they had been making the rounds, trying to narrow down the suspect list. They didn't have any forensic evidence. No fingerprints or DNA. There must have been tool marks on the brake lines, but maybe nothing could be matched to the tool used. Or maybe matched to a common tool that they all had access to.

"There was just swelling around my spinal cord," he explained. "Inflammation. It's mostly gone, now. I just... have to be careful. Think about what I'm doing for a while until it all becomes natural again."

"No permanent damage?"

"No. I was very lucky."

"And your girlfriend? Her injuries were not severe?"

Had she heard that from the police? Or had she checked up

on him through other channels? It wouldn't be hard. A call to the hospital. To one of the reporters who had covered the crash. Not a lot of information had made it into the news articles, but the reporters knew that there had been a second person in the car. They had those details.

"She's... not exactly my girlfriend. We've been out together a few times, but... it's not that serious yet. We're taking things slow." He didn't know why he was telling her so much. What did it matter whether she thought Kenzie was a serious girlfriend or not?

But Zachary didn't like the thought of anyone thinking Kenzie was a serious girlfriend. If someone was out to hurt him, out to coerce him into closing a case, he didn't want them threatening her. Someone who was serious enough to cut Zachary's brake lines might be serious enough to take a hostage.

Surely that wasn't Molly Hildebrandt. She was a little old lady. He couldn't see her crawling underneath his car to cut his brake lines. He couldn't picture her grabbing Kenzie and holding a knife to her throat or a gun to her head. Sometimes it was the least likely suspect, but he still couldn't fit Molly into that role.

"Oh... well, I'm very glad that neither of you was killed or permanently injured. I think we've all had enough of hospitals this winter."

Zachary nodded his agreement. "How is Isabella?"

"She was released December thirtieth. We're still trying to keep a pretty close eye on her. Neither of us believes she's recovered... she's stable as far as the doctors are concerned, but she still won't take the antidepressants they want her to. She's convinced that they will make her worse."

Zachary scratched his knee intently, considering his approach. "I have several concerns about Isabella."

"Yes. We all do," Molly agreed. She avoided his eyes and didn't ask him what his concerns were. Maybe she figured his concerns were the same as hers, or that she had enough on her plate already and couldn't handle anything more.

"I think... that Isabella was the one who gave Declan cough medicine the day he died. Whether she was scared by his reaction, or she had been expecting it... I suspect she was the one who took him to the pond that day."

Molly's eyes went wide and two bright spots appeared in her cheeks. Her voice when she addressed him was not weak or wavering. There was no uncertainty.

"That is the most ridiculous thing I have ever heard. Isabella wouldn't let anyone give Declan cough medicine. She would never give it to him herself. She would certainly not plan his death or do anything that led to it. You are wrong, Mr. Goldman. Your brain must have been addled by your accident. There is no way my daughter had anything to do with Declan's death."

"You weren't there. You weren't with her. The possibility is still open."

"No. It's not. That's ridiculous. Why? Explain to me why she would give him cough medicine when she knew he would react negatively to it. Explain why she would take him to the pond and drown him?"

"She gave him the medicine so that he would be unconscious and not fight her."

"Why? Why would she harm her own son?"

"Because she didn't want to be a mother. She hadn't realized how difficult a job it would be, and how much he would interfere with her job and with the order she and Spencer had developed in the house. She didn't realize how his care would interfere with her routines, day after day. Every day it wore on her. She wanted to paint. She wanted to tape her shows. She wanted to live a predictable, ordered existence. Declan screwed that up."

"No, you're wrong." A tear slid down Molly's cheek. Was it a sign that he'd hit the mark? He had hit too close to the truth, and she couldn't help reacting? "My daughter wasn't like that. Isn't like that. She loved Declan dearly."

"That doesn't preclude her doing something to harm him. She could love him and still decide that she just couldn't handle him

183

anymore. It happens. You read about it in the news. People who are overwhelmed with their children's care. Or with the stresses at work or in other areas of their lives. They decide that they can't go on like that anymore, and they decide to take the child or children out of the equation."

"She didn't do that. She would never do that."

"Drowning is a common method of disposing of unwanted children."

"Drowning is a common method of disposing of unwanted kittens. Not children. People don't just drown their children because they are inconvenient. They get help. I could have helped her. I could have spent more time there. If she wanted me to babysit Declan, I would have been happy to do it. All she had to do was ask."

Zachary sighed. He wasn't sure what to do with his hands and wished that she had offered him coffee or a cookie so that he could avoid fidgeting. He held his hands in his lap but wanted to move them around, to use them to illustrate his point.

"You say that you would have been happy to babysit him, but maybe Isabella didn't feel like she could ask you. You were already doing too much for them. Or maybe she didn't approve of your parenting methods. Kids often don't appreciate their own parents. They think they know better."

"I was a good mother to Isabella!"

Zachary didn't answer for a few seconds, considering it. *Had* she been a good mother? Or had she done the wrong things and damaged Isabella? No one had offered any reason why Isabella was the way she was. Had she just won the genetic lottery? Or was it the result of something traumatic that had happened in her childhood? Or throughout all of her childhood? Most parents, if confronted, would admit that they had made mistakes in parenting. Maybe Isabella wouldn't agree that Molly had been a good mother. Maybe she hadn't been. Maybe Isabella was incapable of parenting because she hadn't had a good example herself.

"I'm sure you were a good mother," he reassured Molly, trying to keep her calm. "But Isabella might not think so. All children think they can do a better job than their parents." He gave her a conspiratorial smile. One that invited her to agree with him about the follies of children and admit that Isabella might not always agree with her.

"Isabella never had any complaints about the way that I took care of Declan," Molly said sullenly. For the first time, Zachary could see another side of her. The person who wasn't always upbeat and positive. The one who had doubts and took offense and who wasn't the perfect example of a loving, devoted parent. A human being.

"How is Isabella as a wife?" Zachary spun the conversation in the other direction.

Molly blinked at him, disconcerted. "What do you mean, how is she as a wife?"

"Does she enjoy being married? Does she get along with Spencer? How have they made out together?"

Molly opened and closed her mouth. She tried several times to approach the question, seeing a minefield and trying to figure out how to navigate it.

"Being a wife is... hard for Isabella," she admitted.

"I know marriage was pretty hard for me," Zachary said. "I wasn't a very good husband. I wish I could say that I always thought of my wife and that I did everything I could to keep our marriage going smoothly. I made a lot of mistakes. In the end... I drove her away." That was what Bridget said, anyway. The story worked for Zachary's purposes.

"Isabella didn't have a good example of a successful marriage growing up," Molly said. "She never had a father, and I didn't have any strong, long-lasting relationships when she was a girl. She was a very difficult child, and there wasn't any space in my life for a man. She needed all my attention. A man would just have felt neglected."

"That makes it hard. You can't just take your example from TV." Zachary smiled at her. "The Brady Bunch might seem perfect, but that's not the way families really work. Husbands and wives don't always agree. They're not always compatible."

Molly got up and paced across the room, stopping to retrieve the photo of Isabella, Spencer, and Declan. She sat back down with it, showed it to Zachary for a moment, and then sat staring at it.

"I thought her marrying someone else with a mental illness was a bad idea. Isabella thought it would be perfect. They would be able to understand what the other was going through. Because their tendencies were opposite, they would each... complete the other. Spencer would complete her. Would fill in the gaps."

"But that's not the way it worked out, is it? Spencer told me about the blue plate."

Molly smiled softly. "She had that plate since she was a girl. She ate from it every day. She had to have it. When Spencer threw it out... I think that was the first sign that it wasn't just going to be a bumpy ride. It was going to be a rollercoaster. Or a bungee jump. It wasn't going to work... not the way they thought it was."

"How did Isabella react to the difficulties with Spencer? How did she react when he did something that she didn't like, or that interfered with her space or her routines? How did she feel when he did something like throwing out her plate?"

"It would send her into a tailspin. She'd be impossible to talk to for days. She needed her therapist on the set or needed me there to help direct her. To work things out so that she could tape the show. The network understood that she had emotional problems, but... they weren't very understanding."

"Her job was in jeopardy? Because of the way things were going at home?"

"No, I'm just speaking generally. They had trouble with her. Not constantly. Things went very smoothly most of the time. I just meant, when Isabella and Spencer were fighting, it spilled over into her professional life."

Zachary pounced on the word. "Tell me about their fighting."

"No… not fighting… not like you're talking about. I mean disagreements. Conflicts. Nothing physical."

"Are you sure nothing ever got physical?"

"Isabella would never have abided anyone who laid a hand on her. If Spencer had hit her, she would have called the police. I'm sure of that."

"And what about her hitting him?"

"Her hitting him?" Molly laughed and shook her head. "She didn't hit him. Never. She isn't a violent person."

"Spencer has broken ribs. I've seen the bruises. Can you explain that?"

Molly's brows drew down. She shook her head at him, scowling blackly. "She never did anything to hurt him. How could she? He's bigger than she is."

"That doesn't mean she couldn't hit him. I've known little tiny women who beat the hell out of their big, strong husbands. Size has nothing to do with it. Women can be just as violent and abusive as men."

"Not Isabella. That's ridiculous."

"How did Spencer get the bruises? He works from home. From what I've seen, he rarely goes out. Who is beating up on him? Who caused those bruises?"

"I don't know," Molly said flatly. "I've never seen any sign of either of them hurting the other. Isabella has never said anything to even hint at abuse. You've got it wrong, Zachary. I don't know where you're getting this, but you've got it all wrong."

"Have you ever seen Spencer with injuries? Bruises or cuts on his face? Unexplained injuries?"

"No!" Zachary could see it wasn't the truth. She *had* seen it. He could tell by the shock in her eyes. Maybe she hadn't registered the thought that her daughter was abusive, but she had seen unexplained injuries.

Zachary let the silence build for a couple of minutes. He didn't ask anything further, but let Molly think about it. Watched her grow uncomfortable with the silence and try to justify it to herself.

"You've never seen him with unexplained injuries?" Zachary prompted.

"Everybody has accidents. Spencer is no exception."

"What kind of accidents did he have?"

"I don't know. He never really tried to explain. He just brushed them off and said it was nothing. Or sometimes he said it was Declan. They'd been play-wrestling, and Declan had kicked him in the eye. Or Declan had been playing a game with him where Spencer was blindfolded, and he walked into something. I don't know. Things happen. People get hurt. I often get bruises and don't know where I got them. On my legs and knees. Sometimes my arms. It's just part of life. It doesn't mean I'm being abused. I don't believe Spencer was either."

Zachary traced figure-eights on the arm of the chair with one finger. "Maybe you really don't know what was going on," he said. "Maybe they both had you fooled, and you didn't realize. You know that things were difficult between them."

"Yes, but they had worked things out. They had set up boundaries and rules. Ways that they could get along with each other. Live with each other without driving each other totally crazy."

"Like Spencer not going into Isabella's art studio."

"Right."

"What would happen if he did go in?"

She stared at him. "What do you mean?"

"Just what I said. The studio was off-limits for him. What would happen if he ignored that rule and walked in? Or moved something? Or took something, because he couldn't stand the mess?"

"He wouldn't do that. He wouldn't go into her studio."

"Because of the way she would react if he did?"

"Because they had agreed on rules and boundaries," Molly growled. "And he wouldn't *want* to go in her studio."

Zachary thought back to the chaos and disorder that ruled in Isabella's studio. He pictured Spencer standing in the doorway, as he had a couple of times. He didn't hover in the door, wishing that he could enter. He didn't look longingly at the disorderly shelves and tables, wanting to straighten them. Rather, he had hung back as if he couldn't stand to enter.

"What about Spencer's office? Was Isabella allowed to go in there?"

"It was his space," Molly growled. "Is his space. I don't know if she is *allowed* or not, but it's his space, and she respects that boundary. You can't think that she would want to go in there and interfere with his things."

"No, I don't think that. But *would* she go in there? To talk to him? To leave the mail on his desk? To pick up a toy that Declan had left in there? What are the rules?"

"You'll have to ask them."

"And what were the rules for taking care of Declan? They each had separate responsibilities?"

"Yes. Of course." Molly nodded vigorously. "They were very good about sharing responsibilities. Spencer took Declan in the mornings. He made sure that he had breakfast and lunch and played games with him. Did chores or went on walks. Then in the afternoon, it was Isabella's turn. She'd take over so Spencer could work in peace."

"What did she do with Declan?"

"What do you mean? Looked after him."

"You listed off things that Spencer would do with him. Make him breakfast. Play games with him. Take him out for a walk. What things would Isabella do with him?"

"Well... put him down for his nap. It's very important for young children to get enough sleep, or they get grumpy. Being chronically short on sleep makes a person sick, overweight, more prone to catching everything that goes around."

"Uh-huh. And?"

"And what?"

"What else would she do with him? Put him down for a nap. What else?"

"I don't know. A hundred different things. Do an art or craft with him. Watch him while he played in the backyard."

"She didn't spend as much one-on-one time with him as Spencer did. She found ways to do other things while it was her time to look after him."

"There's nothing wrong with letting him nap or watching him playing in the back yard."

"Of course not. That's not being negligent."

"That's right." Molly nodded her agreement.

"But it does show a pattern. It shows that she wanted to continue to follow her own routine, and only did what she had to in order to accommodate Declan."

"You're wrong. She loved Declan. She loved spending time with him."

"Maybe she didn't always share her feelings with you. Maybe she felt like she couldn't tell you how inadequate she felt, or how she didn't want to be with Declan all the time. Maybe she was afraid that you would judge her for not wanting to spend as much time with her child as she possibly could."

"I would never criticize her for that. Parents are people too. You still have to take care of yourself. I would understand that she couldn't take care of Declan all the time. She needed time to herself. Isabella has always needed alone time. Time to regenerate, to work on her art."

"And she wasn't getting that, not when she had to watch Declan while she painted. She didn't really get alone, undisturbed time, did she?"

"She did. Mr. Goldman, you're talking in circles. I know she needed time for herself. She had a husband. She had me. She didn't need to do anything to get rid of Declan. If she wanted help for a few hours, she only had to ask."

"But it wasn't just a few hours. It was every day. Every single day, she had to look after him, listen to his inane, childish chatter, clean up after him. She had to make sure he didn't touch any of her precious things. She had to feed him and change him and be there for him. Children take a lot of work."

"You think I don't know that? I raised Isabella as a single parent. There were no breaks for me. No husband, no grandparents. She was a very high-needs child, and there was no one to help me. Don't you tell me how hard it is to raise a child." She shook an accusing finger at him. "You don't have children. You told me that. You can't understand what it's like to raise a child on your own, but I do. And Isabella wasn't on her own."

"Maybe not; but maybe she felt alone. You had raised her by yourself, but she couldn't raise a child with the help of her husband. She felt like a failure. That's why she killed Declan, and that's why she tried to kill herself, overwhelmed with the guilt of it all. The guilt of not being able to be the parent she wanted to be and the guilt of killing her own child."

Molly stood up. "I'm going to have to ask you to leave."

Zachary didn't move.

"Leave," Molly repeated. She motioned to the door. "If you don't leave, I'll call the police and have them arrest you for trespassing. I've had enough of this." Her lips twisted into angry shapes before she managed to spit the rest of the words out. "Please submit your final report to me. By mail. Then I don't want you to investigate anymore. You will be done."

Zachary stood slowly. He walked to the door and let himself out.

18

It had been an emotional day, and Zachary knew that he needed to take the time to complete the final report on the Bond case and get it off to Molly. Then he had to decide what he was going to do about the case. The more he looked into it, and the more he discussed the merits of the case, the more certain he was that the only culprit could be Isabella.

No wandering child killer had happened by their yard and spotted Declan. They hadn't snatched the child or persuaded him to leave the safety of his yard, dosed him with cough medicine, and drowned him in the pond. The timeline was too tight. The killer's goal had to be drowning him from the start. They hadn't tried to kidnap him or harm him in other ways and been thwarted. They had to have gone straight from taking him from the yard to killing him within an hour or so. The crime suggested a parent. A frustrated caretaker overwhelmed with the pressures of taking care of a child.

But he couldn't go to the police and say that he was sure that Isabella had murdered her only child. There was no evidence to clinch it. The case had already been closed and Zachary could offer nothing to change their minds.

He plowed through the written report anyway. He had already

made his opinion known to Molly, so he didn't mince words. He didn't try to phrase the file diplomatically as he had before. She knew what he thought, and he needed to lay it all out without flinching. She could do with it what she liked. Shred it or burn it so no one else could ever read it.

When he was finished—or at least finished the first draft—he sat back in his chair, making it creak angrily in protest. He called Kenzie on an old flip phone he had just activated.

"Are you free for a late dinner?" he suggested.

"I've actually already had dinner. I was starving."

"How about a nightcap, then?"

"Sure," Kenzie's voice was warm, "that would be nice. Where do you want to go?"

His options were getting more and more limited. Nowhere that Bridget might go. Nowhere any of his subjects might go. Not to the inn. Somewhere in town so he could get there easily by bus. Or he could call a cab when he was ready to go home. Maybe Kenzie would offer to drive him home, which might lead to better things.

"How about… there's a little pub called *The Four-Leaf Clover*. Have you ever been there?"

"No… but I know where it is. It's across from *Old Joe's*, isn't it, where we ate…"

"Yes."

"And we're not going to run into Bridget there, right?"

"No. She never went there."

"Let's hope she doesn't start."

The nightcap went well. They were both relaxed, tired after a long day, but happy to have put their work behind them, not still stressing out over it. Zachary was able to stop being so self-conscious about his movements. To stop worrying that he looked like someone with brain damage, and just relax.

"You're glad to be closing the Declan Bond case?" Kenzie asked.

"Yes. I wish I could do something more about it, but that will be up to someone else. I don't have anything new to give to the police, so all I can do is tell Molly my opinion. And that's that."

"Good. I'm glad you're getting that one out of your hair. And the others...? Are you still working on any of the others that... that the note could have been about?"

"I'll have them all closed off soon. I'll start new cases... not have to worry about those other ones anymore."

"Yeah. Good. Because I don't want any more accidents."

"Me neither," Zachary agreed.

Even so, he was still a little nervous when they finished their drinks and went out to Kenzie's little red sports car. Zachary walked around it, looking for anything suspicious. There was no note on the windshield. Nothing attached under the bumpers. He took a good long look under the car for anything that didn't look like it belonged, or any fluids dripping underneath. When he declared it safe and got into the passenger seat, Kenzie didn't tease him about his paranoia.

And he noticed as she backed out and shifted gears that she kept testing the brakes. Pressing down to make sure she still had pressure. Easing out of the parking space slowly and being even more cautious when she pulled out onto the main road, slowing significantly before curves and being unusually careful at intersections. Zachary kept an eye on the mirrors, trying not to be obvious about it. He caught Kenzie's eyes on him a couple of times and knew that she had noticed.

They both breathed a sigh of relief when they made it to the parking lot of Zachary's building, and Kenzie pulled into Zachary's reserved parking stall, empty because he hadn't yet replaced his car. Zachary got out and walked around the front of the car to meet her as she got out.

He swore.

Kenzie looked at him, eyes alarmed, and turned to see what he was looking at. Bridget was striding across the parking lot toward them, and her eyes were blazing. She looked crazed. Zachary checked her hands to make sure she didn't have a weapon. Kenzie backed away and looked at Zachary worriedly. She slid out her phone, and Zachary knew she was dialing 9-1-1, getting ready to press 'send' and get them on the line.

Bridget started yelling and swearing before she reached them, calling Zachary names up and down, her face bright red.

"What's wrong?" Zachary questioned. "What's going on?"

"You dog! You stupid, inconsiderate lowlife! I knew you were a jerk, Zachary, but this takes the cake!"

"What?" Zachary held up his hands defensively. "Tell me what's wrong."

"I took my car in to the shop for some servicing. What do you think they found?"

Zachary swallowed. He glanced aside at Kenzie, then back at Bridget. "Whatever has upset you, we can deal with it," he soothed. "We'll sort it out."

She slapped him across the face. Zachary was too slow and clumsy from his spinal cord injury to react and pull away in time and took the full force of her assault. Out of the corner of his eye, Zachary saw Kenzie moving to place the emergency call and raised his hand to stop her.

"You don't think he deserves it?" Bridget challenged Kenzie. "I should slap him silly!"

"For what?" Kenzie demanded.

"I took my car to the mechanic, and he found something on the inside of the bumper."

Kenzie shook her head. "What did they find?"

"A tracking device! A device that transmits my location, no matter where I go. So that *he*—" she shot a glare at Zachary, "— can know where I am at all times. Any time, night or day, he can look at his receiver, and see where I am. What do you think of that?"

Kenzie looked at Zachary. "Really? Is that true?"

"Ask to look at his phone and computer," Bridget said. "Which is it on, Zachary? Or is it on both?"

He swallowed, keeping his mouth shut. He'd be in trouble if he denied it, and in trouble if he admitted it. There was no right answer. He was glad that all he had on him was his old flip phone, which didn't even have any games on it, let alone the GPS tracker app. The computer back in his apartment was another story.

"Why would you be tracking your ex-wife?" Kenzie asked slowly.

Zachary brought his hand up to his face to rub his forehead. He felt like his hand was disembodied, not actually part of him. He rubbed the furrows between his brow slowly, trying to figure out what to do or say next.

"Bridget. I was just..."

"Just what?" she demanded furiously. "I'm curious. Just what excuse do you think would justify stalking me? What would the police say if I took this to them? You want to go to jail?"

"You were so upset when you ran into me and Kenzie at the restaurant. You made it clear you didn't want to run into me anywhere. If I could check your location, I could make sure I didn't..."

Rather than looking reassured at this, Kenzie looked appalled. "So those times when I asked you if we were safe to go to a restaurant, to the inn, or somewhere else, the reason you knew Bridget wouldn't be there was you were tracking her?"

Zachary could tell by her voice that she did not want an affirmative answer. He looked at Bridget, a quick sideways glance to see just how angry she was, checking her position to make sure she wasn't going to hit him again, even though he knew he wouldn't be able to avoid it if she did.

"I'm taking out a restraining order," Bridget said. "This is going too far. You stay away from me, and you stay out of my life!"

"Wait a minute here," Kenzie spoke up, addressing Bridget. "You're the one who just hit him. You're the one who freaks out if you see him out in public. Who keeps calling me about him. You came to see him at the hospital, acting like you're all concerned. From everything I've seen, there's pretty good reason for him to want to keep track of your location."

"I *had* to go to the hospital. He still has me down as his emergency contact."

"There's no requirement for you to go to the hospital. You just tell them no."

"And you're the one who broke into my apartment," Zachary said tentatively. "There's a police record of that. Are you going to tell the judge that?"

"I didn't break in!" Bridget shouted, taking a step toward him.

Zachary took a step back. Kenzie moved in closer; her hands clenched into fists. "If you hit him again, I'm calling the cops," she warned. "What's all this about breaking in?"

"Christmas Day," Zachary said. "When I was at the hospital with Isabella's family. She came by here. Used her key to get in. I called the police because I thought she was a burglar."

"You are sick; you know that?" Kenzie addressed Bridget. "Maybe you should get some help. Some therapy. Because you're the one who won't leave him alone. For all I know, you're the one that cut the brake lines on his car."

Zachary watched Bridget carefully for her reaction. He knew that her car hadn't been anywhere near the inn that night. What about Gordon? Had he done her bidding? Or had she borrowed his car, knowing that Zachary might recognize hers if he saw it in the parking lot or following him on the street? He had never asked the police if they'd looked into the possibility that she was involved in the sabotage.

"I didn't do that," Bridget hissed. Her face contorted with rage. "I wouldn't do anything to hurt him. If I need therapy, that's his fault too. Do you have any idea what it's like putting up with his crap day in and day out? With his suspicion and paranoia and having to check and recheck everything? He's never had a healthy relationship in his life. I warned you. You don't want to lose years of your life to this creep. He's like a soul-sucking vampire. It's no wonder I ended up getting cancer. The stress of having to deal with his obsessive behavior every day wrecked my health. I got sick because of him!"

Zachary couldn't have been more staggered if she'd punched him. His gut and his chest tightened, and suddenly he couldn't breathe anymore. His legs were like jelly, and the world turned all wavy in front of his eyes. He knew it had finally happened. He was having a heart attack. She had broken his heart. He had suspected she blamed him for her cancer, but it was the first time she had put it into words.

"Zachary!" Kenzie grabbed at Zachary as his knees hit the ground, then his body. He curled up in agony, clutching his chest and unable to draw breath. "Zachary!"

"Look at him!" Bridget jeered. "Look how far he'll go to get your sympathy. You imagine living with a man who has a panic attack any time you have an argument! I stayed with him because I thought he would die if I didn't. I seriously thought he was going to keel over and die if I left."

"Zachary!" Kenzie was clutching at him. "Should I call 9-1-1? Do you need a pill? An inhaler? What can I do?"

He couldn't draw breath enough to answer her. The world was going dark around him. By the time an ambulance got there, he'd be dead.

"He'll have pills in his apartment," Bridget said grudgingly. "I don't know why he doesn't carry them with him. Or have something he can take every day to prevent it from happening in the first place. If we can get him up there..."

Kenzie put her hand under Zachary's arm, trying to coax him to his feet. "I don't think we're going to be able to get him anywhere. Maybe I should get an ambulance."

"If you just wait, it will pass. An ambulance and admitting him to the hospital will just rack up the bills."

"He's turning blue."

"It will pass," Bridget repeated. "It's self-limiting. He'll either pass out or it will start abating on its own."

It helped Zachary to hear Bridget's calm voice repeating what the doctors had always said. She'd seen him have panic attacks before. She didn't see anything to be concerned about.

"What if it's not a panic attack?" Kenzie asked. "What if it's a heart attack? Or a stroke?"

"It's not."

They both watched Zachary. Gradually, his gasping started to slow, and the world began to come back into focus. Kenzie attended to him, rubbing his shoulder comfortingly and repeating soothing words and phrases.

"Better?" Kenzie asked. "Are you okay?"

Zachary cleared his throat. His chest was still hurting, and his throat felt raw from breathing so hard. He still felt dizzy and a little nauseated. "Yeah. I'm okay."

"You should see a doctor," Bridget snapped. "You know you have a problem, so why don't you do something about it?"

"They can't always control it."

"You haven't even tried."

Zachary started to sit up, taking his time. He stopped and put his head in his hands, closing his eyes.

"I have tried."

"Can you get up?" Kenzie asked.

Zachary let her help him to his feet. He leaned on her, trying not to put too much of his weight on her.

"I think it's time for you to go," Kenzie told Bridget.

"I'll help you get him up to his apartment."

"I don't think so! You've done enough damage."

Bridget stood there for a moment, her mouth partway open, looking for something to say. Finally, she raised her hands in a melo-dramatic shrug. "Fine. He's all yours. I don't want him in my life."

"Good. Then go."

Bridget turned halfway around. "He has a few Xanax in his

medicine cabinet. He'll probably want one of them. Then he'll sleep."

"We'll sort it out."

"Fine." Bridget looked at Zachary. "No more trackers on my car. No following or surveilling me. Not personally, not with electronics, and not by hiring someone else. Got it? Just stay away from me."

"Take your own advice," Kenzie snapped.

"If I were you, I'd have your car checked for trackers too," Bridget told her.

Kenzie looked at Zachary. He tried not to give anything away with his expression. He shifted, easing his weight off of her, trying to get his legs working.

"Okay," Kenzie said. "Let's get you upstairs."

They moved together, awkward and slow. Zachary's heart was still beating too fast, and he was reeling with Bridget's words. It was his fault that she got cancer because he was too needy, too much of a strain on the relationship. No wonder she hated him.

At the door, he couldn't get his key out and fitted into the lock properly, so Kenzie took it from him, unlocked the door, and ushered him in.

"Do you want a pill?"

Zachary looked around the apartment, not sure what to do. Entertain her? Sit down in front of the TV? Head to bed? What was Kenzie expecting? What was the protocol when a date ended with the appearance of a raging ex-wife and emotional collapse?

"Zachary? Do you want me to get you a pill?"

Zachary settled on the couch in the living room. There he could sleep, watch TV, or talk with Kenzie. He dug his flip phone and his wallet out of his pockets and put them on the side table.

"No... I don't think I can."

"You can't?" Kenzie frowned and shook her head.

"Because I had a couple of drinks. The doctor said I couldn't mix them."

She went into his bathroom and opened the medicine cabinet.

It was nearly bare after Bridget's Christmas Day visit. She picked up the Xanax prescription, with a few white pills kicking around the bottom. She looked at the bright orange warning stickers affixed to it.

"Yeah, you're right," she agreed. "Is there something else? Anything else that would help?" She looked at a couple of other bottles. Zachary shifted uncomfortably in his seat. He didn't like her snooping through his prescriptions.

"No. I'll be fine," he told her. "Don't worry about it."

After pawing through the cabinet for another minute, she closed it and returned to the living room, sitting down on the couch next to him.

"That was scary," she said. "I thought it was a heart attack. I can't believe Bridget could stay so calm about it."

"She's seen a few anxiety attacks... maybe not that bad, but..."

"It must be scary for you, too."

"Yeah. Sort of."

She took his hand and sat with him for a few minutes in silence. "Do you think Bridget had something to do with the car brakes?"

"No," Zachary answered immediately. "She couldn't ever do something like that. Besides, I checked the tracker. She wasn't anywhere near the inn. She had no way of knowing that's where I was."

"What if someone had a tracker on your car? I don't see how anyone could have known you were there, otherwise. Did you tell anyone?"

Zachary's brain was still in a soup of stress neurotransmitters; he couldn't sort through the question calmly and logically, and wouldn't be able to until he had crashed and recovered. "I don't know."

"You wouldn't have told any of your clients. Any of those cases that you've been working on. Would you?"

"No... I don't think so. I don't remember."

"Someone would have had to have recognized it. Or followed you. Or tracked you."

"Yeah."

"Zachary."

His brain was going fuzzy.

"Zachary."

"Yeah?"

"I'll leave you to go to sleep, should I?"

"Yeah."

"Okay." She got up off the couch and stooped to kiss him on the forehead like a mother might kiss her child. "I'll talk to you tomorrow."

19

His dreams were always disrupted after a panic attack. Like his brain couldn't stop repeating the attack over and over. That was one of the reasons he would normally have taken a Xanax even though the attack had already subsided. He wanted to forget it and sleep, to stop the endless loop of crazy images in his head.

Bridget was a prominent feature in his dreams. So were the images from his distant past. His parents, the fire, some of the subsequent homes that he preferred to forget when he was lucid. Because Kenzie had been present, she was in his dreams too, iterating and reiterating all night.

"He said he'd drop it," Kenzie said, talking on an old-style desk phone with a rotary dial and tightly twisting handset cord. "You don't need to do anything else. He said he's done now."

Zachary couldn't tell who was on the other end of the call. Perhaps his mother, if the twang in the voice was any clue. He couldn't make out the words, just the angry, insistent tone, like Bridget's voice.

"It's over," Kenzie repeated. "I told you that. Just leave him alone now."

Who was she talking to? And why? Who was she reporting back to while he slept?

"He's not going to figure it out. I've told you everything. He doesn't suspect a thing."

Zachary puzzled over her words, trying to unwind the clues. In all the time he'd been investigating the Bond case, he'd never suspected Kenzie of being complicit. She didn't have any connection with Isabella. He'd discussed the case with her openly. All the evidence and his ideas. She'd told him the blood levels were all normal, making no mention of the cough medicine until pressed for an explanation. She had repeatedly suggested he drop the case and not make any waves.

What did she know that he didn't suspect?

"I'll give him something to make him sleep," Kenzie said on the phone. "He won't know anything."

Zachary tried to raise his voice to tell her again that he couldn't take anything. Not after being out drinking. Like in many dreams, especially those anxiety-triggered ones, he had no voice. He was as helpless as a child. Completely at her mercy.

The voice on the other end of the phone continued to squawk. Zachary saw his mother in his mind's eye. It had been so long since he'd seen her that it was only a vague, shadowy memory. He saw long, dark hair like Isabella's. But she was not *The Happy Artist*. Had he ever seen her smile? Their home had not been a happy one. He knew from the time he was small that they were unwanted. All the children. They were vermin, like rats, always in the way, eating the meager supplies of food. They kept her from true happiness and fulfillment.

He tried to compose a speech to his mother in his addled head. To explain to her that he didn't mean to be a drain on her. He was trying to be helpful. Trying to make her love him. Parents were supposed to love their children. That was what everyone said. A mother's love. Like it was the most precious thing in the world.

"He'll sleep right through it," Kenzie promised. "He won't feel a thing."

Zachary started to choke as the smell of acrid smoke curled into his nostrils. He coughed. After that Christmas Eve so many years ago, he was terrified of fire. Just the faintest wisp of smoke would bring it all back. The room was growing warm and then hot around him. He could hear the screams of his family. The blaring sirens and horns, and the shouts of the firefighters. His throat constricted as he tried to breathe, the combination of smoke and heated air scorching his throat.

He tried to scream, but he couldn't.

He couldn't wake up from the dream.

A bright light pierced the thick smoke. Zachary remembered that light from before. The relief of the firefighters finding their way through all the smoke and fire to find him. The relief of rescue from the burning hell he was in.

"Over here!"

Another figure joined the first, spraying down the area around Zachary. The first hefted him up, lifting him out of his seat and carrying him through the thick, burning clouds of smoke. Down a couple of flights of stairs. Out into clear air that was so cold that it caught in his chest and throat making him cough again. There were red, strobing lights everywhere, dark figures hurrying back and forth, shouted orders and discussions and radio chatter.

The fireman put him down on a gurney.

"This one was in the affected apartment. Get a mask on him right away. Keep checking his airway."

An oxygen mask was pressed over Zachary's face before he could say anything. He tried to talk through it but couldn't get out anything coherent.

"Just relax, sir. Lay back, and we'll take care of you."

A blanket was thrown over him. His skin was already cold from the night air.

"Just breathe the oxygen and don't try to talk right now. We'll talk in a little while."

Zachary lay there for a long time, breathing the oxygen and gradually coming to understand that it wasn't a dream. There really had been a fire, not just a memory from the past. He was at his apartment. Outside, in the cold, just like when he was ten. It wasn't Christmas Day this time, but a few weeks later.

"How are you doing there, sir?" A paramedic bent over him, ruffling his hair like he was a little boy. Like they had ruffled his hair all those years ago. "You had a close call. How's your throat?"

Zachary pulled the oxygen mask away from his face experimentally. He was again assaulted by the frigid outside air but managed to avoid coughing.

"It's sore," he admitted, voice strained.

"You might have some inflammation from the smoke and fire. How about the rest of your body? Are you burned anywhere?"

Zachary tried to tune in to his body. He'd been so caught up in his nightmare that he had no idea what else his body was feeling. He had been burned in the first fire, but he didn't know if he'd been burned again. The paramedic was checking him over, not waiting for a response, examining his arms and legs, pulling up his shirt, looking for any burns.

"You're red like you got a sunburn," the man said. "But I don't see anything serious. They'll check you out at the hospital. Unless there's something you're aware of…?"

Zachary shook his head. "No. What happened?"

"You'll have to talk to the firefighters. I don't know. A few people got smoke inhalation, but you're the only one who was in the apartment that caught fire first."

He was glad that no one else had been hurt, but he was confused by the fire. It had started in his apartment? He felt like his dreams had engendered it. That somehow, by dreaming about fire, he had brought it into being. He knew it didn't make any sense, but he didn't understand what had happened.

Eventually, a firefighter came over to talk to him, taking off a blackened helmet and leaning over Zachary's gurney to talk to him.

"Are you able to talk, sir?"

"Yes." Zachary's voice was rough, and his throat hurt, but he wanted to know what had happened. "What happened?"

"You're the one who was in 3C?"

"Yes. I'm 3C."

"Looks like maybe you had been burning some candles earlier this evening and fell asleep. One of the candles burned down, and some papers caught on fire."

Zachary shook his head. "I wasn't burning anything."

"Some candles. Christmas candles."

"No."

The man raised an eyebrow at Zachary, like he was a stubborn child and just needed to admit what he had done. "We understand that it was unintentional. Sometimes things happen. Fires are tricky things. People don't realize how dangerous candles can be. You can never go to sleep while they're burning."

Zachary tried to sit up. "I wasn't burning candles. I would never do that."

"It's nothing to be embarrassed about. People start fires cooking Christmas dinner, smoking in bed, throwing a scarf over a lamp for a romantic atmosphere. Burning candles is just one of those things. It happens."

"I was in a fire as a child," Zachary said, catching the fireman by the front of his uniform and holding on to him tightly, afraid he was going to leave before Zachary could explain. "I *can't* light a candle. They're terrifying."

The firefighter stared at him, his head wrinkling in puzzlement.

"You're 3C."

"Yes."

"That's where the fire started. It started with candles."

"That's impossible. I don't have candles. If I did, they would just be for decoration. I would *never* light them."

"Well, there were, and somebody did. There were apparently no batteries in the smoke detectors."

Zachary's jaw dropped. "There were! I replace them every two months." He could see that the fireman didn't believe him. "I was in a fire," he repeated desperately. "I am very careful. I make sure! I replace the batteries every two months and test the smoke detectors every Sunday."

"Let me talk to my chief. You just stay here." The man sought out a paramedic close by. "You won't take him to the hospital yet, will you? We need to talk to him for a few more minutes."

"Okay."

"Keep an eye on him. Don't let him go anywhere or talk to anyone else."

Zachary was again left alone, sitting on the gurney with his head whirling, trying to understand what had happened. How could a fire start in his apartment? With candles he'd never owned? And no batteries in the smoke detectors?

Another fireman came over to him, this one not drenched in smoke like the first. There was a policeman with him.

"Can I get your name, sir?"

"Zachary Goldman."

The policeman looked startled but didn't say anything, letting the fire chief proceed with his questions.

"And do you want to tell me what happened tonight? What did you do today, before going to bed?"

Zachary tried to sit up straighter. He wanted to look calm and self-possessed. He needed them to believe him and what he had to say.

"I went out for drinks with a friend in the evening."

"You've been drinking?"

"I had a few drinks. Yes."

"And you came back here. Alone?"

"She drove me home and walked me up to my apartment. She didn't stay."

"How long was she here? I'm going to need her name."

Zachary filled in the details the best he could.

"And you didn't light candles for a romantic atmosphere with your girlfriend?"

"No. I was telling the other fireman. I was in a fire when I was a boy. I don't have any candles. I can't stand having them around, and I'd never light one."

"This fire was obviously started with candles. There is plenty of evidence of them in the apartment."

"But I didn't *have* any candles. He said there were no batteries in the smoke detectors. I always have fresh batteries in my smoke detectors, and I test them every week."

"How much did you have to drink tonight?"

"Two, three drinks. Over a couple of hours. I wasn't drunk."

"Did you take anything before bed?"

"No. I couldn't. Because I'd been drinking."

The police chief looked at Zachary and looked at the policeman. "Does that mean that you normally would have taken something?"

"Sometimes I do… a sleeping pill to help me get to sleep. Or a Xanax… because I'd had a panic attack. I didn't take either one because I'd had alcohol and I knew you're not supposed to mix them."

"But even so, you didn't wake up when your apartment started to fill with smoke."

"I… I don't know when I was awake and when I was asleep. I was dreaming about a fire, having a nightmare. I don't know when I woke up. I don't know how much of it was a dream and how much was real."

"How long was your girlfriend there?"

"Just a few minutes. I was tired… she didn't stay."

"Did she want to?"

"I don't know."

"Did you walk her out? Lock the door behind her?"

"No. I was already falling asleep… she saw herself out."

"Are you sure?"

"Yes. I didn't walk her out. I was too tired."

"Are you sure she *left?*"

Zachary felt the cold through his blanket. He was starting to shiver. Another night out in the cold, nearly killed under suspicious circumstances. He thought of Kenzie in his dream. How she knew something. She knew who it was that was trying to kill him. She was helping them. Had he heard her leave the apartment? Or had he merely walked out of the room and waited until she was sure he was asleep? She was the one he told everything to. She was the one who knew about the fire when he was ten. She could have put something in his drink at the Four-Leaf Clover to make him sleep more soundly.

He won't wake up. He'll never know.

"I... I'm sure she did," he protested, but he knew they could hear the doubt in his voice. That they knew very well he wasn't sure. He could never be sure. He'd fallen asleep. He hadn't walked her out. Locked the bolt behind her.

"Mr. Goldman," the policeman said.

"Yes?"

"Are you the same Mr. Goldman who was in an accident a few weeks ago? In a car? Brake lines cut?"

Zachary swallowed. He took in a deep breath. Too sudden; he started coughing and had a hard time getting back under control again.

"Yes. That was me."

"Who is trying to kill you?"

"I don't know."

"This girlfriend. Was she with you before the car accident?"

"She was in the accident with me," Zachary said, sure it proved Kenzie's innocence. "She couldn't have been the one who did it. We both could have died."

"Maybe that was the plan. For the two of you to die together."

"No... I don't even know her that well. We've only gone out a few times."

"Uh-huh. Is there someone else who has motive to kill you?"

"I… the other officers who questioned me after the car accident… they have the details about the cases I was working on… I'm a private detective. I've been getting threatening notes."

"I'd say this goes well beyond threatening notes."

Zachary nodded. He put the oxygen mask over his mouth, both to breathe the warmer air that didn't tear at his throat, and to hide behind it, so he didn't have to speak while he was sorting out his thoughts.

"Anyone else we should be aware of?"

He breathed the warm air, not wanting to answer the question.

"Mr. Goldman?"

"My ex-wife was here tonight too."

"You have an ex-wife? Any reason she might be upset with you? Other than being jealous that you were seeing someone else?"

"She wasn't jealous of Kenzie… but she was pretty mad. She hit me," Zachary touched the cheek that she had slapped. "And she said… that it was my fault that she got cancer."

The policeman's brows furrowed. "And how was it your fault that she got cancer? It's not usually something contagious."

"Because… dealing with me made her stressed. She got cancer because her body's defenses were down… or something. I don't know. Does it have to make sense?"

"When do they?" the fire chief intoned, rolling his eyes. "I've got three exes, and there's no point in trying to reason with them. I'm probably lucky none of them have tried to kill me."

Zachary rubbed at one of the scorch marks on his pants, seeing whether it would come off, or whether the fabric itself was burned.

"She knows… that I would normally take a Xanax and go to sleep after a panic attack. She told Kenzie so."

"So, she had good reason to think you would sleep through just about anything," the cop observed.

"Yeah." Zachary rubbed some more. He was going to have to get new clothes. Not just to replace the ones that he was wearing, but everything. None of the clothes that were in his apartment were going to be salvageable. If they hadn't burned, they would be smoke damaged. "But I don't think it was Bridget. I really... I don't think she would do that. I know she wasn't there when the brakes were cut. She was on the other side of the city."

"Or so she told you."

"No..." He bit his lip and looked at the policeman. "I had a tracker on her car. I know she was on the other side of town."

The cop gave no indication he intended to arrest Zachary for stalking or any other crime.

"With an ex like that, I'd track her too."

20

Zachary was again back at the hospital. After being checked out, he wasn't admitted. He went to the waiting room to sleep in one of the uncomfortable plastic chairs. He didn't have anywhere to go, or any way to get there. At least the waiting room was warm. He was around people, so, hopefully, he was safe from whatever psycho was determined to kill him.

He slept fitfully off and on. More off than on. Eventually, he figured it was late enough in the morning he could call Kenzie. He begged the use of one of the nursing station phones to do so. He was again without a phone of his own, or a wallet, or any other possessions. All he had were the clothes on his back, smelling strongly of smoke and not enough to protect him from the elements.

There was no answer on Kenzie's cell phone, or on her line at the medical examiner's office. He continued to call throughout the morning, growing hungry and crabby and at a complete loss as to what to do next.

Finally, almost at noon, she answered her cellphone.

"Kenzie! I've been trying to get ahold of you."

"So I see. I don't recognize the number you're calling from, though." Her voice was cool. Almost frigid. Zachary's heart sank.

"I'm calling from the hospital."

"Oh. What is it *this* time?"

He didn't understand her attitude. Wasn't she even the least bit concerned? "Well… it looks like whoever cut my brake lines isn't done. Someone started a fire in my apartment last night."

"Oh, did they? Why would anyone do that?"

He tried to figure out whether she was putting on a show for someone who might be listening in on the conversation. Did she not care about the second attempt on his life?

"Kenzie? They tried to kill me. Again!"

"I heard you."

Zachary waited for a few beats, trying to analyze her tone. He tried to picture her in front of him to figure out why she was behaving the way she was.

"What's wrong?" he asked. "Did I do something?"

He didn't need to wait for her answer for it to click in. He should have expected it. He should have known that she, too, would abandon him.

"I took Bridget's advice and took my car to the shop."

He swallowed. "Oh."

"You've been tracking me, too."

"It's not like that…"

"I can understand why you would track Bridget. It makes sense in theory. If you wanted to avoid her, you had to know where she was. But why would you be tracking me? Explain that one."

Zachary concentrated on breathing. He sat down in the chair beside the nursing station, unable to keep his feet. He breathed through his mouth.

"I'm waiting," Kenzie prompted. "Or are you out of excuses now? I'm starting to think maybe there's something to what Bridget's been trying to say. You're not a well person, Zachary. There's something very wrong with you."

"I… I wasn't *stalking* you. I wasn't doing anything sinister or creepy. I just…"

"You just what?" she snapped.

"I have… anxiety. You found that out. There's more to it than just panic attacks. I get… worried about people I have relationships with. I want to know… that you're okay. I know it's sick. You're right. I get scared, and I want to check on you. Just to make sure…"

"To make sure that I'm not seeing anyone else? That I'm not sneaking around behind your back? You don't own me, Zachary. We haven't even talked about dating exclusively. We've just had a few casual dinners together. That doesn't make me your girlfriend, and it doesn't give you the right to follow me around and monitor what I'm doing."

"No. I know that. That's not what I was doing. It didn't have anything to do with whether you were seeing anyone else."

"The hell it didn't!"

He was taken aback by her vehemence. He sat there in shocked silence. The nurse's eyes slid over to him, trying to analyze how much longer he would be. Trying to understand his conversation from the one side that she could hear.

"I'm sorry, Kenzie."

"You think that makes everything okay?"

"No. It's wrong. It was an invasion of your privacy. I was just being… a jerk. A stupid, dysfunctional jerk. I couldn't help—" He stopped and corrected himself. "I could help it. I shouldn't have done it. I should have just put up with the anxiety. Not like it would kill me."

She sniffled, and he realized she was crying.

He had made Kenzie cry.

"I'm sorry. I'm so sorry. I didn't—I did, but—I shouldn't have. I shouldn't have done it."

"You're a really sweet guy, Zachary. I can't understand how you could do something like this. You act like this great guy, all put together, a great catch, but inside, you're like… a little boy… like that little, lost boy who tried to do something nice and accidentally burned the house down."

There was a lump in Zachary's throat. "I don't tell that story to anyone. Especially not someone I'm just dating. I don't think I told any of it to Bridget until we'd been married for a year. Even then... no more than I had to."

He thought of the would-be killer lighting candles to start the fire. Was it someone who hadn't known his horror for candles and fire? Who thought that Zachary having a few Christmas candles lit would be perfectly natural? Or was it someone who knew him, who knew his story and wanted not just to kill him, but to do it in the most terrifying way?

"I'm glad you told me. Because if you hadn't, I don't think I could even begin to understand how you could do something so stupid as to track me electronically."

Zachary just waited.

"That doesn't make it okay, Zachary. It just makes it a bit easier for me to understand why you're so scared of losing the people you love."

Zachary swallowed and nodded, trying to make a noise of agreement.

"You really should be in therapy."

"I have been... but it doesn't make these feelings go away."

"But maybe if you understood them a bit better. Maybe if they gave you some strategies to manage your anxiety..."

"Maybe I need to find someone new. A new therapist. Maybe if I was seeing someone every couple of weeks..."

"Yeah. I think you should try."

Zachary sighed. "I'm monopolizing this nurse's phone. I should probably go."

"Oh. You're at the hospital." She had thawed and now sounded a little concerned about him.

"Yeah."

"Do you have a way to get home?"

"No... but I don't have a home to go to, so that doesn't matter."

She was silent at first, not immediately jumping in to offer him a ride. "What are you going to do?"

"I don't know. I haven't figured anything out. I guess I need to get back to my building, see if I can get in or if anything is salvageable. But then... I haven't got a clue. Maybe a homeless shelter."

"Why don't you get a cab and a hotel room? You'll maybe have to live out of a suitcase for a while, but..."

"I don't have any money. No credit cards, no ID. It was all in my apartment. The only thing I've got is the clothes I'm wearing, and those are pretty ripe."

She sighed. "I've got to work. I've already missed a couple of hours getting my car looked at. I hadn't arranged for anyone to cover my shift. You're going to have to figure things out on your own for now. Call me tonight when I'm off... let me know how you're doing. What you managed to get set up. Okay?"

Zachary swallowed. "Okay."

He had told himself that he didn't expect her to drop everything to pick him up. But it turned out he had. He'd been lying to himself. He needed someone to help him; then he could figure out what to do about getting his identification reissued and finding a place to live. Someone's couch to sleep on for a few nights. When he hung up after the discussion with Kenzie, he put his head in his hands, trying to sort out what to do next.

"What can I get you?" the nurse asked. "Coffee?"

He rubbed his palms into his eyes, trying to soothe the deep ache behind them. "That would be really good," he admitted.

"You just stay there for a minute, I'll get you one from the staff room."

He did as she said. Not that he had the energy to do anything else. He gazed out the wall of windows behind the emergency room chairs. Snow was starting to fall in big, white flakes.

Christmas snow. Magical snow.

Just another reminder that he was again homeless. He didn't

even have a coat to keep him warm on the street. What had changed in the decades since he was ten years old, trying to do something to bring his parents and his family back together? He had ended up in hospital then too. More burns on his body than he had this time. A throat swollen and burned by the smoke and the burning air. It was the same thing all over again.

"Here you go," the nurse said compassionately, setting a ceramic coffee cup down beside Zachary. She also set down a napkin with a chocolate glazed donut on it. "You're in luck; there was a meeting this morning with leftover food."

Zachary took a sip of the hot coffee and picked up the sticky confection. "You're a lifesaver, Nurse Nancy," he told her, looking at her name tag. "You don't know what this means to me."

"I gather," she nodded to the phone, admitting to the fact that she had eavesdropped on his call. As if she could avoid it, sitting right there two feet away from him. "Sounds like you're in pretty dire straits. You get something in your stomach, and then we'll see what else we can do for you."

Nurse Nancy and the coworkers she roped into helping Zachary had found a coat that fit him in the lost and found. "People leave them draped over the chairs and get into their cars without realizing they've left them behind," Nancy said. "And when they try to figure it out, they probably don't even think about the hospital. You should see the amount of stuff we get through here."

Zachary nodded politely. It was strange to pull on someone else's clothes, something that didn't quite fit to his skin and that carried someone else's scent. He was grateful for it. He couldn't even go outside without that little kindness. Several people had donated a few dollars so that he wasn't totally destitute and could at least call a cab or buy a sandwich if he were desperate.

Zachary thanked them profusely. They were lifesavers.

Though the hospital was not close to his apartment, he determined to walk back to it. It was something to occupy him while he waited for Kenzie to get off of work and wouldn't cost him any of his meager cash supply.

While the coat was warm enough that he was sweating after a few blocks' brisk walk, he didn't have any gloves, and his fingers turned numb not long into his journey. He swung his hands and clapped them together and pulled them into his sleeves. Eventually, he settled on pulling one at a time in under his coat and clamping it under his armpit until it thawed out. Then he would put it back out his sleeve and pull the other one in, repeating the process on the other side.

It took several hours to walk back to his apartment, as he had expected. When he got there, he found yellow caution tape blocking off all except for the front door to the building, with a police guard there to talk to anyone who wanted access to the building. He stepped forward and looked Zachary up and down, blocking the way.

"Sorry sir, the building is closed."

"I need to see how bad the damage is. If anything of mine can be recovered."

The cop opened his mouth to argue and repeat the stricture that the building was closed.

"I don't have my phone or my wallet. I can't get a hotel without a credit card. I have nowhere to go. I need access to my apartment to see if anything is salvageable."

"Which apartment?"

"Number 3C."

The cop shook his head again. "That's where the fire broke out. You can't have any access to it."

"Please. I need to at least see it. I need to know how bad it is. Should I start on getting my ID reissued, or will I be able to get it back? Can you tell me that?"

"No, I don't know."

"Could you go up there with me? That way you can make sure

I don't touch anything, but I can see if I'll be able to save anything, or whether it's all gone."

"I don't have clearance to do that."

"Maybe you could get permission. Is there someone you could call? Explain the situation?"

The cop just looked at him. Zachary spread his arms wide.

"I don't have anywhere to go. I don't have any identification, phone, or money. I don't have anywhere to sleep. I don't have a car. Can you explain that to someone? Help me out, here."

"I can't let you have access to anything in the apartment."

"I understand that. I won't touch or take anything. Just look to see it there's anything that didn't burn."

The man gave an exasperated sigh. "Fine. Let me see if I can get ahold of someone."

Zachary withdrew to give him privacy. He sat on the bench outside the building where people sat to smoke when it was warm out. He cleared a spot of snow and sat with both of his hands under his armpits. A few times he looked back at the cop, who was still on his phone. Sometimes they made eye contact, as the cop looked to see if he were still there. It was a long time, and Zachary sensed that the cop had needed to make a long series of phone calls rather than just one to make any progress. He finally called out to Zachary, motioning him over.

"Mr. Goldman."

He hadn't given his name, so obviously, the cop had managed to get ahold of the officers on the case and to talk to someone who knew the details.

"I have permission to walk you into your apartment. You mustn't touch anything. The arson investigator would like to talk to you when he gets here."

"I'd be happy to talk to him. I'm going to need... somewhere warm to hang out. I'm freezing."

The cop grunted. He motioned Zachary into the building and then locked the door that he had been guarding, barring anyone else from entering while he was showing Zachary to his apartment.

The electricity had been shut off, so they were forced to take the stairs. Zachary's throat and lungs were sore from the fire. His ribs were still healing after the car accident. His ability to climb the stairs and know what to do with his feet following his spinal cord injury was impaired. All of which meant that he acted like a crippled old asthmatic going up the stairs, making the cop wait for him every few steps. Eventually, they made it up the stairs and to Zachary's apartment.

The door hung open, the catch broken through the door-frame. At first glance, the interior was completely black, but as Zachary moved in and looked around, he saw that there were varying shades of black. Some things were completely burned, some were scorched, and some were only blackened by smoke. He walked around, the cop right with him, watching with eagle eyes to be sure he didn't lay so much as a finger on anything.

It was such a foreign landscape. Nothing was familiar. Nothing looked like it was his.

Zachary pointed to the remnants of his phone and wallet on the side table by the couch.

"I guess that answers my question about the identification," he said. The phone was mostly melted, and the wallet extra-crispy. He doubted any of the flimsy plastic credit cards had survived the heat. Nor any cash. He didn't try to touch it and neither did the policeman.

Zachary wandered around the apartment. The computer sat under his desk. Like the phone, much of the plastic was melted and scorched. He was sure it wouldn't start up. Perhaps the hard drive would be recoverable, but he doubted even that. It wasn't the black box of an airplane, carefully shielded from the elements and any expected adverse events.

He looked over the rest of the rubble that remained on his desk. "I had a stack of papers here," he pointed.

The cop looked at the table and shrugged. "They wouldn't have survived. Papers burn the fastest, before anything else."

"But... there's no ash. There should be a whole bunch of ash from the burned papers, and there isn't."

"I'm no specialist in arson. I'm just here to keep the building secure. Talk to the arson investigator if you have any questions. I'm sure he'll want to hear anything you might have to say. Anything you notice."

Between the fire, the smoke, and water damage from putting out the fire, there was going to be very little that was recoverable, if anything. Zachary sighed. He looked at the small kitchen as he walked by.

"Oh... something in the freezer might have survived, right? They say to put valuable papers in the freezer, so they'll survive fire...?"

"Maybe," the cop agreed. "Did you put anything in there?"

"A few papers, yeah. I don't remember what all I put in there. At the time, I got together everything I thought I might need if everything else was destroyed..."

The cop looked at the closed fridge. "I hope you put them in plastic bags, because everything in there is melting and going to stink to high heaven by the time they retrieve anything."

"Yeah. I did. Hopefully..."

"With any luck."

"I don't suppose you could open the freezer, just take a peek inside?"

"Nope. My instructions are not to touch anything. You'll have to talk to Darryl Reimer. He's the arson investigator. He'll be able to give you a timeline if anyone can."

The cop, Lawson, conceded to Zachary waiting inside the building, just inside the doors where Lawson could still keep an eye on him to make sure that he wasn't getting into anything. It was still cold, right in the doorway and all the utilities in the building being cut off, but it was significantly more comfortable than sitting on the cold stone bench outside in the snow. What should have been lunch time had come and gone, and the sun was low in the sky by the time Darryl Reimer showed up. He looked down at Zachary, sprawled on the floor inside the door, tired and bored, trapped with nothing but his thoughts in the little alcove.

"Mr. Goldman?" he inquired.

He was a stocky man. He wore a suit, not a uniform, and it appeared that he had been wearing the same shirt for a day or two. His face was red. He had a small black mustache.

"Yeah," Zachary scrambled to his feet. "You must be Reimer?"

"That's me." Rather than shaking hands, Reimer pulled out a shield, held it up for only an instant, and then put it back away again. "Thank you for sticking around to see me."

He headed toward the stairs, and Zachary followed him.

"I've read both your statement to the police last night, and your statement following the car accident on New Year's Eve. I'm as much up-to-date as I can be without talking to you."

"Uh-huh." Zachary focused on breathing. The stairs were just as difficult to climb the second time as they had been earlier. Luckily, though, Reimer didn't seem to be in great physical shape and was happy to take it much more slowly than Lawson.

"First off, do you have any questions or concerns for me? Anything you'd like to bring to my attention?"

"I looked around the apartment... I didn't see a lot of ash from burned papers on my desk."

"How many papers?"

Zachary went slowly through what he could remember of what was in the piles. The sizes and approximate number of pages of each stack. That took the rest of the way to the apartment. They were both silent as Reimer looked around. He had brought a powerful flashlight with him, so the setting of the sun didn't bother him. He played the light over the desk and nodded thoughtfully.

"It does seem like there should be more," he agreed. He played the light on the floor surrounding the desk, humming tunelessly.

"You had been getting threatening notes about one of your cases?"

"Yes."

"And were there documents from that case on the desk."

"Yeah. Sure. From all of my cases."

"There was some question of whether your wife could have been involved?"

"Ex-wife," Zachary corrected quickly. "Well, yes. I don't think she was, but there's a possibility. I know she wasn't anywhere nearby when my brake lines were cut, so it doesn't seem very likely."

"Right. And there is a current girlfriend?"

"A girl I am seeing, yes."

"And she was nearby when both attempts were made on your life."

"Yes. She doesn't have a motive, though."

"If there's both a girlfriend and an ex-wife, there's motive. Believe me."

Zachary stood in the middle of the room, watching Reimer move around, examining clues that didn't mean anything to Zachary. It was all just blackened fragments of his broken life. None of it told him anything.

"I was dreaming before I woke up to the fire," Zachary said. "And in my dream, it was Kenzie, the girl I'm seeing." He paused, letting the words sink in. "That doesn't mean it has anything to do with her. It was just a nonsensical dream."

"Our dreams often derive from the environment," Reimer observed. "Did you dream about a fire before you woke up?"

"Yes. I was in a house fire when I was a kid. I dreamt I was back there."

"Makes perfect sense, doesn't it? And dreaming about the girlfriend *could* mean that she was here while you were sleeping. It's not a forgone conclusion. Our brains aren't just input and output."

"She was here before I went to sleep, but then she left."

"Did you lock up behind her? Walk her out?"

"No."

"You are only assuming she left. Maybe you dreamed about her because she was here before you went to sleep. Maybe while you were asleep. No way to know."

Zachary was glad that Reimer hadn't taken it too literally. Zachary had been honest, and Reimer hadn't overreacted, taking it as an accusation.

Reimer continued to look around.

"I have some papers in the freezer."

Reimer didn't look up. "Next time, invest in a fire-proof safe."

"Okay… do you think we could see whether they survived?"

"When I get there."

Reimer wasn't in any particular hurry. His doggedness probably made him a good arson investigator. Single-minded, not easily shaken from the trail. Zachary was starting to get cold. The building kept out the chilly wind, but he needed somewhere with a furnace or heater to get warmed back up again. He'd been gradually losing heat all afternoon.

After a long time in the living room, the epicenter of the damage, Reimer finally moved on. He looked into the bedroom, where the damage was not as bad.

"Where were you sleeping? In here?"

"No. In the living room."

Reimer stared off into space. Zachary tried to read his expression and figure out what he was thinking. Eventually, Reimer spoke. "That's one audacious arsonist. Lighting a fire with you in the room? Arsonists normally stay far away from people. They light buildings on fire. Not people. Normally unoccupied buildings, but occasionally they will be bold enough to set a building they know is occupied on fire. When they do, they light the far end, furthest from the occupants. Not in the same room."

He stared off into space some more.

"What does that mean?" Zachary asked finally. "What does that tell you?"

"Most arsonists are firebugs first and murderers second. I think this arsonist is the opposite. I think he was a murderer who took the opportunity to light a fire to achieve his ends. I don't think we're going to find a serial arsonist involved here. This may be his first arson, which means that he's more likely to have made mistakes and left evidence."

Zachary nodded. "That makes sense, since he didn't put a bomb or incendiary device in the car. He cut the brake lines."

"Right," Reimer agreed curtly.

Zachary waited while Reimer made his way around the bedroom. When he was done, he looked up. "You wanted to look in the freezer."

"Yes."

Reimer went to the kitchen, and again surveyed the area as a whole rather than going directly to the fridge. He played the light on the floor and the counters, moving slowly and deliberately. Finally, he made his way to the fridge and opened the freezer door with a gloved finger.

As Lawson had suggested, everything was melted and starting to go bad. A foul, sour smell crept out into the apartment, and murky water dripped down the front of the fridge. Reimer shone his flashlight around the interior of the freezer.

"Where were these papers?"

"They might be under something. They were in a plastic zip-bag." Zachary craned his neck to see over Reimer's shoulders and around his head. "Check... under that pizza box."

The box was, of course, sopping wet and tore when Reimer attempted to move it out of the way. He moved the few items in Zachary's freezer around, and both of them could see that there was no plastic bag in the freezer.

"You're sure you left them in here?" Reimer asked. "You didn't change your mind and put them in a safe deposit box? Or give them to a friend to hold? Those are far safer methods than keeping important documents in your freezer."

Zachary felt the sting of criticism. "Yes, I'm sure. I don't have a safe deposit box or a fireproof safe, or anyone that I could have left the papers with. I put them in a zip bag in the freezer."

Reimer shook his head. "Not there now. What papers?"

"My birth certificate. Copies of my credit cards. Important phone numbers if my wallet was stolen. Or burnt to a crisp."

"They're not here."

"Can I look?"

Reimer stepped back and allowed Zachary to step in. He didn't have any gloves on, and the frigid water immediately made his fingers numb. He pushed the thawed goods around the freezer, sure that the bag must just have gotten wedged between them, or crumpled up in the back of the freezer, but the whole time he was looking, his heart sank. They weren't there. Whoever had come into his apartment had not only stolen or burned all the papers on his desk, but they had also taken the documents from the freezer.

"Why would anyone take those? They aren't of any use to anyone except me!"

"Identity theft?" Reimer suggested.

"But what would be the point of that? You don't go into someone's apartment while they're sleeping and steal their identity and set their apartment on fire! If all you wanted to do was steal their identity, you wouldn't want to alert them to that fact by setting the apartment on fire. If it wasn't for the fire, it might have been months before I realized that those papers weren't in the freezer anymore."

Reimer grunted. "Maybe it has been months. Maybe they were taken out of there a long time ago. You don't have any evidence that it was during the fire."

"No... it hasn't been that long... I've seen them the last couple of weeks. They were stolen during the fire!"

"You want motives, talk to a psychologist. I can help with basic arsonist psychological profiles, but this guy wasn't a firebug.

This was something else. He wanted…" Reimer considered, shaking his head, brows drawn down. "This guy wanted to erase you. I don't know. Talk to a psychologist. You're sure there wasn't anything in those papers that was connected with one of the cases you were on? The case that the perp keeps telling you to drop?"

Zachary thought about the contents of the bag and shook his head. It wouldn't be of any use to anyone, except to assume his identity. His identity didn't have anything to do with any of the cases he was investigating. He wasn't an important feature in any of the cases. They were all about other people. It was professional. Not personal.

Zachary called Kenzie from Reimer's phone. She was getting off work and agreed to pick him up at the apartment building. He still didn't know what he was going to do for the night, where he was going to stay, but he could only move one small step at a time. He had confirmed that he was going to need to get all of his wallet cards reissued, and that was going to take some doing. He didn't have anything to prove his identity. No birth certificate, no driver's license, not even a piece of mail with his name on it. Everything had burned up or been stolen. He wasn't sure how he was going to go about getting it all reissued.

But that was a problem for another day.

Kenzie said she would pick him up. She also, at Zachary's request, agreed to bring with her another copy of the medical examiner's report, though she seemed reluctant to do so.

Why did she care so much about him investigating the case? Was it really because she thought everything had been handled the right way and that he would be burning his bridges if he contradicted the medical examiner or any of the officers who had been involved in the investigation? Or was there something else going on?

Zachary shook the questions off. Kenzie didn't have any

connection with the case. The only thing that connected her to the case was the fact that she was an administrator in the medical examiner's office.

He waited in the doorway of the apartment building. Lawson was no longer on shift, but his replacement seemed to have no problem with Zachary remaining there while he watched for Kenzie's car to pull up. It was a relief when he finally saw the familiar red sports car pull into the loading zone.

"Thanks so much for helping me out," he told her, as he settled into the passenger seat.

"Yeah. We'll have to discuss the parameters, though. I talked with Mario Bowman, and he said you could stay with him for a night or two. You're not staying at my apartment."

Zachary was both disappointed and relieved. At least he would have a place to sleep. A warm place. He didn't have to rely on a homeless shelter. "Okay. Thanks. I really appreciate it. I'm just in a tough place now… everything is a little crazy."

"I can sympathize, but I can't let myself be pulled into your problems. We are not a couple, and you are not staying with me, not even on the couch."

Zachary nodded. "Understood." He massaged his hands in the air from the heater, trying to thaw out. He was cold to his core, just like the night of the accident. He was looking forward to spending the next few hours in central heating, no matter where it was.

Kenzie's eyes were on his purple-tipped fingers. She looked back at the road. "You hungry?"

"Starving."

"What are you in the mood for?"

"Whatever you feel like. I can't pay, but I'll pay you back when I get access to my bank account and credit cards."

"No need. I'll treat tonight. Pizza? Italian? There's that buffet place on Hillcrest that has a bit of everything."

"Yeah, let's go for the buffet," Zachary agreed. "Then we can each have whatever suits us." And he'd have no worries about getting enough to eat, making up for a day of nothing but a cup of coffee and a chocolate glazed donut given to him out of pity.

Kenzie nodded her consent.

The ride to the restaurant was mostly silent. Even though Kenzie had agreed to help him out, it was obvious that she was still upset about the tracker on her car. He couldn't blame her; he knew it was not something that he should have done.

They walked into the restaurant, were seated, and went through the buffet. Zachary loaded up his plate and Kenzie very carefully picked and chose small amounts of a few favorite foods. Zachary was a little embarrassed at how his plate compared to hers. It probably wasn't her first meal of the day, though.

After they had sat down at the table, Kenzie slid the familiar medical examiner's report across to him.

"I'm not sure why you need that," she said. "I thought you were closing the case."

"I was. I am. I have to rewrite the final report. All of my materials are gone in the fire."

"You should have saved it in the cloud."

"Where someone else could access it? I never save case files to the cloud."

"Then how are you going to recover all the stuff you lost in the fire?"

"I don't know." Zachary sighed. "I'll have to reconstruct what I can. Request new copies." He groaned as he thought of all his photography equipment and negatives. He had been saying for years that he needed to store stuff off-site. That he needed to find a way to back up his data somewhere safe. He never had. The backups he had made of his computer were in the apartment, just like the computer. A lot of good that did.

Kenzie put a forkful of salad in her mouth and chewed it slowly. "What are your other active cases about?" she asked.

Zachary shrugged. "Adultery. Insurance fraud. Accident reconstruction. Stuff like that."

"The Declan Bond case is the only one about a death."

"Yes."

"Then doesn't it have to be the one that they're trying to stop you from investigating? Who's going to set your apartment on fire over adultery? The only one that makes any sense is the Bond case."

"Only it doesn't," Zachary disagreed. He took a minute to nibble the meat from a buffalo wing before expanding. "I know the principals involved in the case. If it was the mother, which is what I think, it doesn't make any sense that she would try to get me to shut down the investigation. She already got away with it, and no one from the police department is going to reopen the investigation. She wouldn't kill me because I state in my report that she's the only one who had motive and opportunity. Her mother and husband are just going to brush it off. It isn't going to get to her employers or viewers. There's no reason to kill me."

"Why do you think it's the mother and not just an accident?"

Zachary sighed and shook his head. He was starting to get warm inside at last. He wrapped his fingers around his coffee mug while he tried to explain it to Kenzie.

"First, because of the cough medicine."

"So he had cough medicine in his system. That's not suspicious."

"It's suspicious when they all say they wouldn't give him cough medicine. If one of them volunteered and said, 'yes, he was developing a cough, so I gave him some medicine,' then I would be happy with that. No big deal. When the mother says that they absolutely would not give him cough medicine because it knocks him out... that's a different story."

"Tell me more about why she wouldn't give it to him."

"She gave him a children's cold tablet once a couple of years ago. It knocked him out and scared her so much that she's never given him any cold medicine since."

"That's sort of an extreme reaction, isn't it?" Kenzie suggested. She flaked a little fish into her fork and took a dainty bite. "Why wouldn't she just go with a half dose the next time?"

"Because Isabella is all about extreme reactions. She gets stuck and does things that don't make logical sense. Like putting out fresh food for the missing cat every day for eight years. Like refusing to eat off a plate in her own home, because Spencer threw out her favorite. Like not painting the color blue since Declan's death. That's what she's like."

"A little like someone I know who can't listen to Christmas songs and insists on GPS tracking anyone he gets close to."

Zachary scowled, staring down at his plate. He started on a small slice of pepperoni pizza.

"Regardless. Declan reacted to cold medicine, so she was afraid of ever giving it to him again."

"So maybe Spencer gave it to him."

"Spencer obeys his wife's rules. They both have rules to keep the house running. He's learned from the past what happens when he's up against one of her compulsions."

"So, he does it secretly. He doesn't tell her."

Zachary thought about it and shook his head. "He knew how Declan reacted the last time. He wouldn't risk doing it again."

"Like I say, he gives Declan a half dose. The kid is much older now. A half dose would probably be just enough to keep the cold symptoms at bay without knocking him out."

"But then why deny it? Why not just say that he was the one who gave Declan the medicine when I asked him?"

"Because it would get back to his wife. He's keeping it a secret from her at all costs. Because... he doesn't want her to blame him for Declan's death."

"It had to be Isabella," Zachary said stubbornly. It was the only answer that made sense.

"I'm not convinced," Kenzie said. "I think the father could have given it to him, but kept it a secret so they wouldn't get blamed. Or Declan might have drunk out of the dosing cup after someone else took some without anyone realizing."

"At least you're not saying it was a stranger who took him from the yard and gave it to him." Zachary was aware that his tone was sullen. He grimaced at his own reaction. Kenzie was helping him out; he shouldn't do anything to alienate her.

"It's still another possibility," Kenzie said. "You said yourself lots of parents do it to put their children to sleep or make them more compliant. It's a well-known strategy. There's nothing to say a stranger didn't lure him out of the yard with a popsicle laced with cough medicine."

"The *most likely* suspect is still the mother."

"Maybe. That's only speculation. You have no evidence."

"I don't need evidence. They're not going to reopen the case. All I'm doing is making a final report of my findings to the family in a case that is never going to be re-investigated."

"You said she has motive."

"Yes."

"What's her motive?"

"Declan was a pain in the neck. Motherhood is difficult, and she didn't want to do it anymore. She wanted him out of the way."

"That's pretty harsh."

"Not all women are cut out to be mothers." He thought of his mother, of her decision to break up their family and not be a mother anymore. "It didn't fit with her lifestyle. With her mental illness. She just wanted to paint. Not to have to take care of a mewling brat while she was trying to work from home."

"Did she tell you that?"

"No. It was pretty obvious that she didn't give Declan much attention. Even if you believe her story, she lost track of him for an hour or more. Not just two minutes. She wasn't painting facing the window so that she could watch him. She was painting with her back to the window so that she would have to turn all the way around to see him."

"That still qualifies as an accident, not murder."

"If you believe her story. And I don't."

"Did she tell you that she didn't want to be a mother? That she didn't like watching him? That she was glad he was out of the way? Exactly what did she say?"

"Spencer did things with Declan. Read to him, made his meals, played with him. Everything he said indicates he was engaged with Declan. Isabella is the opposite. She put him down for a nap. She sent him out to play while she painted. She was detached. Disengaged."

"They had different approaches to parenting. If she didn't say he was a bother or a distraction..."

"Isabella is OCD. She likes everything done a certain way. A child would just mess everything up."

"Didn't you tell me she's the hoarder? She's the one with the messy studio, and it's the dad who's the neat freak?"

"Yes."

"Then why would she be upset by a child messing things up? She's the one who likes a mess."

Zachary frowned. He switched mid-meal to chocolate pudding. One of the things he loved about buffets was it was not necessary to eat things in order. He could have dessert first. He could have it halfway through. Whenever he wanted.

Spencer would have to eat everything in order. Isabella, on the other hand... she was the one who would be able to mix everything up.

"How does Isabella deal with her OCD?" Kenzie asked. "Is she on medication? In therapy? How does she manage thoughts that intrude in her life?"

"She's in therapy. No meds, as far as I know."

"And Spencer?"

"I don't know which one he's doing right now, if either. He has a sort of unique approach to things that disrupt his life."

"Oh?"

Zachary told her about how he had moved to Vermont because of the billboard sign ban. So that his life wouldn't be overrun by having to count signs all day every day.

Kenzie stared at Zachary. He thought at first that she was done eating and was waiting for him to finish, but she still had food on her plate, forgotten. He looked down at his food, then up at her face.

"What?"

"Spencer deals with his OCD by removing the triggers."

Zachary nodded. "Right."

"He *removes his triggers*."

etting information from Molly about the OCD support group where Spencer and Isabella had met had taken some persuasion. She had been reluctant to even talk to him again, let alone part with any information.

"Isn't it supposed to be anonymous?" she asked. "It's one of those doctor-patient privilege things. Or like AA. Everybody only goes by their first names, and they're not supposed to talk about what goes on in the support group outside the meeting. People don't want everybody knowing that they have OCD."

"Molly, I really need to talk to somebody who knows a little bit more about Isabella's OCD if I'm going to help," Zachary coaxed. "I'm not asking for the name of her therapist. I just want to know what meeting she goes to. The one where she and Spencer met. Do they still meet every week?"

"I don't know." Molly went into her little galley kitchen and fussed around, making some tea. "Isabella only goes now and then, and I don't think Spencer has been in a couple of years. If you want to know more about Isabella's OCD, you can just ask me. Or ask Isabella herself. We'll tell you whatever it is you want to know."

"I really need an unbiased third party."

"You're not even supposed to be investigating anymore. I told you to mail me your final report. I'm not paying any more."

"I'm not charging you any more. I just want to be sure I have all the details right..."

"Isabella didn't drown Declan. It was an accident. She didn't have anything to do with it, other than that she was watching Deck when he wandered off."

Or she hadn't been watching him. Zachary refrained from reminding Molly that if Isabella had actually been watching him, he wouldn't have wandered off.

"Maybe it wasn't Isabella's fault. I'm willing to consider that."

Molly looked unconvinced.

"I just want to talk to someone who knows the two of them. Outside the family. Someone with more experience in OCD."

Molly's eyes went sideways to Kenzie. Zachary and Kenzie had hoped that having a woman along might soften Molly up a little. He hoped she'd open up and be more cooperative with a woman. That had backfired, with Molly immediately distrustful of the stranger. She had hired Zachary. Not Zachary and Kenzie. Even though they introduced Kenzie as Zachary's assistant, she obviously didn't like it.

"Molly," Zachary tried again. "I don't think it's breaking any confidences to tell us where and when they met with their support group. Surely a lot of people must know those details."

"It isn't exactly a secret," Molly admitted.

"Then if you can just give me the information, I'll get out of your hair."

She still dithered, pretending she had to look it up in her notebook. Kenzie looked at Zachary, and he knew she was thinking the same thing. Molly was just stalling. A couple of times she looked at the phone, an older-model landline, and Zachary wondered whether she was going to call Isabella to ask permission or wait until after they were gone and then call to give her a warning.

Finally, Molly pulled out a scratch pad and wrote out the

address and the time of the meeting. She glanced in Kenzie's direction but handed the note to Zachary.

"I don't like this," she warned, just in case they hadn't understood that from her previous objections. "I don't think this is right."

"The reason you hired me was to find out the truth," Zachary said. "And I think I might have found something."

Of course, the OCD group wasn't that day, and they had to wait until the group met again, because a ledger wasn't kept of the individual members with their contact information. Members could exchange information among themselves, but there was no central register kept. It wasn't quite anonymous, but they did their best to respect their members' right to privacy.

The next couple of days were excruciating. While Zachary had plenty to do, trying to start the process of getting his identification reissued when he didn't have any identification to prove who he was, it mostly involved phone calls with long hold times. Bowman was a gracious host, but Zachary knew having a house guest was stressful, and he didn't want Bowman to think that he had to provide entertainment. He just needed a place to sleep and to pick up a few meals until he was able to get back on his feet.

The night of the OCD support group finally came, and Zachary headed over to the meeting place, the basement of a church. There were signs up stating that the group was nondenominational and not associated with the church that provided the space. Zachary stuck his head into the room, reluctant to go in without an invitation.

"Don't be shy," a voice boomed out behind him. "Go on in. Everyone is welcome."

Zachary turned his head to find that the big voice had come from a diminutive, scraggly-blond, thin man who didn't look a day over twenty.

"Uh, thanks," Zachary said. "I don't know…"

"Come on," the young man encouraged. He reached as if to put his arm around Zachary's shoulders to sweep him into the room, and then jerked back before touching him. "Sorry. Sorry. Come on in. There are cookies!"

Zachary stepped in through the door and moved toward the snack table to give himself some space.

"Looks good," he agreed, looking at the sad little coffee station and plates of store-bought cookies.

"My name is Winston," the young man said.

"Uh, Zachary. Good to meet you."

"It doesn't have to be your own name. Just something that people can call you. There's a sign-in sheet over there." He pointed to a clipboard attached to a pen with a string.

"Thanks."

In a few minutes, all the members of the support group had assembled, and they made their way over to the chairs, where introductions were made, and a group leader ran through the usual order of business for the group.

Zachary introduced himself by his first name only, and glanced around the group, trying to analyze all the faces. Who would have known Spencer? Who would have associated with Isabella? Had they made other friends before they had gotten involved with each other? Or had they immediately been drawn to each other to the exclusion of anyone else? Isabella still went to the group sporadically, though she obviously hadn't wanted to show up while Zachary was there.

"I have a friend who used to go to this group. Do any of you know *The Happy Artist*? He's married to her. He told me about this group, said I should come."

They looked at each other for a few seconds, no one saying anything.

"Spencer?" a man with a bushy mustache asked finally. He had introduced himself as Dave. "Long time since I saw him."

Zachary nodded eagerly and looked around at the rest of the

group to see a couple of other nods as people remembered Spencer. "Yes, Spencer. He thought the group would help me."

Dave's mouth pursed sourly. "Really. I don't know how much it ever helped him."

"He came here, didn't he?"

"Yeah, he came, but I don't think he ever really invested in the group. He thought he was better than the rest of us."

"That's not fair," the redheaded woman called Angie spoke up, shifting uncomfortably and darting quick glances at Zachary. "He never said he thought he was any better."

"He didn't have to. It was obvious from his attitude."

"He didn't share with the group?" Zachary asked.

Angie sipped her coffee not from one of the foam cups provided at the coffee station, but from a chipped ceramic mug, reminding Zachary of the story of the plate Spencer had disposed of.

Dave shrugged. "He shared... inconsequential stuff. Fluff. The things that didn't matter. The work that we're trying to do here... it can be pretty painful. Gut wrenching. People dig down deep and bare their souls. Then someone like Spencer comes along, pretending that he's got it all together."

Zachary nodded, trying to work through this. "He did seem like he had it all. Married, good job, taking care of his little boy..."

"Appearances can be deceiving," contributed the woman in a blazer and skirt. Zachary couldn't remember her name. Something that started with an M? She looked professional and perfectly coifed. Was she referring to herself or to Spencer when she said that? Maybe both.

"Did you know him?" he asked her.

"I remember him. He did act like everything was going pretty well for him, but I think he had problems he didn't want to talk about."

"Everybody has things they don't want to talk about," Dave

said. "But we have to share them if we want to overcome them. This *inner work*; it's not for cowards."

"What did he talk about?"

There were looks exchanged around the circle.

"Maybe you should talk to him," Angie said. "We're not supposed to be sharing information about other people."

"I just wondered," Zachary said. "With the trouble he's been having since his son died... I wondered if he ever talked about Declan when he was coming here."

"I heard about that," Angie said with a nod. "Poor Spencer and Isabella. I can't imagine what they must have been going through. They both loved that little boy."

Zachary didn't want to press the question, worried that the harder he pushed, the more they would push back about not wanting to talk about someone else.

"I lost my parents when I was a kid," he offered. "My whole family. I'm just starting to realize how much it affected me..." He paused, and no one said anything. "Not just grief," he explained, "but... psychologically... the fear I carry into other relationships."

There were nods and noises of agreement from around the room.

"It must have been hard for Isabella and Spencer to parent, with both of them being OCD... and so different from each other."

"Spencer didn't talk much about Declan," Dave said. "He was more likely to talk about business stuff than anything personal. Isabella was more likely to talk about the difficulty of being a parent, responsible for someone else. Spencer just stopped coming. Like he didn't need the group anymore."

"He was complaining about intrusive thoughts," M said. "I thought maybe he'd open up, but then he faded out. He hadn't ever been one to come every week, but it got less and less often..."

"It's only been Isabella the last couple of years," Dave agreed.

"What does that mean, intrusive thoughts? Is that like his counting compulsion, before he came to Vermont?" Zachary intentionally dropped another hint that he knew all about Spencer and his history.

Winston was frowning at Zachary. "You have OCD and you don't know what intrusive thoughts are?"

Zachary snorted. "Well, I know what *my* intrusive thoughts are, but I thought that was more... PTSD. Flashbacks. I can't imagine Spencer getting as emotional over his own thoughts as I do. He's so... ordered."

"He was, though," Angie said. "There was one day when he broke down about it. I think he was too embarrassed to come back after that."

Zachary leaned forward. "What did he say?"

She shook her head slowly. "I don't remember what it was... I don't think he told us anything specific. Just that... he had to do something to get them out of his head. He didn't know how long he could keep fighting them."

Apparently, he had kept fighting them for two more years, alone.

And then what had happened?

Finding the name of Spencer's therapist turned out to be easier than talking Molly into giving up the OCD Anonymous group. He told the group that Spencer had suggested he go to a doctor that he had seen for a while. A Dr. Bloom...? Or was it Chen? He had gotten so many different recommendations; he couldn't remember which had been Spencer's.

"Dr. Snowdon," Dave supplied. "I went to him for a couple of years too. He specializes in anxiety disorders."

"Snowdon..." Zachary mused. "I don't think that was it... are you sure?"

"Yes. He works out of the health center in Vermont Plaza. An old guy, but he knows his stuff."

"Is he still around? Maybe Spencer is seeing someone new now. Didn't Snowdon retire?"

Dave grew more vehement. "No. No, I saw him just a couple of weeks ago. He's still practicing. That's where Spencer went. I don't know if he is still seeing him or not, but he was using Snowdon. I'm one hundred percent sure."

So, Zachary had the name of Spencer's therapist. Other members of the group had given him other suggestions as well in case Snowdon wasn't taking any new cases or wasn't a good fit for Zachary.

Zachary went home, back to Bowman's couch, feeling good about himself. He was making progress. The case was going to go somewhere; he would soon be able to lay everything out for Molly and the police. He'd had a couple of cookies at the support group, a treat he didn't allow himself very often.

When morning rolled around, he looked up Dr. Snowdon's address and credentials. He anticipated that getting in to see Dr. Snowdon and getting any information out of him was going to be very difficult. Who else was going to have better insight into Spencer's psyche than his therapist?

He camped out in the waiting room after introducing himself to the receptionist. She said that he would not be able to see Dr. Snowdon, who was completely booked with sessions for the day. When Zachary sat down to wait, she shook her head and ignored him for the first hour. After that, Zachary watched her get more and more fidgety, looking at him when she didn't think he was looking and whispering to other office staff behind her hand. Zachary continued to leaf through magazines, covertly studying the patients who came in for their sessions.

They all looked remarkably normal. At the support group, there had been a few people who were dressed strangely or had an odd personal appearance, and some who were obviously bacteriophobes, constantly rubbing their hands with sanitizer, or wiping down their chairs. At the doctor's office, everyone gave the appearance of perfect normality. Zachary examined himself. He supposed he had some obsessive-compulsive tendencies himself, but he took care to look normal to other people. He had it down pretty well. No one gave him a second look. Most of the time.

The receptionist was talking to a white-haired, heavyset man in a t-shirt and khakis, making frequent glances in Zachary's direction. Zachary turned his head and made eye contact with the man he assumed was the doctor. He walked over to Zachary, his creased face showing his puzzlement.

"Mr. Goldman, is it?"

"Are you Dr. Snowdon?" Zachary stood up and offered his hand.

Snowdon shook it. "Yes. I must confess, I'm not sure why you're here…"

"Could we talk privately?" Zachary glanced around at the other people in the waiting room, who although they didn't look at him, were all ears.

Snowdon sighed and shook his head. "Follow me."

He led Zachary to an office. It was pretty much like Zachary expected. A computer and desk. A couple of chairs and a couch. More magazines, fake plants, a few bookcases lined with books, certificates on the walls, a picture of his family on his desk.

Zachary sat in one of the chairs and made himself comfortable. "This is very nice."

"Now, if you would explain to me what you're doing here…?"

"I'm a private investigator. One of your clients has come up in one of my investigations, and I wanted to talk to you about him."

"You must know I can't do that. Doctor-patient confidentiality applies."

"I didn't say I was going to ask you questions about him. I said I was going to talk *to* you about him."

Snowdon scowled. "Really, I don't see how I can help you."

"One of your patients is Spencer Bond. He has OCD."

"I can't give you any information on any patients."

"Spencer is married to Isabella Hildebrandt, *The Happy Artist*, who also has OCD."

"That may be." Snowdon shook his head. "I am sorry I can't help you."

"They have a son named Declan, or they did until he died last summer."

Snowdon's gaze sharpened and he didn't make any objection.

"I know that one of the exceptions to doctor-patient privilege is when you think that someone might harm themselves or others."

"Yes, of course."

"If you knew that Spencer was going to harm his child, you would have had to speak up. You would have gone to the authorities and had him committed."

"That never happened."

"No. So, I guess you didn't know ahead of time that he was going to harm Declan."

"Do you have proof that he had something to do with his son's death?"

"You didn't say, 'Spencer would never do that.'"

"Is that a question?"

"No. I just think that if I was a psychologist, I would have some idea as to whether a patient was capable of something like that."

"I don't think anyone could claim to know what their patients were capable of. Not one hundred percent."

"No. You didn't think Spencer would hurt Declan, did you?"

Snowdon just looked at him.

"I know some things about Spencer's past behavior," Zachary said.

"Oh, do you?"

"He came to Vermont because of the billboard signs law. He had a compulsion to count billboards, and it was disrupting his life, so he moved to Vermont where there were no billboards to count."

Snowdon cocked his head to the side a little, considering this. Then he sat down at his desk.

"That's what Spencer told you?" he asked.

Zachary nodded. "And I know that he got rid of Isabella's mismatched stuff so that he wouldn't have to look at it, even though she would only eat from one plate. He didn't say that he didn't know it was the only plate she would eat from, but I think that's what he wanted me to believe."

"You don't sound like you believe it," Snowdon suggested.

"No. I don't think he could have helped noticing that his wife only ever ate off one plate. One that was chipped and didn't match anything. It would have been like a big, red, flashing light for him, wouldn't it? Of course he knew it was the only plate she would use."

Snowdon shrugged, not sharing his opinion or his knowledge one way or the other.

"I also think..." Zachary ventured into guesswork, "that he got rid of her cat because he didn't want it shedding and tracking dirt around the house."

"Really?" Snowdon seemed surprised at this revelation. "Did he tell you that?"

"No. I have a suspicion that if we called their friends, the Raymonds, we would find out that he gave them the cat. I assume they swore never to tell Isabella about it. They ended up moving out of town; maybe that's why he picked them. The cat was missing for eight years. Then when they moved back into town, the cat suddenly showed up again. I don't think that was a coincidence."

Snowdon nodded, sucking in his cheeks. He didn't give his opinion one way or the other. Zachary took a deep breath.

"So we come to Declan," Zachary said. "A kid takes a lot more time and energy to keep up with than a cat."

"That's true," Snowdon agreed. "But parents develop a stronger bond. A different kind of bond, with their children. As much as the cat ladies would like us to think it, loving a cat isn't the same as loving your offspring."

"And you can't just give a child to your friends and ask them to keep quiet about it."

"No," Snowdon offered a little smile at this. "I would agree with that."

Zachary couldn't sit still in his chair any longer. He got up and started to pace back and forth across the room. A beep sounded from Snowdon's desk phone. He hit a button in reply. 'I know I'm running late. I should only be a few more minutes.'

He raised his eyes to Zachary. "We do need to move things along, here."

Zachary paced back across the office. "What would make someone with issues like Spencer, with the same kind of coping mechanisms as him, decide that murdering his child was the only thing to do? That's the part I don't understand. If he needed more help, he could have asked for more help. A housekeeper. For his wife to do more. A nanny. They had the money."

"You've taken quite a leap. I'm not aware of any evidence that Spencer did anything to hurt Declan. The child wandered out of his yard and drowned. It's tragic, but there's no reason to suspect foul play. Is there?"

"He had cough medicine in his bloodstream. His mother refused to give him cough medicine. Or to let anyone else give it to him. He didn't take it himself. He didn't find it when he wandered from the yard. He wasn't given it by a stranger who took him from his yard. The only explanation I can find is that Spencer gave it to him. Spencer decided to do what he always did. Get rid of a compulsion by getting rid of the trigger."

Snowdon tilted his chair back. He rubbed his chin, thinking about it. He didn't look at Zachary as he let out a long breath of air.

"There are many different kinds of obsessions and compulsions. Some people have hand-washing compulsions. Or an obsession with everything being straight and square. Or in groups of four. For other people, it's collecting things. Hoarding china figurines, or cats, or pop can tabs. That's another kind of obsession."

"Right," Zachary agreed. "Spencer and Isabella were both OCD, but they had different kinds of obsessions. Spencer was neat and tidy, and Isabella was a collector. It was hard for them to live together, butting up against each other's obsessions."

"But there are also obsessions that are rarely discussed. It's one thing to go to your doctor or support group and say that you washed your hands forty times yesterday, that you're stuck in a rut, and that you need some kind of intervention. Our society is pretty understanding about that kind of compulsion. They may even see it as a virtue. I've heard people say that they wish they were OCD so that their houses would be clean."

"Uh-huh…?"

"No one ever wants to be the crazy cat lady. We still recognize and talk about hoarding. It's still something that you can get help for if you decide it's time."

"Both Spencer and Isabella were going to a support group for a while. Spencer was coming to therapy with you."

"But there is a whole world of obsessions that our society is not as understanding or accepting of."

Zachary cast his mind over what he had learned in the case, and what he had observed about Spencer, trying to find something that didn't fit. Zachary's own compulsions were less acceptable. People didn't think of stalking when they thought of OCD. They didn't think about his constant agonies over relationships as part of a mental illness. That didn't seem to fit into the puzzle. Not Spencer's puzzle.

Dr. Snowdon got up and went over to his bookshelves. He pulled a thick volume down and returned to his desk with it. He opened it and flipped through the pages for a couple of minutes. Then he stopped, marking the place with his finger.

"Obsessions with Sexual Content and Obsessions with Violent Content," he announced. "Intrusive thoughts can cause the sufferer great distress. Patients are often reluctant to seek support for fear of being labeled pedophiles, homosexuals, or wife-beaters."

"*What?*" Zachary was stunned. He stared at Dr. Snowdon, trying to find the words to express his thoughts. "What are you saying? That Spencer—that OCD patients—can be pedophiles? That's one of the obsessions that people don't talk about?"

"No, no, don't misunderstand." Dr. Snowdon held up a finger on his other hand as if lecturing a class. "They have intrusive thoughts. Unwarranted fears that they could hurt a child or another loved one. They are not sexual deviants, but they fear that they could be. Imagine how you would feel if you had thoughts about causing harm to your wife or your girlfriend. Or your child. Imagine how you would feel if you had these thoughts constantly, whenever you were around them. You loved them and would never do anything to harm them, yet you constantly imagined doing them violence."

Zachary tried to understand the concept. "So, it's not that they want to hurt their child, but hold themselves back…"

"No. They have no desire at all to hurt the child, but they keep seeing themselves doing it."

"They don't have a compulsion to hurt them…"

"No. They have intrusive thoughts. Imagine that you don't want to walk to the edge of a cliff, not because you're afraid you'll fall, but because you're afraid that you will jump."

Zachary sat back down. He stared at the big book on Snowdon's desk. "Did Spencer ever tell you he had this kind of intrusive thoughts?"

"People with thoughts like these will rarely go to a doctor for help. It's a taboo topic. Usually, they will go to great lengths to avoid the triggers, or to avoid getting into a situation where they could act out the intrusive thoughts. Statistically, a patient who is having these kinds of thoughts is *less* likely to actually do harm to their loved one, not more."

"Then if Spencer had intrusive thoughts about hurting or

killing Declan, he would be highly unlikely to be the one who drowned him. Which makes Isabella the lead suspect again."

Snowdon didn't smile or confirm Zachary's interpretation. Zachary pressed his lips together and tried to figure out what he had missed.

"Putting aside the statistics," Snowdon said, "your earlier question was what would make someone decide to murder their child? Someone who had, in the past, resorted to drastic measures to *completely eliminate* the triggers of other obsessive behaviors or intrusive thoughts."

Zachary made the connection. "So maybe it wasn't because Declan was messy or disturbed Spencer's order. It wasn't that Spencer didn't want to be distracted or interrupted from his routines. It was because the only way to stop having these violent or sexual intrusive thoughts about his own son was to eliminate the trigger."

Dr. Snowdon slowly closed the book. "Most people never mention these things to their doctors," he reiterated. "A doctor would probably have no idea if his patient was having these kinds of thoughts."

22

W hen Zachary got out of his meeting with Dr. Snowdon, he tried to call Isabella. There was no answer. He looked at his watch. It was late enough in the day that she shouldn't still have been taping. She should have been back at home unless she had shopping or other errands outside the house to be done. He tried several times, and she didn't answer. Finally, he tried Molly's phone.

"I need to talk to Isabella," he said. "She isn't with you, is she?"

"No. She should be home. Maybe she is just painting and doesn't want to be disturbed."

"It's important that I talk to her. Can you call her and see if she'll answer you? She wouldn't ignore your call, would she?"

"Don't count on it," Molly laughed. "When she gets into a work, she could be on another planet. She wouldn't know if a tornado blasted through the house."

"Can you try?"

"Sure, I guess. What's this about?"

"I need to talk to her about Spencer. About whether he's ever had a particular set of symptoms."

"Why don't you just ask him?"

"I don't think this is something that Spencer would want to discuss with me, but he may have mentioned it to Isabella."

"I've spent a lot of time in that house. I could probably tell you anything you're wondering about."

Zachary didn't think Spencer would have told his mother-in-law about having thoughts that were so repugnant to him. It was a long shot that he would even have shared them with Isabella.

"I just wondered about intrusive thoughts," he said lightly. "If you would please call Isabella and see if she'll answer... I really need to meet with her to get her thoughts."

Molly sighed. "I'll do what I can, but if she's lost in a painting, one of us will probably have to go over to the house to get any response out of her."

But Molly couldn't get a response from Isabella. She wasn't too worried but did want to check it out and make sure Isabella was okay. "I think she's been getting better, since the hospital. They finally got her to take some meds that seem to be helping. If she'll keep taking them. Sometimes... suicidal behaviors can be hard to spot."

Zachary made an effort not to laugh aloud at that. In his experience, very few people even knew what to look for. Depression didn't always look like depression.

He called Kenzie to see if she could pick him up to take him to the house. Kenzie yawned in his ear. "Yeah, I was already thinking of clocking out early today," she said. "I don't know why I've been so tired the last few days. Fighting a bug, I guess." There was a pause. "It's three-thirty now. Let me finish up, and I'll pick you up at four."

"Thanks," Zachary tried to put all the appreciation he could into his voice. "I know it's a pain in the neck. Hopefully, I'll have a new car and be able to drive soon. Once everything goes through."

"Yeah. Then hopefully you can avoid getting yourself killed."

She said it flippantly, but he hoped she was right. He'd had enough of threats and near-death experiences. If Kenzie were right, and the case that he was supposed to drop was the Bond case, then he needed to take care in his approach. Walking up to Spencer's door might not be the best approach.

Kenzie picked him up in good time, and they met Molly outside the house.

"Do you have a key?" Zachary asked. "I'm not sure ringing the doorbell is particularly safe."

She frowned at him, shaking her head. "How is ringing the doorbell not safe?" she challenged. "You think you're going to get electrocuted?"

"No," Zachary said lamely, as they walked up the sidewalk. He dropped his voice so that Molly wouldn't hear as she marched up the sidewalk ahead of them. "More likely stabbed in the eye."

Kenzie glared at him. "That's not funny."

"No."

Molly rang the doorbell. When there was no answer after a few tries, she called both Isabella's and Spencer's cell phones, but couldn't get ahold of either one of them. She looked at Zachary.

"I don't know where they could be. They didn't say that they were going on vacation or running any errands. They both like their routines, and this is where they always are in the afternoon."

"You don't have a key?"

Molly finally produced one. "I never use it. One of them is always here…"

"She gave it to you in case of emergencies, right? And I think this is an emergency."

"Just because they're not answering the door, that doesn't mean that it's an emergency," Molly disagreed. She fit the key into the lock and turned it. "You don't think that she's done something, do you?"

"You said she'd been doing better."

"She has. I'm… just not sure…" Molly picked up the pace

and hurried as quickly as she could without losing her poise. They reached the studio right behind her. It was empty.

"Where is she?"

"Maybe she's sick. In bed. Or in the shower." Kenzie rattled off a few possibilities.

Molly looked suddenly drawn and gray, sick with worry. "She would have told me if she was sick…"

Zachary led the way toward the master bedroom, and Molly and Kenzie followed. It was obvious that she wasn't in the bedroom either. The bed was neatly made. It hadn't been touched since Spencer had stretched the sheets taut that morning.

But there was something different. There was an easel set up in front of the window on a carpet of newspapers, the sunlight streaming from outside. Zachary walked around it to see what painting Isabella had been working on. The canvas was untouched.

The three of them stood there, looking around at the rest of the room. Looking for anything that was out of place or might give an indication of where Isabella might have gone.

It all looked as it had last time Zachary had been there, other than the easel. Spencer's side of the closet neat and orderly. Isabella's side looking like a bomb had gone off. Just as it had the day of Declan's disappearance, Spencer's light summer jacket hung in a prominent position.

Spencer wouldn't go out without his jacket. That was what Isabella had said. Of course, it was winter, and he would be wearing a heavier coat at those temperatures.

His blue jacket.

The one that had hung in his closet to give him an alibi the day of the murder.

When Zachary had visited the house the first time, that blue jacket had been hanging on a peg at the front door. It didn't belong in the bedroom closet. That was why it stood out in Isabella's memory.

She hadn't been able to paint the color blue since Declan drowned.

"The blue coat," Zachary said, pointing to it. "He's copying the day that Declan drowned. He had put the coat there so that Isabella would think he was home, but he wasn't. He is the one who took Declan from the back yard." Zachary looked at his watch. "Declan disappeared from the house around four o'clock and died at about five."

"What do you mean he's copying the day of the crime?" Molly demanded. "Why would he do that?"

"Because it worked the first time, and because he's obsessive. If it worked the first time, then he has to copy every detail for it to work again."

"To work again? Declan is dead. Are you saying he's having some kind of breakdown?"

Zachary stared at her. How could she not understand what was going on?

But Kenzie had figured it out. She grabbed Zachary by the arm.

"We'd better find them," she said urgently.

Zachary nodded. He and Kenzie led the way back out of the house. Out the back door. They followed the fresh prints in the snow. Molly followed behind, murmuring in confusion that she still didn't understand what was going on.

23

The snow made it difficult to move quickly to the pond. The sun was already dipping below the horizon. Zachary's heart raced as they followed the trail in the snow to the little pond. It was frozen over. Spencer was in the middle, working at breaking a hole in the ice with a hatchet. Isabella lay beside him, half-sitting and half-reclined.

"Izzy!" Molly shouted out, finally getting an inkling of the danger her daughter was in.

Kenzie prevented her from dashing out onto the ice. "It's not safe," she warned. "We don't know how thin the ice is. You could all go into the freezing water."

Molly froze, her eyes wide, wanting to rescue her daughter, but unable to do anything.

"Stay back!" Spencer ordered, looking up from his work.

"How's it going, Spencer?" Zachary asked casually, as if they had just run into each other by coincidence on the street.

"Just stay back and leave me alone. I have to do this."

"I talked to Dr. Snowdon."

"So what?"

"I learned some things from him that I didn't know before.

About how some people with OCD have intrusive thoughts. They are afraid to go to anyone for help."

Spencer continued to hack away at the ice, enlarging the hole he had started.

"I didn't know that before. About how some people have thoughts about harming their loved ones. When they wouldn't ever do anything like that."

"I can't deal with it anymore," Spencer said. "I can't shut them off. The only way to get rid of the thoughts is to get rid of the triggers." He shook his head, his voice breaking. "I love my family. I can't... I can't keep seeing them like that."

"There are other ways they can help you. There are medications. Therapies. You never talked to Dr. Snowdon about your thoughts, did you? You never gave him the opportunity to tell you that it was treatable. That there were things that he could do to help you. You don't have to fight this alone, Spencer. There are people who will help."

"They can't do anything," Spencer disagreed. "I've already tried everything else. I know the way my brain works. This is the only way to get rid of the thoughts."

Zachary could see Kenzie out the corner of his eye, working away on her phone, using her own body and Molly's to shelter the glow of the screen from Spencer as she called or texted for help.

"You're a pretty smart guy, Spencer," Zachary said in an upbeat tone. "You really thought things through and planned this out, didn't you? You knew that Isabella would be distracted from watching Declan. You knew that the cough medicine would knock Declan out. Keep him from fighting back or waking up while you... took care of him. You fooled Isabella. You did leave the house without your summer jacket. You left it hanging there for her to see. In the bedroom, not at the front door where it belonged. You wanted her to believe that you were still in the house. She knew that you couldn't leave without the coat."

"I *can* leave without the jacket," Spencer offered. "I just don't like to. It's comfortable. I know what temperatures it is good for. I always wear it... but I don't *have* to. Even when I have a compulsion, I still have willpower. I can resist for a while... until it becomes too uncomfortable."

"But her unconscious mind picked up on what her conscious mind didn't. The color blue. It was wrong. It shouldn't have been in the bedroom; it should have been at the front door. Did you know that was why she couldn't paint the color blue anymore?"

"I didn't know for sure."

Zachary could hear the ice creaking as Spencer moved closer to Isabella. He grabbed her arms and dragged her toward the hole. Zachary was holding his breath, waiting for it all to collapse. In his mind, he was playing out what they would do. They would save Isabella first. He would lie down on the ice to spread his body weight across as wide an area as possible. They would need rope. Maybe his coat. He could take off his coat to stretch out to Isabella. If she were able to grab it.

She was murmuring to herself and didn't seem to have any desire to move away from Spencer. He must have drugged her just like he had drugged Declan. Zachary watched Isabella, trying to hear what it was she was saying. Did she have any idea what danger she was in? What was going on?

"Until we meet again, may God hold you in the palm of His hand."

Zachary breathed out, his chest hurting. "Of course, you were the one sending me threats," he observed, still trying to keep Spencer talking. Trying to keep him engaged and occupied. "But you never said which case it was I was supposed to drop."

Spencer looked up at him for a minute, frowning. "I thought you would know."

"Not if you don't tell me, amigo."

"Oh."

"Is this your first attempt on Isabella's life?" Zachary asked. "Or had you tried that before too?"

"She tried to commit suicide before."

"But was it really suicide? Or did you have a hand in that as well?"

"She was depressed. She felt guilty about Declan." Spencer shook his head. "I don't know why when she wasn't the one who did it. I had to live with the reality of what I had done to turn off those awful thoughts."

"You didn't encourage those feelings in Isabella? Maybe give her a couple of nudges toward suicide? You were posting mother and child pictures on her Facebook."

Spencer looked away. "Encouraging someone to commit suicide is against the law," he said. "I never did that, but I might have... manipulated her environment."

He wouldn't encourage his wife to commit suicide because that was against the law, but he would kill her himself. It made no sense to Zachary.

But in Spencer's mind, it did. With his disordered thinking, it was the best he could do.

"You had me fooled. I thought it was Isabella who had killed Declan."

"Isabella? I told you she would never do that."

"You can't always tell what someone is capable of doing."

Spencer looked at Isabella lying on the ice. "I know. There's no way she could have done anything to hurt Declan. She loved him... like a mother. It was different for her. She didn't have those thoughts. Those visions."

"You would have gotten away with it. The police didn't find anything suspicious."

"And then *you* had to come along. Why couldn't you just leave us alone?"

"I was just doing my job."

"They said that you were paralyzed after the car accident, and I thought I was safe. But they were wrong. That car accident should have killed you. The fire should have killed you. None of that worked. The only thing that worked was this." Spencer gestured to the pond and his wife. "I hit on the magic combination the first time, and I didn't even know how lucky I was. Isabella didn't die. You didn't die. Only Declan."

Zachary glanced at Kenzie, trying to get some idea from her as to when help would arrive. She made a wry face and gave a slight shrug with one shoulder. *Who knows?*

"I get it," Zachary said. "I know you think no one else can understand, but I get it."

"How could you?"

"I have… thoughts… too. I have had since I was ten years old." Zachary swallowed hard. "I've never told anyone."

Spencer stopped chopping the ice and looked across the pond at him. "What thoughts do you have?" he asked. In the failing light, his eyes were just hollows. He looked skeletal.

"I think that people are going to leave me. My wife. Anyone I'm dating. My wife did leave me… and I still think about her all the time. I want to know who she's seeing, what she's doing. I put a tracking device on her car so that I could know where she was all the time."

Spencer was standing there looking at him. He had stopped digging the hole and moving around, for the moment.

"I put trackers on other people too," Zachary said, glancing at Kenzie and grimacing. "Sometimes… people I hardly even know. It started with work, with people I was surveilling, but I couldn't stop with that. I had to know where everyone was. Everyone in my life. I stalk them by GPS. I check social media to see what they're doing all day long. I profile anyone they might be dating or spending too much time with…"

"That makes sense," Spencer said. "But the thoughts I have…" He looked at his wife and shook his head. "You can't imagine how horrible they are."

"You need to get help. There are things they can do to help. There are other ways."

"No… the only way to stop the thoughts is to remove the trigger. That's the only thing that has ever worked for me." Spencer looked down at Isabella with a groan. He grabbed her leg and tugged her toward the hole in the ice.

"Until we meet again, may God hold you in the palm of His hand," Isabella repeated.

Zachary stepped out onto the ice.

"Zachary, no," Kenzie protested in a whisper.

"I have to do something."

As he started to slide his feet across the ice, gingerly feeling his way along and listening for the sounds of cracking, he saw red flashing lights coming through the trees. The police were finally there, but Spencer was tugging Isabella those last few inches toward the hole, and the ice he was standing on could break and dump them both into the water at any time.

"Did you ever go ice skating as a kid?" Zachary asked, trying to distract Spencer and fill the silence. "I never had skates, but we used to go out on the pond, like this, sliding across it in our shoes." He was almost within reach of Isabella, which was both bad and good. He was now adding his own weight to the sheet of ice. "I used to love winter then. Sliding on the ice, building snowmen, Christmas…"

He'd almost forgotten that. Almost forgotten that he had ever loved Christmas. Like any other child. It had been a magical time of year. Not because of presents, because they rarely got anything worth mentioning. Not like some of his friends who got new toys, the latest games, the most popular movies, even new clothes, but because it was the season of peace and love. He could remember sitting in the living room with his mother, drowsy, staring up into the fully-decorated, lit-up Christmas tree. She told him stories and sang parts of Christmas hymns, and he felt the magic of the season.

"Come on, Spencer. Let's get you help."

Isabella started to slide into the hole in the ice feet-first. Peacefully, without a sound, just like Spencer had planned. Zachary threw himself down on the ice, sliding the rest of the way on his belly. He grabbed her coat and her arm and kept her from sliding the rest of the way in. The ice crackled under his body.

"Until we meet again, may God hold you in the palm of His hand." Her voice was drowsy and far away.

"Not yet, Isabella," Zachary growled. While she might be ready to meet her maker, he was not ready to let her go.

"Let go!" Spencer protested, his voice rising from despair to anger for the first time. "You're ruining it! Let her go in! It's the only way the thoughts are going to stop!"

"You can't get rid of thoughts of doing something terrible by doing something equally bad or worse." Zachary clenched his teeth with the effort of holding Isabella up. He could hear the police arriving, yelling to one another, coordinating their actions, but he was locked into the moment with Spencer, unable to move his eyes to the right or the left.

"You have no idea. You have no idea of how horrible the thoughts are. You wouldn't believe that I could think things that are so… so depraved. This is a mercy. For her to go peacefully and be with Declan again. It's what she wants."

"They'll help you, Spencer. They're going to get you help."

Spencer seemed to become aware of the police for the first time. He looked around in horror, his eyes getting bigger. He looked once more at Isabella, then finally abandoned his mission, making a run for it.

He didn't get far.

Zachary was relieved to have Spencer's extra weight off the shelf of ice. He breathed out slowly, tightening his grip on Isabella.

"Now it's time to get you out of here to where you're safe."

Hands grabbed Zachary's ankles. Two strong hands on each leg.

"You got a good grip on her?" a voice demanded.

"Yes."

"Hold tight. We're going to pull you back from the hole."

He tightened his grip. "I'm ready."

The voice gave a three-count, and then they pulled. Zachary kept ahold of Isabella.

They both slid easily across the ice, her body completely out of the water.

"That's it," Zachary breathed. "You're safe. You're okay."

24

Zachary and Kenzie stood watching as Isabella was covered with blankets and loaded into the ambulance.

"Glad it's not you this time?" Kenzie asked.

"Very glad," Zachary agreed. He rubbed his arms even though he was dressed warmly enough for the weather. "I'll bet she's colder than a witch's behind."

Kenzie laughed, nodding. "You did good," she said. "You saved her."

"This is not how most of my investigations end. I'm glad she's okay." He shook his head. "I didn't want it to be him."

"No one did."

"Any idea what she was given?" one of the paramedics asked them.

"My first guess would be cough medicine," Zachary said. "But I'm not sure if he could have gotten her to take it. He could have slipped her a prescription for anxiety. Valium, maybe."

"We'll have to get them to run her blood when we get her to the hospital."

"We might be able to find out from Spencer," Kenzie suggested.

Zachary looked at the police car they had put Spencer in.

Hands over his face, Spencer was crying uncontrollably. "I wouldn't count on it. It's probably going to be a while before he can talk."

"You're both all right?" The paramedic looked from one to the other. "How are you feeling?" he asked Zachary.

Zachary brushed at the snow coating the front of his jacket from sliding across the ice. "Yes, I'm fine."

"You didn't get wet?"

"No. Just Isabella."

They watched as the ambulance pulled out a few minutes later. Molly would follow it to the hospital and give them the information they needed to admit her daughter.

"What are you going to do for excitement now?" Kenzie teased.

"I'm looking forward to going back to a non-exciting life. A nice insurance fraud, that's what I'm feeling like right now. Following someone around for three weeks to see if they really do have a whiplash injury."

Kenzie smiled. "Sounds incredibly boring and tedious."

"Exactly."

"And what about… your health?" She stared at the police car Spencer sat in rather than looking at Spencer. "Sounds like you've still got some issues to work through."

"I guess I'm like Spencer," Zachary said. "I always figured I could just keep it to myself and muscle through it on my own, but maybe… the cookies at the support group weren't so bad."

Kenzie gave a smile of approval.

"Cookies are good," she agreed. "That would be a good place to start."

EPILOGUE

Zachary settled into his easy chair with his morning cup of coffee and turned on the TV. He didn't often watch morning TV, but there was a show on that he wanted to check out.

The theme song for *The Happy Artist* started to play, and the opening credits played while showing different angles of Isabella painting in past episodes. It was the first new episode of *The Happy Artist* since Spencer's arrest, and she'd been sorely missed in the intervening months. Then there was a view of Isabella sitting on a stool facing the camera, talking about the painting she would be undertaking for that episode. She seemed calm and relaxed, much more in her element than she had been when she and Zachary had both appeared on a talk show interview the previous day.

Then she had looked small and vulnerable. She seemed uncomfortable in her own skin and looked like she was wearing the wrong clothes or colors. Unlike the producers of *The Happy Artist*, which insisted that she keep her tattoo covered up and her memorial jewelry to a minimum, the talk show wanted to show her off in all of her mourning regalia. She had short sleeves that she kept tugging at, and the numerous chains and pendants made noise whenever she moved. Her mic had to be repositioned several times to find a placement that didn't pick up the clinking.

They had run Zachary through the details of the investigation, more focused on his two near-death experiences and Isabella's suicide attempt and her close call at the pond than they were in how he had developed the case. Then the cameras were focused back on Isabella, stroking the tattoo on her arm, gazing off into space, her lips mouthing the familiar words.

Until we meet again, may God hold you in the palm of His hand.

"And how are you feeling now, Isabella? Have you been able to move on, knowing the truth of what happened to Declan?"

"Yes… I'm doing a lot better now. It's horrible, knowing what Spencer did. At least I know… it wasn't my fault, and that Declan didn't suffer. He just went peacefully to sleep and never woke up."

"Are you getting the help and support that you need?"

"What I didn't know is that for the few months before the arrest, Spencer had been manipulating my environment. He had messed with my social media feeds, blocking out friends and changing my interests to dark and depressing things, so that whenever I went online, I just felt worse and worse. He blocked numbers on my phone and email as well, so that people couldn't reach me. They didn't know he had blocked them." She turned her head to smile at Zachary. "Zachary has been so good in helping me sort it all out since then, so that I have the support of my friends and colleagues again, instead of feeling so isolated and alone."

"That must have lifted a big weight off your shoulders."

"It did. I guess Spencer thought that if he could make me depressed enough, he wouldn't have to do anything directly. I would just kill myself. He almost succeeded."

"And are you getting professional help?"

"Yes. Yes, of course. Things are much better now."

"What would you say to Spencer now, if you were face-to-face with him?"

Isabella bit her lip, her brows drawing down. "I guess... I'd tell him I was sorry."

There was a noise of exclamation from the host, but Isabella went on, ignoring it.

"I wasn't a very good mother. I should have paid more attention to Declan and taken care of him more. I shouldn't have left him for Spencer to take care of all the time. I should have noticed that something was wrong... I should have asked Spencer about what was going on, but I was just focused on myself. On my comfort and my profession."

She sighed and stared pensively off. Her fingers brushed over the tattoo again, and she looked down at it as if she hadn't been aware she was touching it.

"He's here with me all the time, now," she said. "He can't ever wander away now."

Isabella stopped speaking, but he could still see her lips mouthing the words.

Until we meet again, may God hold you in the palm of His hand.

Isabella gave a brave smile and brushed a few stray cat hairs from her dress.

She was much better on her own show. She sat on the stool she was comfortable and familiar with and chattered to the camera about colors and tones and shades. She was wearing the clothes that suited her, even if she did have to wear long sleeves to cover up her tattoo. And just one necklace and ring. Nothing that would be too distracting as she painted.

Zachary sipped his coffee while he watched her begin to daub the canvas. A beautiful seascape started to appear. Cerulean blue waves and fluffy white clouds scudding across a sky of celestial blue.

Did you enjoy this book? Reviews and recommendations are vital to making a book successful.

Please leave a review at your favorite book store or review site and share it with your friends.

Don't miss the following bonus material:
Sign up for mailing list to get a free ebook
Read a sneak preview chapter
Other books by P.D. Workman
Learn more about the author

Sign up for my mailing list at pdworkman.com and get Gluten-Free Murder for free!

JOIN MY MAILING LIST AND

Download a sweet mystery for free

PREVIEW OF HIS HANDS
WERE QUIET

1

Mira Kelly put the pictures of her son down on her kitchen table, one at a time, like they were precious treasures she thought Zachary might try to run off with.

Photographs were Zachary's passion. Ever since Mr. Peterson, his foster father at the time, had given him a used camera for his eleventh birthday, he'd been taking pictures. It was that passion that had eventually led him to his profession. Not a department store photographer or a wedding photographer, but a private investigator. It gave him the flexibility to set his own hours, even if many of them were spent sitting in a car or standing casually around, waiting for the opportunity to catch a cheating spouse or insurance claim scammer in the act.

Zachary ignored the lighting and framing issues in Mira's pictures and just looked at the boy's face. He was a teenager, maybe thirteen or fourteen. Still baby-faced, with no sign of facial hair. Dark hair and pale skin, like Zachary's. Quentin's hair was a little too long, getting into his eyes in uneven points. Zachary couldn't stand hair getting in his face and ears and kept his short. Not buzzed like foster parents and institutions had always preferred, but still easy to care for. The first few pictures of

Quentin didn't give a clear view of his eyes. His eyes were closed, hidden by his shaggy hair, or his face was turned away from the camera. Then Mira put one down on the table that had caught his eyes full-on, looking straight through the camera. Blue-gray. Clear. Distant.

Mira kept her fingers on the photo, reluctant to release it to him. "Quentin was a beautiful baby," she said. "Everyone always said how beautiful he was. Not cute or handsome, *beautiful*. He could have been a model. But he didn't smile and laugh when you smiled or tickled him, like other babies. He laughed at other things; the sunlight filtering through the leaves of a tree, music... I didn't realize, in the beginning..." She wiped at the corner of her eye. She'd been resisting tears since she had first greeted Zachary.

Isabella Hildebrandt had said that Quentin had been autistic when she asked Zachary if he would meet with Mira. The boy had been living at the Summit Living Center, some sort of care facility, when he had died suddenly. 'Died suddenly' was a euphemism that Zachary particularly hated.

Mira was convinced that Quentin's death couldn't have been suicide. "He wouldn't have done that," she insisted again, looking at the picture that showed Quentin's eyes.

"Why not?" Zachary asked baldly.

He could see that his bluntness surprised her. She was used to people talking about her son's death in veiled terms. Coming at it sideways and trying to comfort her. But that wasn't Zachary's job. Zachary's job, if he took the case, would be to find out the truth about Quentin's death. And if he was going to do that, he needed Mira to speak plainly instead of soft-pedaling euphemisms.

"He... he couldn't." She stumbled over the words, looking for a way to explain it. "That just... wasn't something that he would have been capable of."

"Physically, you mean?"

"No, he was healthy physically, mostly, but... he had autism. He didn't have the ability... mentally... to decide to do something like that, and plan it out, and follow through." She shook her head. "The idea is ridiculous."

"Because he was mentally handicapped."

"No... not handicapped. I just don't think... I don't think he could have understood what it meant, to kill himself. And I don't think he could have planned it out. There is other stuff that can go along with autism... His executive planning skills..."

Zachary wasn't sure what that meant. He looked at the other angles of the case. "Was he depressed?"

"He was happy at Summit. It was a good place for him. The only place that had been able to manage his behavioral issues."

Zachary looked at the haunting eyes that looked up from the photograph. "This is a recent photo?"

"Yes." Mira looked down at him. "I know he's not smiling for the picture. But he never smiled for pictures. He *was* happy at Summit. They were able to get him off of all of the meds that the other places had put him on. So that he could be himself and not a drugged-out zombie."

"Sometimes depression isn't obvious. People are often taken by surprise by suicides." Zachary looked away from her uncomfortably. Other times, depression was obvious, and friends or family members did everything they could to head it off. Like with Isabella Hildebrandt, when her mother had hired Zachary to look into her son Declan's untimely death, hoping to bring Isabella some peace. They'd been unable to prevent her suicide attempt. Only luck and quick-acting professionals had been able to bring her back. As they had done for Zachary in the past. "When you say they took him off of his meds... did that include antidepressants?"

"No, he was never on antidepressants. He was on other medications to keep him quiet. I couldn't have him at home anymore, because he was too much of a danger to my younger sons. And me."

There was a snapshot on the fridge of Mira with two younger boys, maybe eight and ten. Mira was a slight, small woman. The ten-year-old was almost her height. There were no pictures of her with Quentin, but Zachary suspected he was taller than she was by a few inches. Even though Quentin had a slim build, a child in the midst of a meltdown could be very strong. Looking down at the pictures of Quentin on the table, Zachary saw another child in his mind's eye.

Annie Sellers had also been autistic, and well-known for her rages. He had watched, through the narrow observation window of his detention cell, as several members of the Bonnie Brown security staff had tried to bring her under control. She was slim and small, but even three guards together could barely hold on to her to get her into a cell.

Zachary blinked, trying to focus on the case at hand. Annie was in the distant past. He couldn't do anything for her. No one could.

"How long had Quentin been at Summit?"

"Two years. They turned him around completely. He was not the same child."

"And you hadn't noticed any changes in behavior recently. Anything at all."

Mira bit her lip. She was a strawberry-blonde with a pixie cut. She kind of reminded Zachary of a forty-year-old Julie Andrews. The same shape to her face. But there were fine lines that told the tale of a hard life. There was no sign of a man in the house. Raising three boys as a single mother was not an easy job, especially when one of them had behavioral issues. Summit was a good two hours' drive from Mira's house, which meant that she wasn't visiting him daily.

"He'd been agitated the last few times I went to see him," Mira said finally. "They said it was probably just hormones, and they were increasing his therapy sessions to address it."

Zachary scratched a note to himself in his notepad. "What do you mean by agitated?"

"More... anxious... more... behaviors..."

"Describe to me what that looked like. What exactly was he doing?"

"Picking at his skin... flapping... He was voicing and didn't want to sit down to visit with me. He wanted to walk around to visit, but they said... his therapist said he needed to work on sitting quietly to visit. When they forced him to sit down, he started banging his head or got angry, and they had to take him out and cut our visit short."

Zachary wrote down each of the behaviors. "He didn't usually do those things?"

"No, he'd been pretty good at Summit, they could usually suppress them."

"Is there something that triggers them? When he lived at home, did he do them all the time, or just sometimes?"

Mira ran her fingers through her hair. There were bags under her eyes, camouflaged with makeup. She looked exhausted. She probably wasn't sleeping.

"Yes, when he was frustrated about something... Before he died, I felt like he wanted to tell me something. But it's difficult for him. If I'd been able to walk around with him, talk with him some more, I might have been able to figure out what it was. But they said he had to go back to his room."

"So he *could* talk...?"

"He was mostly nonverbal. He had a few words. He would take my hand to show me something or ask me to do something for him. But Summit said I needed to force him to use speech." Mira sighed heavily. "They said that if I ignored his nonverbal communication... he would use words more..."

"Oh." Zachary nodded. "Then he could, if he had to?"

Mira frowned and tugged at a lock of hair. "Well... it was hard for him. They said that if he could speak some of the time, then he could speak all of the time, if he just worked at it. When he was at home, we would use pictures, gestures, whatever we could." She wrapped the lock around her finger. "It wasn't like he was just being willful or lazy when he wouldn't speak. That's what Dr. Abato says, but I always thought... Quentin was doing the best he could, and that we should let him use PECS or signs or whatever he needed to communicate..."

"That makes sense," Zachary agreed, giving her a nod of encouragement.

"They said that I was just babying him. Keeping him from progressing. They said if he was ever going to get out of Summit, maybe on a work program or something, he would have to be able to speak. To get along in the real world and be treated like everyone else, he needed to be able to speak."

"And it was working? You said that his behavior had improved at Summit. Did that include his speech?"

Mira picked up one of the photos from the table and stared at it, her eyes shiny with tears.

"Scripted speech," she offered finally. "They were very proud of how well he was doing with scripted speech."

"What's that?"

"I would come to visit him, and he would say, 'Hi, Mom.' And I would say hi to him. He would ask me how I was doing, and I would tell him and ask him how he was. He would say, 'fine' or 'happy' or 'well.' But that was it... if I asked him what he had been doing, or who his friends were, or anything like that, he would fall apart. He would cry and mope and shake his head at everything I said. Then when it was time go, and I would say goodbye and hug him, he would pick up the script again. He'd say, 'Bye, Mom. Love you. See you next time.' They'd taught him how to say hello and goodbye..." Mira's voice cracked. "But they had just trained him to say the words. He still couldn't have a conversation. He still didn't have a script for what came between hello and goodbye."

"Maybe that would have come."

"Maybe... but conversations are complicated. I don't know how many different scripts he could have learned. There are so many different pathways a conversation could have followed."

Zachary looked at the yellow envelope at Mira's elbow that she had not yet opened. She was assiduously ignoring it.

"Do you want to take a break?"

Mira looked relieved. She let out her breath. "Yes. How about some tea? Can I get you a drink?"

"Tea would be great," Zachary agreed. He was not a tea drinker, but it was a soothing ritual for those who were. It would help Mira to calm down and move forward again.

She got up from the table and moved around the kitchen, putting the kettle on and rattling the cups and saucers and other bits. She opened the kitchen window a crack, letting in a breath of fresh, cool air.

"How long have you known Isabella?" Zachary asked her.

Isabella, *The Happy Artist*, beloved local TV personality, had connected the two of them. Zachary had been the one to investigate her son Declan's death and, in spite of the hell she'd been through as a result, she seemed to be grateful to Zachary.

"I've known Isabella a long time. Since we were both in school. We weren't really close friends. But I watched her when she started painting on TV. Quentin loved to watch her show. I knew Isabella had used a private investigator, so I called her…"

Zachary nodded.

Mira set their cups on the table and filled them. Zachary stirred his, not really interested in drinking it.

"I can look at those when I get home," he said, nodding to the unopened envelope. "There's no reason you have to look at them again."

Mira hesitated, considering his offer, then shook her head. "No. I can do this."

She took a couple of determined gulps of piping hot tea and picked it up.

2

"Oh, that poor boy," Kenzie sympathized.

It wasn't the first time Zachary and the attractive brunette had looked at photos of dead bodies together over dinner. Being attached to the local medical examiner's office, Kenzie had a strong stomach, so things that would have made a normal woman queasy didn't bother her one bit.

Not that Quentin Thatcher's photos were gruesome. Strangulation was bloodless, and his body wasn't bloated and swollen like Declan Hildebrandt's had been. But they were still stark and depressing.

"His mother saw these?" Kenzie asked. "She's a stronger woman than I would be. I could never look at photos of my dead child like this."

"She had a pretty hard time with it," Zachary said. "But yes... she's strong."

"The poor woman."

Zachary had a sip of his soft drink and nodded. "I feel bad for any mother who has lost a child."

Saying it brought back painful memories of his break-up with Bridget. The loss of the child he had expected to raise with her.

Kenzie looked at him, her brows drawing down. "I hear a 'but' in there somewhere…"

"No, no, not at all. I do feel sorry for her."

"Okay."

They were silent for a couple of minutes until the waiter brought their meals. Kenzie poked at her phone, not speaking to him, and he got the feeling she was waiting him out, trying to force him, by not asking questions, to say what was on his mind. Just like Mira had been told to ignore Quentin's nonverbal communication so he would be forced to use speech.

Zachary cut into his steak, pretending that he was checking to make sure it had been cooked to his specifications. It had been, of course, and he really wasn't that picky as long as it wasn't bleeding. He just wanted to look at something other than Kenzie, patiently waiting for him to spill his guts. Outside, it was raining, the intermittent traffic passing the restaurant with that familiar swish of wet roads.

"I guess she just irked me a little," he admitted. "She did what the institution said to, even though she didn't think it was the best thing for her son."

"But they are the professionals."

"Sure… but I've dealt with a lot of doctors. They're not always right. In fact… they are frequently wrong when they're dealing with messy stuff like mental illness. Or autism and the other conditions that go with it. They have so many patients to treat. They only have a few minutes to spend on each case. But Quentin's mother only had to deal with him. She raised him for the first twelve years. She knows him and what he needs better than they do."

Kenzie twirled her fork through spaghetti marinara, her movements smooth and dexterous. "But she doesn't have the training. The doctors and therapists have studied the best way to treat kids like this. All of the latest research. All of the different methods. The mother doesn't have that."

"Maybe not… or maybe she does. Parents have a lot of

resources available now. Internet, support groups, millions of books. They can spend hundreds of hours researching what's best for their particular child." He paused, chewing a couple more bites of steak. "But… I don't get the feeling she ever did any of that. She just let the institution dictate what she should do."

"Do you think the doctors were doing something wrong, or do you just not like his mother toeing the line?"

"I don't know yet. I'm trying to go into it with an open mind." Zachary looked down at the pictures of Quentin still on the table, the dark bruises around his throat. "If nothing else… they didn't stop him from killing himself."

Kenzie nodded. "He should have been closely supervised. They should have known if he was suicidal and have had him on a watch."

Zachary took another sip of his cola, wishing that he had something stronger. When he started to get anxious, like the case was already making him, he liked something to take the edge off. Kenzie watched him put the glass down. He wondered whether she could tell what he was thinking, whether she knew that he was craving a real drink. He breathed out, long and slow, trying to release the knot in his belly.

"She feels guilty for institutionalizing him," he told Kenzie.

"Of course. I'm sure every parent who has a child like that does. But she did what she had to do."

Zachary laid down his fork, unable to pretend that he was interested in his steak anymore. "She also said that when she took him there, when she had to go home and leave him behind… she felt relieved."

Kenzie looked at Zachary, her eyes traveling over his face like she was reading a book. "That sounds pretty normal too. He was probably exhausting to take care of. Getting bigger and harder to control. Maybe even violent."

"Yes. He was. She said she feared for her other children."

"And herself, even if she didn't say so. Even a child can hurt you when they're in a rage. More so when it's a teenager who doesn't understand how much damage they could do."

"Yeah." Zachary looked down at his plate. He picked up his napkin and dabbed at his mouth, covering up the grimace he couldn't check.

"What is it?" Kenzie asked, when a few minutes passed in silence.

"Nothing. It's nothing."

"I think I know you well enough by now to tell you're upset about something. Why don't you tell me about it before it builds up into something worse?"

He tried to swallow a lump in his throat. Kenzie let him sit and stew for a while longer. Her eyes went to the photos and she picked through them with two fingers, moving them around. She didn't point out anything suspicious.

"My mother," Zachary said finally. "I told you that she didn't want me. She had me put… into a place like that."

Kenzie put her hand over his. "Oh, Zachary…" She shook her head. "I still don't understand how she could have done that. I really don't. I don't think that any child deserves to be locked up for making a mistake. And that's what it was. A mistake."

"I did things I knew were wrong. I knew, and I went ahead and did them anyway. I wore her ragged. She couldn't manage all of us. It wasn't just her. I never lasted long in any foster family; no one could manage me. No matter how many meds they put me on, no matter how much therapy I did, I always ended up back at places like that."

"But you made it. You're okay now. You turned out alright. You might have had the childhood from hell, but you're not a child anymore. Everything turned out okay."

He wondered if she really thought that he was okay. Whether he could pass as normal to her. His past always plagued him, floating in his peripheral vision, clouds of darkness that threatened to overcome him the moment he let his guard down. People could tell, even if they didn't understand what it was about him. They could always tell that he was different.

He swallowed hard. "I just couldn't help wondering, when Mira said that, how my mother felt when she told the social worker to put me away. I always wondered if she regretted it. If she ever felt the least bit sorry about breaking us up. Abandoning us like that. But what Mira said she felt..." Zachary struggled mightily to keep his cool and not allow his voice to crack, "...was relief."

Kenzie's hand squeezed his more tightly. "I'm sure she felt all of the other things that Quentin's mom felt too. Guilt. Regret. Sadness. No parent wants to institutionalize their child."

"*She* did."

"She said she did. But I'll bet she cried."

Zachary thought about this. She thought about all of the times she had screamed at Zachary or his siblings. Hit them. Punished them unfairly. She hadn't been exaggerating when she told the social worker she was at the end of her rope and couldn't do it anymore. He had done that to her. Had she regretted it? Had she cried, once she was out of sight? Once it was all over and she could let down her guard? He honestly couldn't picture it. The last thing he had seen of her was her unrelenting anger.

"I don't think she cried," he said finally.

But Mira had.

Order His Hands Were Quiet now at pdworkman.com

ABOUT THE AUTHOR

Award-winning and USA Today bestselling author P.D. (Pamela) Workman writes riveting mystery/suspense and young adult books dealing with mental illness, addiction, abuse, and other real-life issues. For as long as she can remember, the blank page has held an incredible allure and from a very young age she was trying to write her own books.

Workman wrote her first complete novel at the age of twelve and continued to write as a hobby for many years. She started publishing in 2013. She has won several literary awards from Library Services for Youth in Custody for her young adult fiction. She currently has over 50 published titles and can be found at pdworkman.com.

Born and raised in Alberta, Workman has been married for over 25 years and has one son.

Please visit P.D. Workman at pdworkman.com to see what else she is working on, to join her mailing list, and to link to her social networks.

If you enjoyed this book, please take the time to recommend it to other purchasers with a review or star rating and share it with your friends!

facebook.com/pdworkmanauthor

twitter.com/pdworkmanauthor

instagram.com/pdworkmanauthor

amazon.com/author/pdworkman

bookbub.com/authors/p-d-workman

goodreads.com/pdworkman

linkedin.com/in/pdworkman

pinterest.com/pdworkmanauthor

youtube.com/pdworkman

CPSIA information can be obtained
at www.ICGtesting.com
Printed in the USA
FSHW011009161220
76934FS